CIRCLE
OF
SECRETS

KIMBERLEY GRIFFITHS LITTLE

CIRCLE
OF
SECRETS

Scholastic Press / New York

Copyright © 2011 by Kimberley Griffiths Little

All rights reserved. Published by Scholastic Press, an imprint of Scholastic Inc., *Publishers since 1920.*
SCHOLASTIC, SCHOLASTIC PRESS, and associated logos are trademarks and/or registered trademarks of
Scholastic Inc.

Library of Congress Cataloging-in-Publication Data
Little, Kimberley Griffiths.
Circle of secrets / Kimberley Griffiths Little. — 1st ed.
p. cm.
Summary: A year after her mother has deserted the family, eleven-year-old Shelby goes to stay with
her, deep in the Louisiana bayou, where they both confront old hurts and regrets.
ISBN 978-0-545-16561-7
[1. Mothers and daughters—Fiction. 2. Guilt—Fiction. 3. Ghosts—Fiction. 4. Bayous—Fiction.
5. Louisiana—Fiction.] I. Title.
PZ7.L72256Ci 2011
[Fic] — dc22
2011000889
10 9 8 7 6 5 4 3 2 1   11 12 13 14 15
Printed in the U.S.A. 23
Reinforced Binding for Library Use
First edition, October 2011

Book design by Kristina Iulo

To my lovely nieces,

Tehya, Eden, Avery, Casey, Brandilyn & Alexis.

May there always be a touch of magic and

the miracle of love in your lives. . . .

The summer I turned eleven, I found out that ghosts are real.

Guess it's hard to rest nice and easy in your coffin if you got stuff on your mind. Your soul stays chained to Earth instead of zipping up to heaven to sing in one of the angel choirs.

Sometimes ghosts show up in the most peculiar places.

Sometimes ghosts fool you.

Then there are those ghosts that hang around because we have unfinished business. Business that stinks like old crawfish left in a bucket for a week. That's some nasty smell, let me tell you.

But the most important thing I learned is that ghosts can help you spill your guts before guilt eats you up and leaves a hole that can't never be fixed no matter how many patches you try to steam iron across it.

CHAPTER ONE

SOON AS MY BIRTHDAY PRESENTS ARE UNWRAPPED AND THE chocolate raspberry cake gulped down, Daddy packs my stuff in the Chevy and slams the trunk. Inch by inch, I slowly slide into the front seat, waiting until he tells me to buckle up before I snap the seat belt.

Then he drives sixty miles to Bayou Bridge — where we rent a boat that takes us deep into the swamp. I sit in the prow of the motorboat, worms jiggling my gut the whole way, fat and sassy on all that cake I just ate.

When we get to the swamp house, I watch my daddy tie the rope around the dock piling, get my suitcases out, and set them on the scraggly lawn. Wind moans through the giant cypress trees surrounding the house, making the Spanish moss float in the air like mermaid's hair.

Daddy holds out his hand for me to take, but I just stare at it and don't budge from my seat.

"Come on, Shelby, you gotta get out of the boat."

I'd suffered through miles of dark, scary swamp, past a spooky abandoned beaver dam and cypress stumps lurking like monsters under the water, and I wasn't about to get out of that boat.

"Your mamma's expecting us."

"I didn't ask to come here." I peek through my hair at the weather-beaten house sitting on stilts, the windows blank and empty. What if I got left here for the rest of my life? What if I never saw my daddy again long as I lived?

"No, but where you going to go instead? Our house is closed up, locked tight, until Grandmother Phoebe gets out of the hospital."

"You could quit that job clear over there by Russia. Whatever it's called." I'd made a point of not remembering exactly which country because I didn't want my daddy's leaving to be real.

"The timing is bad, but you know I gotta go. It's only for six months, and it's the best job offer I've had in ten years."

"I heard Grandmother Phoebe calling her a swamp witch."

"That's ridiculous, Shelby Jayne, and you know it. 'Course,

that might be better than calling her nothing," he adds pointedly. "It's harder to pry 'Mamma' out of your mouth than to open a trap sealed with Krazy Glue."

I stopped calling her Mamma when she left a year ago. Then I started calling her Mirage like we were both grownups. Now I don't call her anything.

I stare down at the muddy water, wondering what lives underneath that I can't see. I want to curl up in the bottom of the boat and never get out. Make my daddy turn it around and head right back to dry land where the Chevy's parked at the town docks.

I haven't seen Mirage in three months.

Haven't lived with her for a year.

When she walked out of the house right before my tenth birthday with only a single suitcase, I got so mad it felt like sucking on sour grapes all day long.

When she telephones I listen because Grandmother Phoebe taught me manners, like how to be a proper young lady by bringing in the lemonade and cookies during Garden Club meetings, but sometimes I watch the clock to see how long I can go without answering any of Mirage's questions.

Folding my arms across my chest, I wonder how long I can sit here before Daddy physically hauls me out himself.

Then I notice that there's an inch of dirty water floating in the bottom of the boat. Finally, I climb out, sighing a lot so he knows for sure I'm still mad.

"That's gotta change, Sweetie Pie," Daddy goes on as we climb the porch steps to the swamp house. Cypress trees drip so much Spanish moss the stuff sweeps the ground like those plantation draperies that lay in folds on the floor to show just how rich a family used to be before the Civil War. Grandmother Phoebe likes to point them out when we go on plantation tours along the Mississippi River Road.

"What, Daddy?" I ask, pretending I've forgotten what he's talking about.

"You're being silly with all this 'Miz Mirage' or 'Yes, Miz Allemond,' on the phone. Allemond is *your* name, too, you know. She's not a stranger."

I gnaw on the inside of my cheek where I have a permanent scab embedded there. My throat gets all hot and scratchy as my feet move slower and slower up the steps. "Just being polite, Daddy," I manage to whisper. I stare at the boat bobbing up and down at the dock so he can't see my face as I try not to cry.

It hits me real bad that I'm not going to see him for six whole months. Might as well be forever. All kind of worries mix up inside my brain. What if Grandmother Phoebe dies in the hospital? What if my daddy decides he doesn't miss me or forgets to come back for me? My chest squeezes so tight I can't suck in any air. Little black spots float across my eyes and I get dizzy.

Mirage left me. What if my daddy leaves me, too?

He lets out a sigh, and I can tell he doesn't want to get mad when we're saying good-bye. "Well, it ain't polite to say 'Miz Allemond' when it's your own mamma."

I fight real hard to keep my voice normal but it's not cooperating. "Tell those embassy people you can't go because you have a crippled child who needs you."

He lowers a knee to the rickety porch where the cypress boards don't meet quite right and looks me in the eye. "You aren't crippled, Shelby Jayne. And you're gonna be just fine."

I finally tell him the thing I've been worrying about ever since Mirage left that night in the rain, leaving me on the front porch all by myself. "What'd I do wrong?"

"What're you talking about?"

I look into his dark blue eyes, wondering if I can really tell him the truth. "I must have done something to make her go away and never come back. Maybe she never really loved me."

He opens his mouth in surprise. "Shelby — I don't know

what to say — no, it was never your fault. It was mine. Mostly mine. Nope, *all* mine. So you can just quit your grudge against your mamma, you hear?"

I glance away from him and swallow hard. I'm out in the middle of nowhere with only water far as I can see. Soon there's going to be a million miles between me and my daddy. The fear that I'll never see him again closes around my heart in a death grip. "Then why don't you fix it?"

"It ain't so easy, Sweetie Pie." He looks down at the porch planks and the gooey, squishy mud swirling below. I don't like how those planks aren't fitted right. Any second I might fall right through.

Daddy takes my shoulders and looks me straight on. "Mirage — your mamma — loves you and she's gonna take good care of you."

I'm not so sure about all that love and stuff. "How many mothers leave their children to go live in a swamp? Isn't that proof she don't want me?"

His eyes drop away to stare at his shoes. "There's more to the story, but it's tangled up and hard to explain."

"And," I spit out, "my heart does too feel crippled! Like it has two broken legs and a stomach disorder."

My daddy starts to laugh, then turns it into a cough.

Right then, the front door cracks open.

Mirage is standing in front of us, but all I can see is wild black hair writhing in the wind like serpents.

My pulse goes so fast I swear that heart attack's gone full blown. Maybe Daddy should take me to the hospital and I can get a room next to Grandmother Phoebe. But he isn't paying attention no more.

Mirage looks so different, like she really is turning into a swamp witch. I remember her wearing slacks and blouses to classes at the college, and her hair up in a ponytail. Sometimes she wore glasses to read the tiny print in the textbooks better.

Now her black eyes sink into mine like she can read my deepest thoughts. Like she has a crystal ball and uses it regularly. Maybe my *grand-mère*, the old *traiteur*, gave her one. She was ancient and always smelled like icky medicine, so she scared me. Don't think I'd seen her since I was eight or nine so my memories are sort of mixed up and jumbly.

A shivery ribbon of fear runs down my spine and curls my toes. Meeting at a restaurant is easier with other people around. Now it's just going to be Mirage and me — alone. For months on end until I shrivel up like one of those prunes Grandmother Phoebe cooks for breakfast.

I turn around to see how fast I can run back to the boat,

but the porch is missing a plank. A pair of beady red eyes lurks in the mud underneath.

I almost fall right over my suitcases. "What's that?"

Daddy says, "It's only a frog, Shelby."

Instantly, those creepy red eyes jump away, but that doesn't make me feel any better.

"Hey, Mirage," he says as she pulls the door wider.

She sticks her hands into the pockets of a purple gypsy skirt like she's nervous, but I have no idea why she'd be jumpy. "Hey, Philip." Silver earrings in the shape of herons look ready to take flight as they brush against her neck in the gusty wind. I like those herons, and I wonder if they tickle. I want a pair of earrings like that, but Grandmother Phoebe won't allow pierced ears until I'm eighteen. She says I could get an infection — and "why would you want to put holes in your body anyway?"

My daddy and Mirage eye each other. This is the first time I've seen them face-to-face in a year, but they don't do a thing. Just stare at each other for a really long time. All kinds of stuff is clunking around in their minds like rusted cans on an empty road — I can practically *hear* their invisible thoughts — but they don't say a thing. I notice that Mirage has dark circles under her eyes, like she's sick or been crying.

"Last time I saw you was at the funeral," Daddy finally says in a somber voice.

She nods and runs her hands through her wild, curly hair like she's tired. "Still trying to get everything together out here. It's all so much. Some days too much."

"I'm sorry," Daddy says. "You two going to be okay?"

She tries to put on a smile. "'Course we are. Shelby comin' has been somethin' good to look forward to."

Maybe to her, but not to me.

When Mirage left, it was the worst day of my life. Today is the second worst day. Thinking about staying out here alone without my daddy makes my palms itch and my throat tickle. I don't know what she's going to do or say and I don't feel like talking to her. I don't know what to believe when she says one thing, like she loves me, then does something entirely different.

"So here's your stuff, *shar*," Daddy says, setting my box of books inside the door and pushing the suitcases in after it. He kisses me on the cheek, whispers good-bye, and I close my eyes, squeezing back all the hot tears so Mirage won't see.

I throw my arms around him, sticking to him like a leech as he tries to leave. I hold on so tight, he ends up lifting me off the ground. My feet dangle in the breeze. With my face buried in his neck I can feel his scratchy cheek and smell the aftershave he put on before we left home. He gives a laugh and tries to set me down.

"Okay, Sweetie Pie, you can't keep doing this," he says in my ear. "You're so clingy these days, it's embarrassing."

"Please, Daddy!" I whisper right back. "Don't leave me here! Don't go so far away without me."

"Sweetie Pie, I gotta go, you know that. That's how the bills get paid." He leans over, me still dangling from his neck as I hang on tighter than ever, my sneakers bumping his bony knees. Maybe if I just never let go, he'll have to take me with him.

My chest gets a queer bubble of anxiety as he pulls my arms one by one from around his neck. Setting me firmly down on the porch, he takes a step backward, looking at me with his serious eyes.

My throat is closed up so tight, I can't even speak.

I'm partway going on twelve now, but I'm tempted to wrap my arms around his legs so he can't walk down the steps and back to the dock without me.

While I'm debating the pros and cons of doing that, Daddy digs into the front pocket of his jacket and pulls out a white envelope. "Here, Mirage."

She takes the envelope and tucks it into one of her deep skirt pockets. "Appreciate that, Philip."

"Let me know if you need more," he adds, glancing up at her face.

Their eyes lock and it's like their secret conversation starts up all over again. I know there's money in that envelope. Money for taking care of me.

Daddy gives me another quick hug — so fast I can't even get a good grip this time — then clomps down the porch steps. "I'll call you every night, *shar*, or as often as I can get through on the phones."

The lump in my throat has grown to humongous proportions.

Just then, a monster wind comes roaring down the bayou. Empty cans, pieces of fishing line, and bits of rope rattle across the yard and scoot underneath the house to get buried in the mud when it floods. I'll bet there's all kinds of things the wind's blown under that house. I try not to think about nests of snakes and spiders hiding there, too.

Stiffly, I stare out toward the water, at my daddy climbing back into the boat, rain clouds inching closer every second.

"Best hurry back to town," Mirage calls out. "Storm comin'."

Daddy nods and rips the cord on the boat engine. He lifts his hand and a rush of panic comes over me like I got sucked into a tidal wave.

As I finally wave back, the tail of the boat starts to disappear around the bend of the cove. "Daddy!" I shriek, but he doesn't hear me.

Two seconds later, he's out of sight. Just like that. Gone. Until Christmas.

CHAPTER TWO

I WATCH THE BOAT'S CHOPPY WAKE FLATTEN OUT ACROSS THE water, looking almost like it sucked my daddy under, and I try not to burst into tears.

"Come on in out of that wind, Shelby Jayne," Mirage tells me, scooting my belongings into the front room next to several racks of drying Spanish moss.

I force my feet across the threshold and the front door closes. We stare at each other, but I drop my eyes real quick, wondering if she can read my thoughts.

After she moves my suitcases and boxes into the spare bedroom, raindrops start tapping overhead. Guess the storm caught up with us because within seconds, they're coming down loud and fast, like tiny fists beating at the tin roof.

Slowly, I follow Mirage into the kitchen where the curtains over the sink are flapping wildly, letting in a spatter of raindrops.

"Hope you're still partial to gumbo," she says, peering into a pot of okra roux filled with chunks of chicken and sausage. I've always liked her gumbo real good, but I don't say a word. I can't tell if she's trying to bribe me into loving her again, or if tonight's supper is just a coincidence. Like fixing your relative's favorite foods when they come to visit. Even if you're mad at 'em.

"Go ahead and take a load off, Shelby Jayne. Rice is 'bout ready, but I gotta doctor up Mister Lenny first."

"Mister Lenny?" I echo, glancing around for someone else in the room. But it's just us. All I see are dingy walls that need painting and the old-fashioned refrigerator in the corner.

"Sit yourself right there," Mirage says. A breeze full of rain swirls through the window before she leans across the sink and slams it shut.

Something suddenly dive-bombs at my head.

I let out a screech. "What's that?"

"That's jest Winifred. She won't hurt you."

"What *is* it?"

Mirage holds out her palm and a sparrow flits down and

grabs hold of her finger, cocking her head at me like I just landed from Pluto.

I wonder if Grandmother Phoebe packed my bottle of hand sanitizer.

I wonder if the forks are clean.

"Ma petite shar," Mirage coos, releasing the sparrow, which flits back into the front room and disappears behind a bookcase. Next, she reaches up to a branch above the sink and brings down a blinking owl.

"Mister Lenny," Mirage says, "meet Shelby Jayne."

I don't say a word.

My mamma has a pet owl.

Doctoring him up at the kitchen table no less.

Grandmother Phoebe would have a first-rate hissy fit.

"Mister Lenny is a barred owl, Shelby," Mirage tells me, like we're having a science lesson and I'm her C+ student. Her eyes come alive for the first time since I got here.

"A barn owl?"

"Nope, a barred owl. Instead a spots, he has stripes along his neck, like bars of color. And he's jest a *bébé*. Look how sweet, like a teddy bear."

"Um, yeah, I can see the fluffiness."

"Found him this spring, fallen from a nest, his mother disappeared. I hate to think hunters might have got him. . . ."

I know all about mothers disappearing. "What are you doing to his wing?" I ask as Mister Lenny starts making a strange barking noise.

Mirage smoothes the bird's feathers with her fingers and Mister Lenny cocks his head, then pecks her on the nose. Mirage just laughs. Then that owl starts hooting and gurgling.

I grip the table like I'm clinging to a life preserver. "He isn't choking, is he?"

"Nope, jest wants in on our conversation. He gets jealous."

"Never heard of no jealous bird before," I tell her, rolling my eyes. I hear my own voice and wonder at how easily I'm talking like Mirage again. Grandmother Phoebe's been trying to squeeze the swamp speech out of me all year long, teaching me how to speak more proper like ladies in the big cities instead of a bayou girl. Even though I lived out here when I was real young — before my memories kicked in. And grew up with a mother like Mirage. "So what're you doing?" I ask again.

"He got a broken wing, and I been usin' my healing spells on him."

"Healing *spells*?" I wonder if she does that hoodoo magic stuff like folks in New Orleans. Does my daddy know where he's dumped me? My gut starts to jump around like I got a mullet in my belly.

16

I want to grab a boat and follow him back up the bayou, but I don't know how to row. Or which direction to point the boat. He's probably getting soaked in all this rain. I start worrying that he'll catch pneumonia and die before he can come back and get me.

"Today is Mister Lenny's last prayer day."

Mirage closes her eyes, puts her hands on top of the owl's fluffy little head, and begins to pray, murmuring French words in a soft, quiet jumble.

At first I bow my head like for Mass, but then I peek through my hair so I can watch. If she goes into a trance and the owl starts pecking my eyes, I better stay alert.

But there's no trance or candle lighting or incantations at all. When Mirage finishes praying, she lifts her head. "You ready for supper, *shar*? We're havin' crawfish gumbo. Winifred is quite excited. She loves crawfish, and I left some raw 'specially for her."

"Thought it was chicken and sausage."

"Caught some crawfish today and couldn't help throwing it in, too."

I lick my dry lips, rubbing my hands against my jeans. "What *was* that — that praying stuff? Are you really a swamp witch?"

Her black eyes turn dark and stormy. "Who said I was a swamp witch?"

"Um, I don't remember."

"Grandmother Phoebe, I s'pose," she says, and I get the feeling it bothers her, but I'm pretty sure she and Grandmother Phoebe haven't spoken two words in the past year. She always makes me answer the telephone when Mirage calls.

I think about all that icy silence in our house before Mirage left for good, and I can't help shivering. After Daddy started traveling more with his new job, the house was dead quiet. We even started eating dinner separately.

Then Mirage started taking trips out here to the swamp to tend her own mamma, my *grand-mère*, who got sick. I'd always heard my *grand-mère* was a *traiteur*, too. I guess she couldn't heal herself like she could other people.

After that last terrible fight, Mirage just never came back.

Grandmother Phoebe pretended Mirage never existed.

I was supposed to act like everything was normal.

Now Daddy's left.

I think about my daddy getting farther and farther away and my stomach starts to hurt. I stare at the blue flame of gas under the pot on the stove. A dented pot sits by the back door, catching drips from a brown stain in the ceiling.

"Grandmother Phoebe says," I start to tell her, and the words are like little darts of pain in my throat, "that's the whole reason you and Daddy split up."

Mirage tries to reach for my hand, but I move it off the table and stick it in my lap.

The kitchen falls into a sudden hole of silence while I stare at a tiny rip in my jeans.

She clears her throat and puts Mister Lenny back on his perch. His head swivels around as Mirage dishes up two bowls of gumbo and sets them on the table with the pot of rice. I secretly admire her purple flowered skirt and the sparkly rings on her long fingers, but mostly I'm watching her eyes, her face, wondering what she's going to do next.

Tiny little pieces of crawfish float to the top of the roux, but I hunt down the chicken and sausage instead and take a bite, burning my lips it's so hot.

Rain sheets the kitchen window like gray dishwater. "Bad storm, ain't it?" Mirage says with a small smile. "Hope your daddy made it back to his car okay."

"Me, too." I stare at my gumbo again, fishing out some okra to chew on.

"Shelby," she tries again. "There's a whole long story you wouldn't understand, but I ain't a witch. That's an old wives' tale. I'm a *traiteur*. That's French for healer. *Traiteurs* go way back when Cajuns first got to Louisiana and had no doctor for fifty miles."

"You're a doctor?" I say, blowing hard on my next spoonful.

"Oh, *non*, I ain't no doctor. A *traiteur* just has a special talent for healin' folks. I learned about plant medicine and the special healing prayers from my mamma before she died. Certain people liked to call your *grand-mère* a swamp witch because she was old and kept to herself, mostly because of arthritis that knotted her up the last couple a years. Calling a *traiteur* a swamp witch is jest plain ignorance. Most a town didn't understand her ways, but she had a friend in her mailman who brought out her letters and groceries couple times a month. No amount of gossip or rumors could stop her from helpin' folks." Mirage gives a small laugh, but her voice sounds funny, almost like she's gonna cry. "Folks liked my mamma's cough syrup remedy better than anything on them store shelves. And after she laid her hands on your head and whispered her prayers, you felt a hundred percent better."

"Sounds like magic," I say, wondering if it was really true or just a story.

"Not magic. Faith in God. She had a spiritual gift, jest like the Bible says. But the healing comes from God, not her, not me. Never me."

She gets real quiet like it's important that I understand what she's saying.

"So what happened to her? How'd she die?"

"She got real sick. That's why I came out here so much last year, and then just stayed. Got so bad, she finally couldn't get out of bed at all. Passed a few months ago in her sleep. By then she was just a wisp of a thing, but she knew just about everything there was to know about healing. I got her recipe book to keep forever. And the prayers in my head."

I want to know why Mirage never came back to New Iberia after Grand-mère's funeral was over and done. Why she left me and Daddy forever. But I can't get the question to come out of my mouth.

Besides, she should be giving *me* the answers without me having to ask.

I push the spoon around my bowl, thinking about the night she left when I screamed at her to come back, to stop walking down the steps to the car.

She'd paused, then knelt to take my hands in hers. "Shelby, Grand-mère is real bad sick and I gotta go."

"You coming back, right?"

She shook her head, but she wouldn't look me in the eyes. Just kept staring back at the house, back at Daddy standing on the porch. "If I don't leave now and get away from here, I'm gonna die myself."

"That don't make no sense," I'd told her.

"I love you, Shelby Jayne. Wish so bad I could take you

with me, but you got school here, and everything you need. I can't take care of you for a while. Grand-mère is gonna take every ounce of strength I have."

But I didn't believe her. I stopped believing anything she said.

I once wrote her a letter, but she just said it was too complicated to explain. Which wasn't an answer at all. One of those things grown-ups do when they don't want to talk about something. Or don't want to admit they did wrong.

Maybe I really don't want Mirage telling me the truth. I don't want to know that her love was fake, that I wasn't worth it. That she'd been pretending her whole life.

I feel a shudder go right up my spine and into my brain. Even though I want answers, I'm afraid of them, too.

At that moment the sun bursts through the clouds, wiping the darkness away as if the sun's rays were long golden hands.

The chattering rain stops.

The trickles of water running in squiggly lines down the window slow.

And on the other side of the kitchen windows, the air is suddenly filled with an extraordinary blue light.

CHAPTER THREE

"WHAT IS THAT?" I ASK, SHOVING BACK MY CHAIR. "IT'S LIKE the entire world turned into the sky."

Mirage points to the back door. "Go on out. Door's unlocked."

In two seconds, I'm standing on the back porch — which is more stable than the front porch — and I just look and look and look.

A giant tree grows up from the center of the yard, the top of it reaching the sky. And it's filled with dozens and dozens and dozens of blue bottles. Every single branch, big and little, higher than a cypress and lower than a weed, has a blue bottle stuck on it.

A pillar of sunlight pierces straight down through the

storm clouds, almost like a spotlight. The light catches all those hundreds of bottles, throwing a blue tinge of color over everything in the yard. The tomato plants in the garden look blue, the lawn chairs, a set of old tires, fishing nets stacked against the exterior of the house, a wobbly card table off to one side of the porch cluttered with work tools, and an old chipped ceramic fountain, filled with rainwater. Even the water in the fountain is puddled into a soft, pretty blue.

Mirage's whole yard is surrounded by cypress trees and hanging with curtains of moss, and the blue glow of all those bottles makes it look just like a fairyland. Never seen anything like it in my whole life.

"It's a blue bottle tree," Mirage says, coming up behind me.

I start laughing, even though I don't want to act happy around her. The name Blue Bottle Tree is so obvious. And perfect.

"Go look, Shelby," she says, leaning against the porch railing and wrapping her arms around herself like she's cold.

I jump down the steps and walk closer to the tree.

Raindrops are running down the sides of the bottles, dripping off the ends. There's a plinking noise as all that rain drip, drip, drips onto the bottles below, like the tree is creating its own magical rain shower.

I throw a look over my shoulder. "Who made the tree that way? Where'd all those bottles come from?"

Mirage's face looks sort of red and splotchy, but maybe it's just the light from the clouds and the rain. She clears her throat. "My daddy was the one started it when he and my mamma got married and moved out here. We been adding bottles ever since I was a girl. One a your *grand-mère*'s favorite things to do was collectin' blue bottles at garage sales and on the side a the road."

"I don't remember ever seeing it before."

Mirage shoves her hands deep into her pockets and sways on the top step of the porch, and I notice that she doesn't come any closer. "You haven't been out here since you were real little."

"You really grew up way out here?"

"Yep, spent my whole childhood here, fishin', gardenin', trappin'."

A thought suddenly occurs to me. "How do I get to school?"

"Used to be a school boat came for all us kids when I was growing up, but there are more roads in Bayou Bridge now, although I'll have to take you to school by boat."

"Oh. Boats make me seasick, you know."

"Hmm," she murmurs. "Glad you didn't get sick coming out here today."

Without looking at her, I say, "I could stay back at my house in New Iberia, you know. Then you don't have to boat me to school. I can take care of myself while Grandmother Phoebe is in the hospital."

I feel Mirage give me a quick glance. "I'm sure you're real capable, Shelby Jayne, but eleven-year-old girls can't stay alone in a house for weeks at a time. Against the law, for one thing. You'd get lonely, for another. And you can't drive to the store to get groceries. Besides, I don't mind rowing you. Grew up surrounded by water, as you can see."

It occurs to me for the first time in my life that I know almost nothing about my own mamma before she married my daddy, and I'm not sure I want to know more. Even if I do like her silver heron earrings and that blue bottle tree. I'd forgotten that she used to wear unusual jewelry. Grandmother Phoebe would call it costume jewelry. That the only proper jewelry was a string of pearls or modest gold studs, if a woman had to wear it at all.

"Can I call Grandmother Phoebe tonight and see how she's doing?"

"You can call her and your daddy anytime you want."

I wish she wasn't trying to be so nice. I wish I could yell at her. I've spent a lot of time the last year wishing I had a different mamma. That Grandmother Phoebe was my real mamma. That I didn't have to think about Mirage out here in the swamp, staying away on purpose.

I didn't want to think about the good memories all mixed up with the bad. Like her leaving right before my birthday last year — after she promised to make me a castle cake for finally turning double digits — ten. I stuck the picture I'd been saving from the cake-decorating magazine under my pillow and cried. A castle cake with a moat and a drawbridge and gold candies to make it look fancy. She'd promised to take me to lunch with LizAnn and her mamma on a special outing to Lafayette, too.

Instead, I got a plain white cake in a square pan with vanilla ice cream.

Grandmother Phoebe doesn't like to bake, and that year Daddy said he didn't have the energy. Later, he apologized for giving me a terrible birthday, but I remember how he sat in the chair every night and moped and didn't talk to no one.

I'll bet Daddy bribed Mirage to take me while he was over there by Russia and Grandmother Phoebe was having her hip surgery and rehabilitation.

That's what all that money in the white envelope was for.

We stand there, me under the tree and Mirage still on the porch, and don't say a word.

I listen to the drip, drip, drip of rain plinking on all those blue bottles hanging from a hundred branches. I shield my eyes and squint into the sunlight to see the very top of the tree.

Something brushes against my legs and I almost jump right out of my clothes. "It's a alligator!" I scream, running toward the tree. I wonder how fast I can shimmy up the trunk even if it means I might break a few bottles on the way up. I can practically feel that gator ready to chomp on my toes.

"Shelby Jayne," Mirage calls. "It's okay!"

I hit the bark of the trunk and look for a place to stick my foot. "Can gators climb trees?" Another stupid question, but it just pops out of my mouth.

"Shelby, stop running, it's only Miss Silla Wheezy."

Gripping the stringy bark of the tree, I steal a quick glance backward. A pure white cat slinks around Mirage's ankles. Her swirly purple skirt poofs out like a parachute as she crouches down to stroke the cat.

"Miss Silla Wheezy is a funny name," I say, my heart still pounding.

"She's real old now, but when she was a baby she was a

silly kitty, bumping into things and sliding on the floors when she got to running too fast."

A second cat, this one all black except for a tiny white patch on its throat, lifts its head from the bottom of a turned-over wheelbarrow under the eaves of the house.

"That's Mister Possum Boudreaux and he's taking shelter in the barrow because rain puts him in a sour mood."

I've always liked cats, but Grandmother Phoebe does not. No pets allowed in her house and that is for certain.

"So why do people put blue bottles onto a tree anyway?" I ask. "It's kinda strange."

"The tradition comes from the African people long time ago. Folks believe the blue bottles will trap bad spirits floatin' around their yard and keep 'em from comin' into the house. The blue bottles hold the bad spirits inside so they can't get out."

"What kind of bad spirits?"

"Oh, things like imps or fairies or haunts, gremlins and critters that'll play tricks on you, bring bad luck or evil into your life or your house. Maybe even ghosts."

I look at her and swallow hard. *Ghosts?*

"Nowadays, folks mostly make blue bottle trees for fun, to decorate their yards."

Inside the house, the phone begins to ring.

29

"Expect that's your daddy on the phone, Shelby Jayne. Me, I'm also expectin' company so I gots to get ready for 'em."

My stomach gives a little twist at the thought of other people, strangers I don't know, here with us. "What company?"

"Not really company, more like a customer, if you want to call it that. Except I don't charge and I don't get paid. It ain't right and I wouldn't want it."

"I don't get it."

"Someone's comin' who wants some healin'."

"Do they make an appointment?"

"Not usually, but sometimes I just get a feelin' come over me. Sooner than later, someone's at the door. Rain seems to bring folks, too."

The phone keeps on ringing as I back away from the trunk of the tree.

"You get the phone, Shelby Jayne, and I'll get the door."

Mirage bounds up the porch steps as I take one last look into the blue bottle tree.

A dizzying array of light- and dark- and medium-colored blue bottles reaches up to the sky. My eyes go cross-eyed, with all kind a blue as far as I can see. I want to get a blanket and sit under it, although the ground is sopping wet now.

Then I see something very peculiar. One of the bottles has something inside. Maybe it's just a trick of the light and the rain. I figure it's a bug or some dirt, a rock, maybe, but the closer I look I'd swear there's a *piece of paper* inside there. Like a *note*. Like in a movie when a bottle washes in from the ocean with a note that turns out to be a map for a treasure hunt.

The telephone stops ringing. "Shoot!"

I do want to talk to my daddy. I wonder if he's already in New Orleans checking in for his flight. I'm surprised that much time has already gone by. He'll probably call right back, but that means I only have a few seconds.

Stretching as tall as I can, I grab the branch overhead and pull it down, my arm practically popping a tendon, it's so high up. My toes are cramping by the time I slip the blue bottle off the branch and peek inside. Sure enough, there's something in there.

I put my eye to the opening, and then shake it. A piece of paper, all folded up, is inside that bottle, but the neck is so narrow, it's tricky.

I angle the bottle this way and that, slipping that paper all over the place.

The phone starts to ring for the second time.

Holding my breath, I slowly tilt the bottle just so and the

note slips down right through the mouth. I grasp the end with my fingers and pop it out. The phone stops ringing and I hurry to stick the blue bottle back onto its branch fast as I can.

My heart's beating so loud I can hear it in my ears.

"Shelby Jayne!" Mirage calls from the screen door. "It's your daddy!"

"Coming!" I gulp as my heart keeps whopping inside my eardrums like an echo. I want to read that note bad, but I want to talk to my daddy just as bad. Maybe he's decided he'll miss me so much he's gonna come and get me. I mean, *going* to come and get me.

I'm trying to remember all those words Grandmother Phoebe taught me to swap out for better ones, but here in the swamp it's harder than I thought it would be. It's like all my growing-up language got programmed into my brain permanently and I'm short-circuiting.

The shadow of Mirage's figure moves away from the door. I keep my back to her and quickly unfold the paper.

There are words, written on yellowing notebook paper, fading like it's old.

Don't forget! Tonight's the night! Come to the bridge — and hurry!

A note in a bottle! How strange, and exciting. My head fills with a bunch of questions. What does the note mean, and who's it for, hanging up in that bottle in the tree?

The lettering is partly squiggly, partly printed, like someone writing in a hurry. I shiver with the mysteriousness of it, and the knowledge that blue bottle trees are meant to trap evil gremlins or imps or fairies.

I fold up the note again, stuff it into the pocket of my jeans, and run for the porch, darting around Miss Silla Wheezy and Mister Possum Boudreaux.

An ancient, green, rotary dial phone is off the hook and lying on the yellow tablecloth. A long cord runs along the floor and up the wall, like a phone out of an old movie.

Mirage already answered it and left the receiver on the table for me. I can tell she's with someone in the front room. She really does have a customer.

Instead of talking in the kitchen where they can hear me, I grab the phone and slip around the corner of the hall, using every inch of that twisty old-fashioned telephone cord. I go into the bedroom Mirage stuffed my suitcases in and perch on the edge of the patchwork quilt. "Hello?"

"Shelby, you there?" My daddy sounds happy, relaxed, and I get a funny tickle in my throat. He's supposed to miss me dreadfully, and tell me he's coming straight back to get me. Instead he asks, "Are you getting settled at your mother's house?"

"Um, sort of." I glance at the unopened suitcases and the box of books and school stuff still sitting on the floor.

"Bet you had some of Mirage's famous chicken-and-sausage gumbo, huh?"

"Nah. Crawfish," I tell him, half lying to make him feel sorry for me.

Mirage and the visitors drift into the kitchen. I want to spy on them something fierce. Will she make her customer drink potions out of a cauldron? Or wave a wand over their head? I can't seem to concentrate on my conversation with Daddy.

"What did you say, honey? The connection suddenly went full of static."

"Crawfish," I say. "I said crawfish."

He gives a laugh. "Crawfish is probably easier to come by out there than boudin, *shar.*"

"I guess." I bend over to look for critters or bugs hiding under the bed. All I see are dust balls of crud.

"What I mean, Shelby, is that Mirage sets traps below the water in the mud and hauls some up every couple days. Easy eating."

"How do you know all that?" And why was my daddy

talking about *her* and not *me*? I thought they hated each other.

"She and I used to go fishing all the time. We lived at that house when we first got married and had you; we moved in with Grandmother Phoebe when we decided we better go to college. And, then, well, we just never left."

"How come you didn't stay out here and go to college?"

"Well, lots of reasons. First, the school was a mighty long commute, more than two hours. Your grandmother was lonely, too. And sick a lot. Plus, well, this is all grown-up stuff not to worry about, but my daddy's money ran out and I helped keep up the mortgage for my mamma. Never had enough money to pay for two mortgages, and while that old house I grew up in was in a nice neighborhood, it needed so many repairs I thought it was gonna kill us for sure."

"Never knew all that, Daddy," I whisper, but I'm not sure he hears me.

Storm clouds move across the sky, covering up the sun. A lone trickle of rain dribbles down the bedroom window, making the bedroom gloomy and depressing.

"I'm sorry you're unhappy there, *shar*. I wish this assignment wasn't going to be so long, but I do miss you very much. Good news is, this better job is helping get us out of debt and save up for our own place. If I can pry you out of Grandmother Phoebe's hands."

I think he's right, although I never thought about it like that before. I don't think my grandmother would like the idea of us leaving. In fact, I think she's gonna fight it hard.

"I miss you, too," I whisper. I picture him in the bright, cheery airport, people overflowing with luggage as they check in for flights to the Bahamas or Egypt or Rome. And me left behind.

After Daddy tells me he loves me, I return the phone to its cradle then tiptoe back to my room, and stare at a big old wardrobe standing under the corner eaves. It's dark and sinister-looking, like something out of medieval times.

I wonder if I should start unpacking and whether my clothes will fit in that thing. It looks like the wardrobe from the Narnia books. I wonder if it could take me back home or someplace more interesting than this swamp.

The phone starts ringing again, and the sound makes me jump.

"Can you answer that, Shelby Jayne?" I hear Mirage call from the front room.

My stomach skitters as I run back to pick up the receiver and say hello.

"Shelby, is that you?"

36

My breath goes out in a whoosh. It's Grandmother Phoebe.

"Darling girl, I just wanted to see if you were settling in down there."

"Yes, I'm fine." Not really, but I probably shouldn't complain to my grandmother. She doesn't hold with whining.

"We will have to make the best of it, all of us. Unfortunately," she adds.

I don't want to think about making the best of it, so I ask, "How's your hospital room?"

"Adequate. The food is terrible. I think I'm living in a cafeteria."

"Are you scared about the surgery?"

"Surgery is a necessary evil, I guess. I do want my hips back in working order so I'll do what the doctors tell me and live with the consequences." She pauses, and then says, "I suppose we both have to live with less-than-pleasing consequences. I'm sorry you have to be there, Shelby darling. You used to have this fantasy where everything worked out again between your parents, but it's time to stop living with make-believe and face reality — and the reality of who your mother really is."

I take a gulp as my throat burns and tears spring to my eyes. "Why?" I whisper, stubbing my toe into the rug as I clench the phone.

Grandmother Phoebe sniffs. "Under the circumstances, I think this past year our family is working out for the best. Chin up, now. This little setback of your living with Mirage is just temporary."

"Okay," I tell her, and nod my head even though she can't see me.

My grandmother harrumphs. "I'm afraid I didn't hear you correctly, Shelby."

My face burns. "I meant, yes. Yes, ma'am."

After we say our good-byes I hang up the telephone for the second time and go back to my room, throwing myself across the bed. The bedroom is shabby and musty and the floor slants at an angle, almost like it's running downhill. Feels like this house will break into pieces during the next bad storm.

Our house in New Iberia may be old, too, but at least it's been kept up and Grandmother Phoebe makes me dust and vacuum every week.

I lie on the bed wishing I'd run away to LizAnn's house. She and I should have planned my getaway before I got dragged here.

I hear a noise come from the kitchen, which makes me curious to see what's going on out there. This might be a good chance to see Mirage in action.

I take off my shoes so I won't make any noise, then flatten myself against the wall as I tiptoe down the hall and peer around the corner.

A black umbrella lies drip-drying in the sink while a young woman wearing damp jeans and a wet hooded sweatshirt sits at the table. She's biting her fingernails while a small boy perches in her lap. He looks about three or four years old and he's wiggling like he's got ants in his pants and whimpering.

Mirage is arranging bottles of various ointments on the table. A carved wooden box sits next to the pile of medicine bottles. There's also a crusty-looking book with rough-edged pages and stuff spilling out of it, leaves and pieces of string and jotted notes on scraps of paper. The binding is cracked and ready to fall apart. Like a witch's book of spells.

The boy's got a hundred red spots all over his face and arms and he's scratching something fierce. I'm pretty sure it's the chicken pox.

Mirage rubs her hands over his hair, murmuring soothing noises.

"I'm sorry to disturb you, ma'am, Miz Mirage," the woman says. Her face is pale, and there are dark smudges under her eyes like her mascara dripped from the rain on the boat ride over. "Don't got no money for a doctor."

"You come on any time," Mirage tells her. "I'm most always here."

Then she goes quiet as she bends over the little boy, making a circling motion around all those angry red spots. One by one, Mirage circles each red blister, murmuring the whole time in French. Then she lays her hands on his head, closes her eyes, and says a prayer, in French. I have to admit, Mirage's French words are so beautiful, it almost sounds magical.

After she's done praying, she picks up one of the bottles of pinkish liquid. "Now put this ointment on before bedtime and I promise you he'll be feelin' better by mornin'."

"Oh, Miz Mirage, you are so good," the boy's mamma tells her, rising from her chair. "What would we do without you? His itchin' and scratchin' get so bad, they start to bleed. Didn't get no sleep last night at all."

I start remembering the stories I'd heard at school about *traiteurs*. They could cure warts and rashes and sunburns. Sometimes they could pray a fever right out of your body. But sometimes all you got was smelly medicine to drink.

Now I wonder if all those stories are actually true. Did Mirage do that circling with her finger and praying when I had chicken pox? I think I was only three years old, too, so I don't remember.

It's a good thing I'm healthy now and don't need no heal-ing. Grandmother Phoebe doesn't put any store in all that "mumbo-jumbo," as she calls it. She's much too prim and proper. A regular Garden Club lady, getting her hair washed and set every Friday morning like clockwork.

My grandmother's words bounce around my brain like popcorn on a hot skillet. How in the world did Grandmother Phoebe and Mirage ever live together for all those years? They are total opposites. Like Hot and Cold. Salty and Sweet. Pickles and Candy.

Safe and Mysterious.

CHAPTER FOUR

WHEN THE CHICKEN POX BOY AND HIS MAMMA GET UP to leave, I run back to my room and lock the door, balancing on the edge of the fraying quilt. The blanket is made up of patches of material with faded azaleas and hyacinth, stripes and circles, stitched together probably a hundred years ago.

I grip the edge of the mattress and stare under the dark recesses of the bed again to double-check. There's those same clumps of dusty crud, but at least no spiders or cockroaches scuttling around. I have a lamp, but the bulb is so dim, the room feels not only old and shabby but spooky, too. I'd never admit that to anyone but LizAnn, though.

LizAnn's mamma is the kind of mother that pulls warm

cookies out of the oven after school and lets us play hide-and-seek in the house on rainy days. Mirage was always at class or studying — or avoiding Grandmother Phoebe.

A scratching noise slashes across the window and I jump two feet in the air, my heart grabbing at my throat. Quickly, I shut off the light and sneak up to the glass panes so I can see better. Mirage doesn't have neighbors. I hope it's just a branch from the cypress squirreling too close.

An orange haze glows above the cypress as the sun sets. I can still make out the giant blue bottle tree standing in the center of the yard, all those hundreds of bottles quivering on their branches.

Jerking the curtains shut, homesickness jabs me right in the heart. I wish I could shut my eyes and wake up in my own bed in my own room. I miss the bright lamps and my glossy white bedroom furniture with gold trim. I miss the gardens and I'll miss getting it ready this year with my grandmother for the Spring Show. I even miss Grandmother Phoebe making me practice the piano, but that only lasts about five minutes.

Digging into my box of stuff, I try to find the book LizAnn gave me for my birthday. We always shop at Books Along the Teche, searching for the funny parts, the romantic parts, giggling like we're off our rockers. When I find the shiny book that smells like new paper and glue, I press it tight against my chest.

Missing LizAnn is the worst. I think the lump in my throat is going to burst into a hundred pieces.

Setting the volume on the bed, I peek out the bedroom door. Silence fills the hallway. Taking quick, careful steps, I glance into the kitchen. Empty. The front room is empty, too. Don't know where Mirage went to. Guess her bedroom. I grab the phone again, cursing the long cord that twists around my legs as I scramble back to my bedroom.

After I dial LizAnn's phone number, I listen as it rings four times. Finally, she picks up and my breath goes out in a whoosh. "LizAnn, that you?"

"Shelby!" She sounds excited. "Where you callin' from?"

It's so good to hear her voice, I feel weepy. Feels like weeks instead of just a day since we said good-bye.

"I'm out in this dumb swamp."

"With your mamma?"

"Yeah."

"Is it weird?"

"I can't even begin to tell you all the strange things out here. Like she has a pet owl."

"A real live owl?" LizAnn sounds much too interested. "Does she let you hold it?"

"No!" Leave it to LizAnn to get excited about a wild animal. "It's got a broken wing. And she's got cats with funny names."

"So does half my neighborhood."

"Well, she's got a gigantic blue bottle tree, too. Takes up practically the whole yard."

"Oh, I like those bottle trees. My aunt in Mississippi has one. She makes it 'grow' every summer by adding branches and bottles she finds in the trash. Think I could come see your mamma's tree sometime?"

"You mean Mirage? But you'd be coming to see me, right?"

"You silly, of course. The bottle tree would just be a nice extra."

I keep trying to impress her with Mirage's weird way of dressing and her broken-down house and bizarre pets and going to school in a boat, but LizAnn just takes it all in stride. Maybe Mirage should have been *her* mamma.

When LizAnn has to go do the dishes, I hang up the phone feeling more depressed than ever. I'm stuck. And nobody seems to care how terrible it is.

I want to get out of this room, but it's coming down crawfish and lobsters again, rain smacking against the window so hard I wonder if it'll crack the glass. If I ran outside, I'd probably end up with pneumonia and Mirage would pin me down to do a healing on me.

I wonder if this little island inlet will get so soggy it'll float down the swamp while I'm sleeping and nobody will ever be able to find us again. Especially my daddy.

Finally, I start unpacking, putting socks and underwear in the empty dresser drawers, my brush and comb and mirror on top of the doily sitting on the bureau like I'm at a little old lady's house. Maybe the doily belonged to my *grand-mère*.

I zip open my backpack of school supplies just as a screeching "Mreowww!" yelps behind me. Papers and notebooks spill out, pencils rolling into the corners, my ruler, calculator, and pack of brand-new colored pencils tipping over one another.

Miss Silla Wheezy and Mister Possum Boudreaux go flying around the bedroom like wild things, then race into the hall, slipping on the loose carpet runner. Miss Silla Wheezy darts back inside for safety, stopping dead at my feet. Her white fur seems to light up the room.

"What're you doin', little Miss Silla Wheezy?" I say, scooping her up in my arms. When I scratch behind her ears, she begins to purr, sounding just like a jet engine. "Do you want to help me unpack?" I ask, trying not to agonize over Daddy flying across the Atlantic Ocean, and Grandmother Phoebe in the hospital waiting for surgery. I have no idea what Mirage is doing right now. Talking to that owl, Mister Lenny? Conjuring up a spell from her magic book?

The anger crawling up and down my neck won't go away. Nobody will listen to what I want, or where I want to live. It's more than wrong; it's downright unjust!

Glancing around the bedroom, an idea begins to form in my mind. I set down Miss Silla Wheezy, who slinks off to the corner to wash her paws, and dig underneath my stack of shirts, pulling out several pairs of socks. I lay four socks on the lampshade so they dangle down, throw the rest across the bed, and then pull out the bureau drawers, draping T-shirts over the edges.

I stare at the spilled papers and pencils and notebooks on the floor, and then leave them right where they are.

I'd never dare make a mess at home. Grandmother Phoebe would give me a dressing down. I wonder what Mirage will say. I'm hoping it'll bug her to pieces. Show her how mad I am and what I think of her weird old house.

My gaze settles on the mahogany wardrobe standing in the corner like a haughty queen. The pretty swirls in the wood are like eyes watching me, and the burnished gold handle is beautiful.

As soon as I reach for the latch, I can't help thinking about witches and lions, even if there is a solid back wall to the wardrobe.

I count to three, fling open the doors, but there's absolutely nothing inside. Just a row of bent wire hangers. No fur coats pressed together, no piles of pointy black umbrellas. Just dust.

I was hoping for wondrous, exotic things, but I'm more relieved there aren't spiders creeping in the corners or a loose snake slithering along the rod.

A set of small drawers with matching gold knobs sit in rows along the bottom of the wardrobe.

I can smell something sharp and musty, like mothballs and old socks. Yuck. Grandmother Phoebe has an old cedar hope chest from when she was a girl, and when she opens it, it stinks bad.

Kneeling on the floor, I pull out each of the cute little drawers, but they're all empty. Except the last one makes a jingly sound when I start to close it.

I pull the drawer all the way out, but it's shorter than I expect and the whole thing pops out and falls to the floor. The jingling object falls, too, and a glint of silver catches the lamplight.

It's jewelry, a bracelet. A silver double-looped bracelet with all sorts of dangling items hanging from the loops. It looks really old, the silver dark with age, although the charms are newer and cleaner.

Laying the bracelet across my jeans, I turn over each of the items for a closer look.

There's a single red-colored stone like a jewel, a Cajun French fleur-de-lis, a little owl, the cutest baby gator ever, and a little wooden box carved with tiny hyacinths painted purple. The box opens on two tiny brass hinges, although it's empty. It reminds me of Mirage's box in the kitchen. The one with her *traiteur* stuff in it. In the center of the charms hangs an oval-shaped locket. And there's a little blue bottle, too. Just like the bottles on the tree outside.

I finger each charm, wondering who they belong to. Putting the bracelet on top of the dresser, I keep looking at it while I pull on my nightgown.

Then I hear another noise and press my ear against the bedroom door. Mirage is talking to herself. Or Mister Lenny and Winifred.

Before I can turn off the lamp and pretend I'm asleep, there's a light tapping at the door.

Mirage stands there with Mister Lenny on her shoulder. He flutters his one good wing awkwardly, obviously not liking the bandage she put on the other wing and taped to his body.

"How long will his wing take to heal?" I ask.

49

"Couple a weeks." She strokes his head and then looks at me. "Thought I'd say good night, Shelby. I can help you unpack, too."

"Already did."

She glances inside the bedroom, at the clothes hanging everywhere, the mess of stuff on the floor, and looks at me sideways. "Don't remember you keepin' your bedroom like this before."

I shrug my shoulders and bite the inside of my cheek. "What's it matter? You haven't cared all year."

"I'm sure you're missin' your daddy and your home," she says in a quiet, solemn voice, but I can't tell if she's mad or sad.

Something starts stinging at my eyes like little needles.

Mirage clears her throat and goes on. "You remember comin' out here when you were real little? We'd collect moss and make dolls, take walks, feed the birds, all kind a stuff like that."

I shake my head and wince at the place inside my mouth that always hurts. I'm sure she's talking about a different girl altogether.

"Can't believe you're eleven today and goin' on twelve now. There's times I feel like I've lost you." She turns away, but not before I see her eyes filling up, like I'm supposed to feel sorry for her.

She steps over the school papers and brushes aside the curtains, looking out the window. It's almost pitch-black now. "Used to be a swing in that big, old oak tree there on the edge of the property. You wanted me to push you for hours. My arms would wear out from all that pushin' and swingin' and runnin' 'round the yard. Later, we'd end up napping in the rocking chair. You were my beautiful baby, Shelby Jayne."

Silence fills the corners. I wish she'd leave so I can go to bed and forget about where I am.

"Jest give me a chance, Shelby. We gotta lot a history the past year, you and me. But I want you in my life real bad."

I rub my hands against my nightgown and stare at the floor, then glance up at the charm bracelet sitting on top of the dresser. Wish I'd hidden it in one of the drawers until I'd had a chance to look at it closer.

"You brush your teeth?" she says, making her voice cheerful like my daddy on the phone.

"Yeah," I lie, biting my cheek again and tasting blood.

Mirage looks up and sees the light catch the charm bracelet. "You found it!" Going over to the dresser, she runs a finger along each charm real slow, studying it.

"It was in one of the drawers in the wardrobe. Are you mad I got it out?"

"Mad?" I watch her swallow and glance around the room. "'Course not, *shar.*"

"Looks old."

"It is that. The silver bracelet belonged to Grand-mère on my side a the family. Think it's from one of our ancestors going back to the Civil War. It's tarnished, ain't it? My mamma gave it to me when I was twelve and — and I started putting charms on it. It's a very special charm bracelet, and charms can be powerful objects."

"You mean like that *traiteur* stuff you do? I don't remember you doing any of that healing stuff back home."

"I didn't really. Didn't talk about it much in Grandmother Phoebe's city-folk neighborhood. Her people go to doctors, not *traiteurs.* Plus I was still learnin' 'bout it from your *grand-mère*, slowly, little bit at a time. Past year she taught me all she could before she died. Good thing, too," she adds. "My mamma couldn't speak hardly at all the last month."

Right then, thunder rumbles overhead, making me jump. I wonder if the wind or the rain ever breaks those blue bottles outside on that tree.

"This here bracelet don't have nothin' to do with being a healer. The bracelet is powerful and special because each charm has a unique meaning. Charms tell a story. Almost like memories comin' to life. The bracelet tells me who my family is, and where I come from."

"How'd one of your old-time ancestors get such a pretty silver bracelet so long ago if they lived out here so poor and didn't have much money?"

"It was a gift from my great-great-great-grandmother's owners. The Mistress, they used to call her. Mistress of the plantation. Give it to her when she was freed when the war was over. The mistress probably thought my grandmother would sell it to help her get somewhere in life or move away, somethin' like that, but she never did. Knew this bracelet was worth more than just money, that it could be a family heir-loom, somethin' very special to give to her daughters to come down through the years. Passed it along the generations ever since."

I stare at her, my stomach jumping around with a queer flopping. "You mean my great-great-great-great-grandmother was a slave?"

Mirage nods, gazing right back into my eyes.

I break off the stare and chew on my cheek. That explains her black, curly hair, I guess. And mine. "So what happened to her?"

"Married a Cajun fisherman and they lived out here somewheres."

"Right here?"

"Not in this house, it wasn't built yet, but somewheres in a little shack probably, crawfishin', living off the land, hunting squirrels and possum."

That was a life I could hardly imagine living, so far from town, no roads, probably not even a horse. Just boats. And nets. And fish.

"You see why this bracelet is special and powerful? Lots of generations and memories tied into it, so many mammas and daughters putting their own special charms on it. My mamma took off her charms when she gave it to me and kept them in her *traiteur* box."

"Where's her box now she's died?"

"Packed away. Stuff I'll keep until I pass it on to you someday when you're a whole lot older."

"I guess that bracelet might be worth a lot since it's so old, but how can the charms make it *powerful*?" That seemed silly to me.

"The charms represent memories, and they're tied to special people and special reasons —" She stops and I glance up. Her eyes are suddenly rimmed in red and she wipes her nose.

I shift on my bare feet and hope she doesn't start crying for real.

Mirage takes a breath. "Giving a gift or a charm to some-one is about both people — the one giving the gift and the one receiving it. A gift is powerful because of the hearts of the giver and the receiver."

"You mean like if they give it with good intentions, it could help you?"

Mirage runs her fingers along the silver, making the charms tinkle together. "Good gifts are given with love; just remember that, Shelby Jayne." She stretches the bracelet out, watching all the little charms sway on its chain. "When you're twelve I'll officially give it to you and it will belong only to you. For now, you can keep it here in your room, but make sure it's safe. Next year I'll take off my charms, put them away for safekeeping. Maybe you'll receive some spe-cial charms of your own one day to put on it."

My stomach jumps as she steps toward me. Haven't been this close to her in so long. I can smell a hundred different scents on her skin, along the strands of her black hair: that owl, chicken pox medicine, burnt roux, along with sham-poo and a faint perfume. Memories come at me like a tidal wave. I remember her digging with a spade in the dirt in Grandmother Phoebe's garden, shelling pecans at the kitchen table, frying catfish for dinner, staring into space with a text-book in her lap.

I remember all those times Mirage was quiet. Not saying nothing. Like she was sad a lot of the time and couldn't stop herself from being sad.

Now she wraps the bracelet around my wrist and snaps the clasp in place.

"It fits perfectly, Shelby," Mirage says softly, stepping back again.

I drop my eyes, pretending to look at the bracelet real hard. I don't say it, but I love the feel of the silver charms tickling my skin.

"That red teardrop charm," she says, pointing it out. "That's a ruby for July, my birthstone. But it's your birth-stone, too."

I know our birthdays are only three weeks apart, but I don't say nothing. Three weeks ago, I didn't even call her to wish her a happy birthday, but she doesn't say anything about it. Daddy was upset with me that I wouldn't acknowledge it, but I remember that night — it was the night he told me about the plans for me living out here in the swamp with Mirage for six months. I was so mad I'd stomped upstairs and didn't even come down for supper.

Now I clear my throat. "The red is so dark it looks almost like blood, but it's real sparkly, too."

"Ruby stones are beautiful. And it's kinda like blood

kinship for you and me, eh? When I turned twenty years old I got the best birthday present of my whole life — *you*."

I just keep staring at the charm bracelet so I won't have to look into her eyes.

"The charm bracelet will be yours next year on July thirty-first when you turn twelve. Kind of unexpected you finding it, but I guess not too surprising. This room used to be mine when I was a girl."

I feel sort of shivery thinking about her growing up here, and wonder if she ever used to think the wardrobe was spooky, or hide inside pretending it opened up into Narnia. But I'm not gonna ask.

"I do got somethin' special for your eleventh birthday today. Be right back."

She goes to the kitchen and returns almost instantly with a cake on a foil-covered piece of cardboard. A castle cake with a moat and a drawbridge and turrets made of gold candies. "It's never too late for a castle cake, is it?" she asks.

I chew on my cheek and shrug. "I don't know."

"It's chocolate inside, your favorite. I made it myself. Almost forgot to clean your room I was so busy getting it done in time." She pauses. "I know the cake is a year late. But I hope it's not too late for us, *shar*."

I get this strange yearning to throw myself into her arms and start bawling like a baby, but I don't. I hold myself real still and think about all the things she missed because she left and only cared about herself and not me. Not only my birthday, but the story I wrote that got voted best in the class, the Christmas Choir Program where I got to sing two lines all by myself, LizAnn's new baby sister. All kinds a things. Things I'm not going to tell her. Because she doesn't deserve to know.

"Don't eat it all at once," she says, trying to smile at me as she backs out the door and shuts it behind her.

I let out my breath, and it suddenly feels like I've been holding it the whole time she was here.

I stare at the cake and it's pretty, just like a bakery could make. White frosting is spread on the ground around the castle walls like snow and there's a walkway made of sparkly glitter and red hearts framing the double castle doors made of chocolate candy bar pieces.

I set the cake on top of the bureau and just stare at it. Lick a dab of the frosting with my finger. Wish Daddy were here to share it with me. I want to eat some right now because I love chocolate and it looks delicious, but I don't want to spoil the architecture.

I can't figure Mirage out. Is the cake a peace offering or is she just trying to get rid of her guilt for everything she's done? A cake won't take away any of the last year. Not by a long shot.

Kneeling down to replace the drawer from the wardrobe, I see that the back panel of the drawer broke off and has fallen into the empty space underneath.

I tilt the lampshade up so the bulb shines better into the black hole and see something else — something that dropped to the bottom of the wardrobe.

Reaching in with my hand, I pull out a key, an old-fashioned brass skeleton key. It's small, just like a charm, and a little bit faded and rusty. With a silver loop at the end exactly like the loops on the charm bracelet.

Taking the bracelet off my wrist, I finally find a spot where there's an empty silver loop, half open. I slip the key through the loop, then close it up tight so it won't fall off again.

A key. I wonder if it's just a charm — or if it actually opens a lock.

I try the key in the wardrobe but it doesn't fit. I try my bedroom door, but it doesn't fit there, either. There aren't any keyholes in the nightstand or the bureau. No jewelry boxes or latches or padlocks that I can see.

Setting the bracelet on the dresser, I put the drawer back together best I can, then crawl into bed and flop my head down. Grandmother Phoebe told me to bring my own pillow and I'm glad I listened to her.

The rain drums against the roof and I jump up again to retrieve the bracelet from the bureau. The charms slip around my wrist, tickling my palm. A flash of lightning illuminates the ruby-red birthstone against my pillow's white slipcase and the stone seems to glow like fire.

My fingers dart out from under the sheet and I reach for the note from the blue bottle. I unfold it and look at the words in the dark.

Don't forget! Tonight's the Night!
Come to the bridge — and hurry!

It's a message to someone. But who? And what bridge is the note talking about?

A funny tingle crawls up my legs.

A sense of ancient history seems to float on the night air. The bedroom grows stuffy so I jump out of bed to crack open the window.

I can't believe my eyes when I see the figure of a girl move out from behind the blue bottle tree. She's wearing shorts and a blouse and she's barefoot.

A moment later, she starts dancing under the silvery half moon, whirling in circles, leaping around the yard.

Who is that?

When I press my nose against the glass the girl stops dancing and looks straight up at me. I freeze, not daring to breathe. We stare at each other and then she disappears behind the trunk again.

The mysterious shadowy girl looked at me, saw me. *Watched me!*

I can hardly gulp down a decent breath, but I have the crazy notion to run right out the back door in my nightgown.

There's a girl out there, and I get the strangest feeling that she's waiting for me.

CHAPTER FIVE

A SPLIT SECOND LATER, QUIET AS I CAN, I'M RUNNING DOWN the hall, slipping through the kitchen and down the porch steps. My feet sink into the soft, wet grass, mud sticking to my toes. At least it's not raining any longer.

Ducking under the bottom branches of the blue bottles, I peek around the tree trunk and my breath rushes out like a gust of wind. The yard is empty.

The shadows of hundreds of cypresses circling the house seem to watch me. A breeze lifts the dripping moss and I watch it float in the air like invisible hands are running their fingers through it.

Had I fallen asleep and dreamed the girl? Was it only a trick of the moonlight and the bottle tree? No, I'd swear I saw her. But where'd she go?

Shivers of excitement run up and down my neck, and rain-drops keep plinking down from the blue bottle tree onto my head. I run fast as I can back to the safety of the kitchen, the sound of the bottles clinking together like they're talking to one another behind me.

When I jump back in bed, I wrap the hem of my night-gown around my damp toes, thinking about the girl, the note, the charm bracelet, and lie wide awake for hours.

The next morning I huddle on the bank and wrap my arms around myself while Mirage bails three inches of rainwater from the bottom of her boat. Mist rises from the surface of the bayou. Rain drops from the cypresses and oaks, plopping on the metal boat, the elephant ears, and the metal roof of the swamp house.

My stomach clenches and the grits I ate settle in my gut like concrete. The fog is eerie, and it feels like the real world is a million miles away.

"Is the boat going to sink?" I ask.

"We'll be jest fine. Long as no gators got lost after that rain last night and ended up in my cove."

"Gators? We're going to be followed by alligators? Do you have a gun? Grandmother Phoebe says you shouldn't live in the swamp without a gun."

Mirage glances up at me, her hair hanging wildly in her

eyes. "Jest teasin', Shelby Jayne. Actually, me and alligators have a Mutual Admiration Society out here. We admire each other and stay as far away as possible. Only critter you might see is Harvey."

"Who's Harvey?"

"Well, looka there! He's speeding past right now."

I watch an animal, sort of like a big beaver, beelining through the water, ducking under a spread of hyacinth, and then popping back up again. "That's Harvey?"

"Yep. He's a nutria and he knows his name, too. Looks up when I call to him. Nutria are pretty smart."

"You're not going to call him over here, are you?"

"Nope, not today. Now jump in and grab that oar."

I can't believe we're going to town in a boat. I know there's no road out here, just water, but still. It's the principle of the thing.

"Is anybody going to see us when we get there? To town, I mean."

Last night she was barefoot, but today she's wearing home-made socks inside a pair of hiking boots and a crazy-colored skirt with a man's windbreaker to keep off the rain.

"You look like a swamp witch wearing those clothes."

She purses her lips and gives me one of those pinched mother looks, like Grandmother Phoebe does when I don't hurry fast enough or comb my hair for dinner.

"Thought we'd gotten that whole swamp witch thing outta the way last night. I may live in the swamp," Mirage says quietly, "but that don't mean I'm uneducated, Miss Smarty-Pants." Her face is red as she gets busy untying the rope around the dock piling while I gnaw on my cheek.

Folding my arms across my chest, I look down at the boat.

I look at the water.

I don't look at her.

Mirage leans over to pick up the oars, not looking at me, either. "Jump on in," she finally says.

I sloooowly count to five, then put one foot inside the wobbly boat and perch on the damp seat, then the other foot, trying not to tip the boat and fall into the murky water. Everything's wet and muggy, and the moisture seeps through my jeans in ten seconds flat, making me feel all sticky.

Mirage pushes off from the dock and pulls her paddle through the flat brown water.

I glance behind to see which side she wants me to paddle and find that Mirage is staring right at me. Her dark eyes hold mine, but she doesn't say anything. A breeze moves through her long hair like invisible wings.

I turn around, pulling my windbreaker closer, then touch the folded note deep inside my pocket. The blue bottle note was real, not a dream. Was the girl from last night real, too?

Where did she live? Why didn't she stay and talk to me? Why'd she run away? She must have had a boat. A boat I couldn't see on the other side of the cove.

Mirage's boat cuts through the water with a slurping noise. Herons and egrets rise from the rushes. Wind tickles the hanging Spanish moss and breathes down my neck. Seems like there's not a soul in sight for a hundred miles.

Finally, I dip my own oar into the bottomless water. "You ever get lonely out here?"

When Mirage doesn't answer, I sneak a peek over my shoulder.

She gives me a shaky smile. "I'm only lonely for you, *bébé*."

"Don't seem like it to me," I mutter, still feeling hurt over her calling me a smarty-pants. I'm not the one who moved away and stayed away. I never left. I'd stayed right at home where we'd always been.

"It's true, Shelby Jayne," she goes on softly, almost cautiously. "I miss you terribly. I know you don't believe me. You got a lotta stuff in your head. Stuffed in there by other people. Maybe some of it's true, but some of it ain't. I did some stupid things. Like staying away for your grandmother Phoebe's sake. It was easier for her if I wasn't around — easier for me, too — but that don't excuse the fact that I got chicken and didn't come visit you enough or send for you after your *grand-mère* passed."

My face flushes and I squirm when she says that. I don't want her talking pretty about her feelings for me. I don't want to believe her. And I don't want her to be right, either — about Grandmother Phoebe, whom I love, but who does have a hankering for gossip.

My ears burn thinking about all the things Grandmother Phoebe has said since Mirage left. Her voice keeps filling my head fatter and fatter, so I think about the mysterious folded note instead and the words written on the lined paper:

Don't forget! Tonight's the Night! Come to the bridge — and hurry!

Mirage said people put blue bottle trees in their yard to keep away bad spirits. Was one of those evil spirits trying to lure me into the swamp?

I'm sitting in a canoe in the middle of the bayou, too far from shore, and I start sweating. Maybe those blue bottles were actually working! The note had been inside the bottle, trapped, but I'd let it loose by taking it out. Had I let out an honest-to-goodness haunt or ghoul or imp?

What would that evil phantom do — tip the boat over and dump us into the water? I just *know* there's gators roaming right underneath us, crawfish snapping their claws, nutria, and all kind of fish I can't even see.

My brain starts running wild as I keep rowing in the prow while Mirage steers. Feels like all the rowing will never end, but I'm eager to get somewhere safe — and the faster the better. I start counting how many times I pull that oar through the water and lose track after a hundred. My muscles ache something fierce and the burning makes me want to cry, but I suck it down.

By the time I finally see the edge of town I can hardly lift my arms they're trembling so bad. All kind a houses are set back inside groves of oaks and cypress. The streets are lined with older buildings and storefronts, Ozaire's Laundromat and the post office and Sweet Ellen's Bakery.

Mirage ties up at one of the city piers on the edge of the bayou. I crawl up the elephant ears and try to catch my breath.

Mirage stares down the main streets of town, not saying a word. Finally, she says, "Head on this way, Shelby Jayne." She tramps up Main in her boots, turning a couple of corners until a weather-beaten three-story frame house comes into view.

A wide, cluttered porch runs the length of the house. Nailed across the front hangs a board that had once been painted white. The name BAYOU BRIDGE ANTIQUES is cut into the sign, the letters edged in archaic, flaky paint.

"Let's find us some Christmas lights," Mirage says as we climb up the wooden steps.

"But it's August!"

She either doesn't hear me or ignores me.

Two floors and an attic bulge with old furniture, tools, and clothing. The place smells musty with a moist, earthy scent. A few people browse racks of baby clothes and dig through boxes of outdated *Life* and *National Geographic* magazines.

A man in overalls sits in a rocking chair in one corner smoking a pipe, with a baseball cap stuck on his head. I figure he must be the store owner from the way his hawk eyes watch the customers.

A woman with plain black clips holding back her flyaway hair stands behind a counter ringing up a sale on an old-fashioned cash register.

Never seen a place like this before in my life. The antique stores Grandmother Phoebe goes to have fancy, polished furniture and paintings in gold frames and statues and figurines.

I wander down the cramped aisles, past wooden barrels and ancient farm equipment. There's even one of those monstrous sugar pots they used to use on plantations in the olden days to cook the cane syrup.

I leave Mirage digging through some old chests for

secondhand women's clothing and climb to the second story. When I reach the landing, there's a set of open suitcases, filled with dirt — a garden of wildflowers planted right into the dirt.

Grandmother Phoebe would probably laugh and roll her eyes, but I think the garden suitcases are pretty, like nothing I've ever seen before. I can imagine Mirage doing something like this. I wonder if she'd let me dig up some of her flowers to put into a suitcase. Then I wonder what's wrong with me. I'd never plant flowers in a suitcase at home!

I skirt around some antique furniture, a bin full of old bedding, and a bookcase stuffed with ancient paperbacks, their covers dusty and ripped.

Behind a massive cherrywood wardrobe, I stop walking and just stare and stare and stare.

A glass case has been pushed into the corner, almost forgotten, and it's overflowing with dolls: rows of chubby baby dolls, rag dolls, antique porcelain dolls, and old stiff-legged Barbie dolls.

In the center of the case, a little apart from the rest of the dolls, sits the most exquisite porcelain doll I've ever seen. She's got perfect features in a heart-shaped face and big blue eyes with super-long black eyelashes.

I get on my knees to look closer, amazed at how beautiful she is in her rose-colored lace dress and a feathered hat tied under one ear with pink ribbon.

She's got a tiny chip on her chin, but otherwise the doll is in perfect condition. A piece of cardboard sitting in her lap states that she's about one hundred years old and not for sale. How could they have a doll sitting in a case and not let anyone buy her?

I crouch on the floor, my nose almost touching the glass.

For one crazy second, the doll's crystal-blue eyes seem to look right into mine. A funny tickling runs up and down my arms and I glance around, wondering if someone is watching me.

Finally, I tear my eyes away and go look for Mirage. It's hard not to get lost as I end up winding my way through heaps of stacked chairs and tables, and bumping into a blackened woodstove just like the one Mirage has in her kitchen.

I find her next to an oval-shaped bathtub with huge claw feet, an inch of dirt and dead bugs covering the bottom. Then Mirage holds up a box of white and blue Christmas lights like she's just won the jackpot. Her hair is messy and there's dirt on her face.

I gnaw on my cheek and try not to tell her how crazy she looks.

"Since I was a girl I been wanting to hang real lights in my blue bottle tree. They're solar lights, too. The sun'll heat 'em up all day and then, after dark, they'll make a spectacular show for us while we eat our supper on the porch."

"Oh," I say slowly. "I get it now. I guess that could be okay."

"Don't be a stick-in-the-mud, Shelby Jayne."

"I ain't a stick-in-the-mud!" I protest, and then stop, Grandmother Phoebe's voice ringing out rules of grammar in my head. "I mean, I'm *not* a stick-in-the-mud."

Mirage murmurs, "Well, I'm doin' my best to move past the pain. Look to the future, so to speak. Do something I always planned to do with — well, never you mind. I'm probably not makin' much sense."

"You mean Grand-mère? Before she died?"

She gives a little shake of her shoulders like a devilish imp is creeping up her neck right then and there. "Somethin' like that."

"Where's she buried?" I ask, wondering if it was okay to ask or if she'd get mad at me talking about it.

"Bayou Bridge Cemetery."

I swallow hard and slowly edge the question out of my mouth. "What'd she die of that was so bad you had to leave me?"

Mirage flicks her eyes at me. "Cancer, Shelby. Spread through her whole body. Never seen somebody suffer so much in all my life. Had to bathe her, carry her from room to room, her body just a bag of bones and skin, like a skeleton." She stops and looks around, lowers her voice. "Let's not talk about this here in public. But I hope you'll know why I had to come out here. My mamma was all alone, only had me in all the world."

"Grandmother Phoebe only has Daddy and me, too."

Mirage holds herself real still for a minute. "That's true. And I never begrudged Phoebe her son or her granddaughter in all these years, but sometimes enough is enough."

"Is that why you seem so mad?" Even as I say the words, I think about how, mostly, she seems sad and gloomy.

"I ain't mad, Shelby. I'm glad you're here, more than anything. But I am tired. Watching my mamma die, gettin' through the funeral. I'm exhausted and it's been hard being back here again. Too many memories . . . sad memories. And it's lonely out here, like I told you. Thinkin' 'bout selling the house, but don't know where I'd go."

"You mean you'd sell that swamp house?"

She eyes me. "Guess you'd like that, huh?"

I shrug like I don't care one way or the other, but she shakes her head like it's too much to think about.

After Mirage makes the purchase, she says, "Now that I have these lights, they'll probably jest sit in a box on my own back porch. Don't have the energy to put them up. Maybe you could."

"Me?" I have no idea why she'd buy them and then not put them up, but I'm too tired to ask. The rowing from earlier this morning hits me hard and all I want to do is sit down. Mirage doesn't make much sense most of the time and that just makes me feel mad all over again.

Then again, if I put up the lights, maybe I'd find more notes in the bottles.

I suffer through a few more errands, but Sweet Ellen's Bakery *beignets* sort of make up for my suffering as I lick the sugar off my fingers when we pull up at our own dock again. The sun is finally out, blue sky breaking through the clouds.

I jump out, and the boat teeters dangerously as I hit the bank.

"Tie up the line please, Shelby," Mirage calls.

Quickly, I tug at the rope, jerk it around the piling bobbing up and down in the water, then run around the side of the house, past the rickety porch and the woodpile, scaring Miss Silla Wheezy and Mister Possum Boudreaux out of their afternoon naps. They stretch and yawn and arch their backs, then settle back down, eyes half closed, watching me.

I stop running when I get underneath the blue bottle tree. I just have to be alone for a little while. I'm tired of answering Mirage's mother-y questions.

Nothing's gonna help. I think it's too late. I lost my real mamma a year ago. I used to have a mamma that went to college classes and wore her hair in a ponytail with butterfly clips. She used to fix fried chicken and mashed potatoes for dinner on the nights Grandmother Phoebe was gone to City Council meetings, then got her homework done in front of the television while I did mine.

She's not the same person I used to know at all. Now her hair is loose and wild, she has animals for pets in the house, and heals people like a swamp witch — even if she calls herself a fancy name like *traiteur*.

Tears start coming on and I wipe them away with the back of my hand. Then my nose starts running and I rub my face with my sleeve. I'm not going to cry over her. If she didn't want me back a year ago then she can't change her mind now and make the whole year just disappear like it didn't happen.

Seems like the swamp stole her away. Made a new person called Miz Mirage Allemond. A healer who talks to God and owls and has dirty toes to boot.

A sob fills up the corners of my throat.

Then I hear her calling my name. I don't want her to see me crying so I pretend I'm deaf and press my forehead against the cypress trunk. Closing my eyes, I listen to the wind whistle across the open mouths of all those blue bottles above my head.

After a minute, I wipe my face and lean back. The bottles are dancing and swaying and the sun shines right through them, making them glow.

Some of the bottles have rainwater still inside, but three

branches over my head, there's a bottle with something besides rain lying in the bottom.

Something white and folded.

My heart hammers at my ribs and my breath catches like a frog leaped into my throat.

I glance around. No sign of Mirage. I guess she gave up — or is she spying on me from the kitchen window? Maybe she's ignoring me because I ignored her.

Turning, I look for something to stand on. Aha! I run to the porch and grab an old folding chair from a stack behind the old hot water heater standing in the corner. Then I run back to the tree. After I make sure the chair is steady, I scramble up and reach as high as I can to grasp the branch with the bottle.

Once the blue bottle slips off, the branch pops back like a whip, almost cracking the bottle next to it. I hold my breath waiting for a shatter of glass to rain down, but it doesn't break.

First I close one eye, peering into the bottle's mouth, then the other eye. Sure enough, there's a folded piece of paper inside.

It's harder to get out than the first, the paper slipping back down every time I think I've got my fingers pinched around it.

"Oh, heck!" I grumble as I try for the fiftieth time.

Tilting, tilting, tilting, the paper finally slips out at just the right angle and I hurriedly unfold it.

I'm breathing so hard with anticipation, I'm practically gasping.

I can't find you! Are you lost?

This time the handwriting is different.

CHAPTER SIX

Just the mere thought of a new school makes my stomach tilt and whirl.

Two weeks after I arrived, I stare at the muddy, cocoa-colored water and try not to throw up.

I wish school didn't start until September so I could just hang out under the blue bottle tree, play with Miss Silla Wheezy, and find all the secret notes inside the bottles. I hope there are more. I'm desperate to know who wrote them and what they mean.

Like secret notes passed back and forth in class.

Mirage spends most of the trip to town pointing out meadows of purple hyacinth, duckweed, and a flock of herons. I let out a tiny yelp when I see a gator watching us from the banks, but he doesn't move as we pass, even though my heart stops for about five minutes.

"Won't hurt you, *shar*," Mirage says in a calm voice. "He's more 'fraid of you than you are of him."

"Can we move more to the middle?" I ask, flapping my hands to get the boat to move away from the bank. Quick as I can, I pull down my long-sleeved blouse to hide the charm bracelet I snapped around my wrist before I left the house. I know I'm not supposed to wear it, but I can't bear to leave it at home. Long sleeves is hotter than heck, and I'm already sweating, but I don't want Mirage to know I'm wearing the bracelet.

"'Course, we can," Mirage says, then pulls her oar to move the boat deeper into the center of the bayou. The current ripples against the sides of the boat, and I make sure not to look at that big ole gator watching me like he wants to eat me up in one big gulp.

After we tie up at the town docks, I unclench my aching fingers. My palms have red, puffy blisters from gripping the paddle so hard and my arms feel ready to fall off my shoulders again. But I was ready to knock a gator in the head if he tried to take a bite out of the boat.

"Pick you up right here after school. There's a lunch in your pack, too."

My hair is wet and stringy as I hunch inside my jacket, the paddle high over my head. When I step out of the skiff, I'm grateful once again that I've made it to civilization. "Do I have to do this boating thing every day until Christmas break?"

"You'll survive," Mirage says as she steps off the swaying pier and ties the rope.

I feel sick. "You going with me to school?"

She grabs a pack from under the seat of the boat. "I gotta sign them registration papers. Your daddy gave me your shot records, stuff like that."

I freeze like a Popsicle when I see the line of yellow buses and the clusters of kids on the sidewalks. Wish so bad I could hide out in a washtub at Ozaire's Laundromat. Ducking behind a hedge of rain-speckled shrubbery, my heart thuds so hard I'd swear I swam the bayou to get here.

"Come on, Shelby Jayne. Might as well get it over with." Her lips are pressed tight and Mirage almost looks more scared than I am.

"What's wrong?" I ask, even though I don't want her thinking that I care all that much.

"Don't like comin' to this part of town much. Too many sad memories lingering around these parts."

"Like what? How can a town be sad?"

"Oh, there's the bell," she says, ignoring my question as the school bell sounds.

Students stream through the front doors. Within seconds, the school grounds are empty. The rain comes down harder, like punishment for being tardy.

The Bayou Bridge Elementary School is muggy, smelling of old barbecue sauce and rotting carrots, like someone forgot their lunch in their desk over the summer.

My jeans are soaked by the time I step inside the school office and a blast of moist, warm air hits my face.

The office is small and quiet, emphasizing the sound of my squeaky, wet shoes. I swipe a hand across my bangs and discover that the ends of my hair are dripping like melting icicles. I'm sure I look like a drowned nutria and I can feel the red stain of embarrassment creeping up my face.

A woman in a swivel chair uses her feet to wheel across the floor from a desk to the copy machine to retrieve the stapler. She rides that swivel chair all over the office.

She clicks her tongue sympathetically. "I'm sorry to say, but you look like someone dunked you in the bayou, honey. Did you miss the bus? You must be new because I know everybody here since before they were born."

"This here's my daughter," Mirage says, fidgeting with the zipper on her backpack. "Shelby Jayne Allemond."

"Nice to meet you, Shelby Jayne."

Real fast, I say, "Just Shelby."

She smiles and picks up a mug of steaming coffee and

skims the top with her lips. It reminds me of the way my daddy drinks his and I don't want to think about him so my eyes roam across her messy desk. Stacks of green files, papers and memos, a spilled box of paper clips, and a stapler she's in the process of refilling. A nameplate sits askew: MRS. FLORENCE BENOIT.

"Got her paperwork right here," Mirage says, handing the envelope across the desk.

Mrs. Benoit uses her heels to push her chair to a filing cabinet. "Go ahead and sit in those chairs while I see which class has space."

I sink into a chair next to Mirage, who frowns over the blank registration papers and gets out a pen.

A few student aides go in and out, running errands. A couple of other women dressed in pantsuits walk out of the principal's offices discussing something boring.

I close my eyes and pretend I'm not really here at Bayou Bridge Elementary School, but back home in my new class with LizAnn.

A few minutes later, Mirage hands over the paperwork and Mrs. Benoit's eyes dart across each line like a speed reader. "I plopped you into Mrs. Jenny Daigle's class. The students like her real well." She looks up at Mirage. "You forgot your address on this line, dear."

Mirage turns a little red. "I — I don't really have an address."

"Oh, dear," Mrs. Benoit says, and her face goes even redder than Mirage's.

"We ain't homeless," Mirage says quickly. "Jest don't live on a street. Bayou Teche swamp out near Cypress Cove instead."

Mrs. Florence Benoit sizes up my limp clothes and my straggly hair and I'm ready to run straight back to New Iberia — even if I have to use my own two feet to get there. I'd planned on starting sixth grade with LizAnn in Mrs. Bergernon's class this year.

I chew on my cheek and taste blood. My eyes get all watery so I stare at the wall until I can see straight again. Where's Grandmother Phoebe when I need her? I know she has to have surgery, but I wish so bad I wasn't in this dinky little town in this pathetic school in the middle of nowhere.

Mrs. Benoit says brightly, "I'll make you up a file right quick, Shelby Jayne, and request your records from New Iberia. Meanwhile, here's a map of the school — we only have two main halls, cafeteria here in the middle, and fields and track behind us. Mrs. Daigle's classroom is just a couple of turns away. You better scoot on over — and oh! If you get lost, come back here and I can get some students to escort you."

I see one of the women from the rear offices start to walk toward us, and Mirage quickly reaches a hand out to me but stops when I take a step back. In a low voice, she says, "See you this afternoon, Shelby Jayne. You'll be jest fine."

Mirage is out the door and gone before I can hardly turn around. After a year, she's perfected her talent at leaving. A mix of mad and sad tangles up inside my chest. I never knew homesickness was a real disease before. It's like a stick is stabbing at my heart, although I suppose a stick jabbing at your heart isn't a disease, more like a terminal condition.

The woman in the pantsuit stops in front of me. "New student?" she asks Mrs. Benoit.

"Mrs. Trahan, this is Shelby Jayne Allemond," the secretary says. "Daughter of Mirage Allemond."

The woman's eyebrows lift so high on her forehead, they're lost in a poof of teased curls and hairspray. She extends her hand for me to shake, which makes me feel like I'm here for a job interview. "I'm Maureen Trahan, the principal. So you're the *traiteur's* daughter."

I feel a little ping of surprise. "You know Mirage — I mean — my — ?"

Mrs. Trahan searches my face. "You look just like her. All

that dark curly hair and those big brown eyes. She and I went to high school together."

"Really?" All I can do is stare at her and blink. Mrs. Trahan seems normal. Mirage used to have normal people friends. 'Course, I knew that already. At least I knew that a year ago, but not anymore. Everything is so different, so strange now, Mirage most of all.

"It's a small town and everyone knows everybody else, Shelby. She's a wonderful *traiteur*. With your *grand-mère* passed on, we really need her. She's helped a lot of folks lately, 'specially the Mouton family down the bayou."

I'm so surprised I can't think straight.

After I leave the office and follow the map to my classroom, I wonder about the principal in her regular pantsuit and hair fixed real nice knowing Mirage and talking about her like she's any other normal town citizen.

I can't think about all that anymore because Mrs. Daigle's room looms in front of me.

I hate walking into a new class by myself.

I gear up my nerve and take lots of little breaths and right then the door swings open and almost smacks me in the face. A boy with a round face and streaked blond hair darts out. "Sorry!" he calls back at me as he runs down the hall.

I grab the door before it closes and every student looks up from their desk as I cross the threshold. My stomach cartwheels. Sweat breaks out on my palms.

Everyone stops working and I can hear a buzz of murmurs. The teacher, a woman with dyed red hair and glasses perched on the lower half of her nose, puts down her grade book and walks over to reach for my paperwork. "You're Shelby Allemond then?"

A fresh burst of whispers breaks out behind me and Mrs. Daigle cocks her head at the class. "You should be writing, class, not talking."

The room goes quiet as Mrs. Daigle retrieves a textbook from a metal cabinet and points to an empty chair in the middle of the room. "That will be your seat. We're writing our first essay. Something unusual you did over the summer. Write at least a page by the end of the hour. We'll share our stories tomorrow."

My sneakers keep squeaking as I make my way to my assigned desk. I cringe, slipping off my backpack where it thuds loudly to the floor.

No sooner have I taken out a notebook and a pencil than the boy who almost knocked me over whooshes back into the classroom like he's been sprinting the whole way. He grins around at everybody, then takes his seat in the far row.

The girl behind me taps me on the shoulder. Her breath is in my ear, and I see a flash of long brown hair and baby-blue eyes from the corner of my vision.

"That boy there is Jett Dupuis," she tells me.

"Oh."

"Jett's Bayou Bridge's school track star. He bumps into everybody, so don't take it personally. He can't do nothing slow. He's also the cutest boy in the whole sixth grade."

"That's nice." As if I'll be here long enough to care. "Where was he going?"

"Forgot his lunch and his mom brought it to the office. He probably burns a thousand calories a day with all that running so he eats constantly. I mean, *constantly*. You'll be amazed."

I can't help smiling at the way she talks but any second now Mrs. Daigle is going to yell at us.

The girl switches sides and attacks my other ear. I swear she's as good as a ventriloquist because her lips barely move. "Jest in case you get any ideas, Tara has already claimed him, so stay away."

Oh, so this was a warning message, I realize, and my stomach sinks just a little. "Who's Tara?"

"Only the prettiest girl in sixth grade. And the daughter of the president of Bayou Bridge Garden Club. And my best friend."

"Oh." I'm not sure what to say so I whisper, "Congratulations."

She snickers and taps me again. "Me, I'm Alyson."

"Twenty minutes," Mrs. Daigle says. "When you're finished, drop your essays in the basket and do silent reading for the remainder of the period."

"I gotta get started," I tell Alyson, not wanting her to quit talking to me because I like that someone has noticed me. Maybe this tiny little school won't be so bad if all the girls are this friendly.

"Um, Shelby. Take this." Alyson rummages in her pack and hands me a tissue. "You've got black drips under your eyes."

"What is it?" I hiss.

"Just a moldy leaf or something streaked down your cheek. Spit on that and wipe," she advises.

I rub at my face, feeling heat shoot up my neck, knowing everyone saw me walk in like that.

I do a quick glance across the room. Jett Dupuis isn't even out of breath. I catch a flicker of his smile toward a girl sitting across the classroom from me on the far row.

She gives him a slow smile, and then bends over her paper again. Silky dark hair spills like a waterfall over the edge of her desk. She looks like a girl in a shampoo commercial.

Jett taps his pencil as he stares off into space, his right knee shaking up and down a hundred miles an hour as if he's about to explode out of his chair.

The girl with the waterfall hair finishes writing, puts down her pencil, and rises from her chair. She places her essay in the basket on the teacher's desk and glides back to her seat.

My eyes zero in on the girl sitting behind Pantene Princess. Pantene Princess acts as if the girl, who isn't even a foot away, doesn't exist. Like she's invisible.

I can't help stealing a second look, shocked at the bad scar on the side of the invisible girl's face. Looks like she had a mess of stitches. Her cheek sort of sinks in right there, too. The girl frowns at her essay, then rubs her eraser across the page over and over again.

I turn sideways and whisper, "Who's that girl?"

"What girl?" Alyson asks.

"The one behind Pantene Princess."

Alyson giggles. "Pantene Princess! Oh, you mean Tara. That's pretty funny."

Alyson said Tara is the prettiest girl in sixth grade. I guess it's true because she is the prettiest girl I've ever seen in my life.

"So who's the girl behind Tara? She must have been in a terrible accident."

Alyson frowns at her paper. "Don't know. Just some girl."

"She's sitting right behind your own best friend!"

Alyson's eyes flick away as we head into social studies and Mrs. Daigle starts passing out books, enlisting the help of Jett and Tara. "Can't remember. She was new last year."

The next moment, Tara stands in front of me and drops a thick textbook on my desk. Her eyes are so green I swear she received a set of emeralds at birth.

"World studies. We're gonna be learning about Egypt and Rome and China." She's so cool and elegant. Like she's already grown-up or something.

"World History through the Ages," I say, reading the book's title.

Alyson turns around in her seat, jumping into the conversation. "This is Shelby, Tara. And, Shelby, this here is Tara, like I told you a minute ago."

"Where you from, Shelby?" Tara asks.

"New Iberia."

Her green eyes narrow at me, like she's already figured me out. "Thought you were some city girl. Why you here?"

I'm surprised at the way she says it, as though I'm not supposed to be here. As though she needs to give me permission first.

Tara gives her head a little shake. "I mean, where do you live?"

"Uh, sort of near the swamp."

"Near the swamp, huh? Near or in?"

A bell rings and my stomach gives a little jump. "What's that?"

"Morning recess," Alyson says, jumping up to get in the front of the line at the door.

Tara puts a hand on Alyson's arm. "When the end of recess bell rings, we gotta come right back to the classroom. You're bad about that and I don't want detention."

Alyson makes a funny face. "You've never had detention in your life, Tara Doucet."

"That's right. And I intend to keep it that way."

The class stampedes out the door and I slowly follow, wondering what I'll do during my first recess here. Don't know if they play games or have a jungle gym or tetherball or hopscotch.

I barely take two steps into the hallway when suddenly, standing right in front of me, is the scarred girl from my class. Goose bumps prickle along my arms. I wish I could stop staring at her face, but I can't. Her skin is red and crinkled around the scar. Looks awful, like it hurts bad.

"You should stay away from them," she tells me, her voice dropping. She moves closer and her arms are so skinny, I wonder if she's eaten in a week.

"What are you talking about?"

"You heard me."

Her hair is brown and thin and floats in a spray around her head. The sides are held down with a row of plain black clips. Which remind me of someone, but I can't remember who it is.

"Stay away from who?"

"Alyson Granger and Tara Doucet. Don't talk to them. Don't have lunch with them. Pretend they don't exist."

I take a gulp. "But why? They seem nice."

"It's dangerous, believe me."

She's so intense, I get a spidery feeling in my stomach. Then she steps closer. "And whatever you do, don't go to the cemetery pier with them."

I take a step backward. "What cemetery pier? Don't know what you're talking about."

She glances around as if she's terrified someone will hear her. She's also clutching her world history textbook in her arms like she forgot to leave it in the classroom. Maybe she reads it for fun during recess. But I notice that her arms are trembling a little bit so I also feel sorry for her. I don't know whether to hug her or tell her to get lost.

"It's this stupid secret the kids in this town have," she whispers. "But ssh! Bad things happen at that cemetery pier.

If I tell you any more, they'll make my life miserable. But I had to warn you."

I feel her fear and my own fear level rises, too, when she talks about bad things and warnings. "What'll they do? And what's your name anyway?"

Her eyes go big like I just asked the worst thing in the world. I can't help wondering why my questions seem to make her so scared.

"I'm not tellin' you. You'll tell *them*."

Before I can say another word, she turns and flees, her skinny spider legs stuttering across the floor.

I brush my damp hair out of my eyes. She sure is odd. Or is she right about those other girls? I don't know what to think. Maybe she's just jealous of Tara and Alyson, wants them to be her friends, and they ignore her instead. It is a sad but true fact that when it comes to school popularity, the prettiest girls never hang around the plain girls, or girls with unusual characteristics — like strange and ugly scars.

I dig out the school map from my pocket, wondering which is the fastest direction to the playground. Wondering if I just want to go back inside the classroom and read the history book.

Two seconds later, the school fire alarm goes off.

CHAPTER SEVEN

THE FIRE ALARM SEEMS TO GET LOUDER THE LONGER IT GOES on, seeping into my brain so I can't think in a straight line. I need to get back to my homeroom, but I stand there in the middle of the corridor covering up my ears and feeling like I've just gone stupid.

Classroom doors bang against the walls and the kids who'd made it back to class before recess ended start emerging again in long, snaky lines.

My stomach is seesawing when I realize that I have no class to walk with, no buddy partner. I'm one of those lone fish, swimming in the wrong direction, looking for any familiar face.

Suddenly, someone grabs my arms on either side of me — Alyson and Tara — and my feet start walking with them.

"We won't let you burn up," Alyson says with a giggle, and then gasps as someone bumps into her and all three of us almost fall over.

"Hey, watch it," Tara mutters, holding out her arms so the crowd has to walk around her, like she's the queen of the corridor.

Maybe she really is.

A teacher blows shrilly into a whistle behind us, and a bunch of boys start yelling up ahead just to hear their voices echo.

"Boys are so silly," Tara says, sighing like she's a teacher. "They think they can get away with it because it's so crowded and nobody will know who's yelling."

Me, I just want to get out of the crush. "You mean there really is a fire?"

"Nope, just a drill. Happens every month like an alarm clock." Tara laughs as she flings her long, silky black hair over her shoulder and gives us a smirk. "Get it? Alarm clock?"

"Oh," I say, trying to smile back. "Right."

"Never saw a fire alarm on the very first day of school," Alyson says. She leans in close. I can smell Tabasco sauce on her breath, like she pours it on her eggs for breakfast. "Hey, after school, our group is going down to the piers along the bayou. We play games and stuff. Want to come?"

The voice of the scarred girl rings in my head. Her warnings about the piers. Almost like she knew this was going to happen.

Finally, we get past the heavy doors and break through the mob.

I can breathe again. Alyson and Tara drop their arms from mine and start whispering together, leaving me out of their conversation. I hear something about Jett and some other boys, but at the moment I'm just glad we don't have class.

It's still cloudy, but there are breaks of hazy blue peeking through. Maybe it'll stop raining finally.

Since I don't know anybody else, I follow Tara and Alyson out to the field where students are standing in clusters, talking or kicking at the grass. I see that Jett Dupuis kid running in circles yelling, "I'm free, I'm free!"

Tara watches him from under her eyelashes.

Alyson gives a happy sigh. "I love getting out of class."

I stare at the main road in front of the school. "Look at that!"

There are sirens and fire trucks in the distance, coming closer every second. The noise on the field grows louder as everyone starts pointing and yelling. Teachers are trying to blow their whistles and keep their classes together, but it's getting harder to keep everyone under control.

Alyson's big eyes get bigger. "Looks like there really *is* a fire."

Long red fire trucks pull up in the bus circle, followed by a couple of ambulances.

"I wonder what happened," Alyson goes on. "Don't see no smoke."

"You're lucky you started school today, Shelby," Tara murmurs with a half smile, watching the cluster of boys who are now competing with one another to see who can jump the farthest.

What am I supposed to do if school lets out early and Mirage is out in the swamp and doesn't know to row back for me? I guess I could call her from the school office, but I don't want to. A fire drill always feels like a free day. It did back home. And what if the office is on fire and the telephones are all burning up?

A ripple of murmurs moves through the crowd of students. I notice that the first graders are sitting in a circle playing Duck, Duck, Goose. Teachers cluster in knots gossiping about the fire trucks.

Jett breaks away from his friends and runs up to us, like he's hog wild ecstatic to be the first to tell the breaking news. "Fire in the kitchen," he says, not even breathless from jumping across the grass twenty times and running around like a maniac. "One of the cooks got burns from the oil."

"Oh, wow," Alyson says. "A real fire."

"She'll be okay," Jett says, his eyes darting to Tara over and over again. I guess boys can't help staring at the prettiest girl in the school every five minutes.

But then Jett gives me a wink, real quick, his brown eyes smiling as he pretends like he didn't do anything.

Tara glances at me, like she's not sure she saw what she just saw. I press my lips together, trying not to smile back at Jett. I know better than to make an enemy out of Tara on the very first day. I'm the new girl. I'm nobody. I'm just glad the most popular girls are even paying attention to me. Maybe the next few months won't be so bad. Now if I could just figure out how to stay away from the swamp house and Mirage for most of the day.

A few minutes later, the official announcement comes from Principal Trahan. She tells us that school is shutting down for the day, and the air is filled with whoops and hollers of joy. "Your parents are being informed and buses will be here shortly. The students who walk home will be allowed to leave as soon as you check out with Mrs. Benoit over here, who has the rosters."

Just like that. My first day at Bayou Bridge Elementary is over.

"Well," Jett says, grinning, "I think it's a good day for the pier."

Tara laughs and Alyson hops up and down on her toes. "Yeah, it might be our last chance for a while."

I clear my throat, not wanting to get forgotten. "What'll I do about Mir — my mamma — coming to get me? How will she know school's canceled?"

"Who *is* your mamma?" Jett asks. "Didn't you just move here?"

"Um." I pause, not wanting to admit it. Real quiet I say, "Mirage Allemond."

"You mean that swamp witch lady?" Jett asks, throwing an arm in the direction of the bayou and gazing into my face like he's figuring out the resemblance between the swamp witch and me. When he looks at me, I get funny tingles in my stomach. Like I just drank five fizzy sodas in a row.

"She's not a swamp witch," I tell him, surprising myself by defending her. "Least I don't think so," I add, trying to sound intellectual. "I'm still studying the matter."

Jett laughs and Tara says, "You're funny, Shelby."

"Does she do that hoodoo magic like in New Orleans?" Tara asks. "My mamma and my aunt took me to some hoodoo shops on our last trip for fun. And that voodoo museum in the Quarter."

Alyson is staring at me, her blue eyes so big I swear they're gonna pop out of the sockets.

I picture Mirage the night Daddy dropped me off, circling the chicken pox on the boy's arms and face with her finger, giving him medicine, saying her French prayers. "She's more like a doctor and a priest combined."

"Didn't know girls could pray like priests," Alyson says, her forehead wrinkling.

"Anybody can talk to God, can't they?" I say, trying to think fast and hoping they don't probe for details. I don't want to admit that I haven't lived with her for over a year, that she left me, that my own mamma is the strangest mother in town. "Men don't have a monopoly on that."

"My mamma prays all the time," Jett says, his hands on his hips, looking tough and cute all at the same time. "She drives me crazy with all that praying and crossing herself and going to Mass. Having a *traiteur* for a mamma can't be worse than that, right, Shelby?" He grins real big and pokes me in the arm.

Tara sidles closer to Jett, her eyes dark slits of green, like a cat. She tosses her hair again and carefully ignores me. What a princess.

"Well, thank you very much for your permission," I say, pretending to be indignant. That just makes Jett laugh even more. I feel embarrassed and brave and foolish all at the same time. Is this how other girls feel around boys?

"Are you planning on becoming a *traiteur*, too?" Tara asks, bumping her shoulder against Jett like they're best friends. Her eyes bore into mine like she's examining my brain.

I try to act indifferent. "Um, *no*. Why would I do that?"

Tara arches an eyebrow. "Like mamma, like daughter."

I give a little shrug, like I don't care what she thinks. I find myself touching the charm bracelet on my wrist, rubbing the little carved spell box and the cute silver snout of the baby gator. I don't know what the charms mean, but they're like an anchor to hold on to around these new kids.

It feels like I'm treading on ground that's gonna move out from under me without warning. Like a magician snatching at the tablecloth, but the trick doesn't work and all the dishes crash to the floor in a hundred sharp pieces.

"You gonna be president of the Garden Club like your mamma?" Alyson asks Tara.

Tara looks startled, as if her own best friend just punched her in the arm. Like Alyson is talking back to her, or questioning her position as Pantene Princess aka Most Popular Girl in Bayou Bridge. She lifts her chin. "Only if I get to live in the biggest house in town."

"You already do live in the biggest house in town," Alyson

tells her with a giggle. "So we going or not, everybody?" she adds. "The whole school just about left now."

She's exaggerating, but most of the students have returned to the front of the school, milling about as they wait for the buses to return and take them home.

Parents are already pulling up in cars and trucks to pick up kids when we race back across the blacktop to retrieve our school packs from our classroom. Since the cafeteria is in a different building, the firemen allow the staff and students to get their belongings.

"So how do I tell my mother to pick me up later?" I ask Alyson as we hit the main sidewalk of town. "I'm supposed to meet her down at the water."

"Just leave a note at the docks," she suggests.

"How do I do that? She probably took the boat back home."

"Just pin it to the pier. Come on, we'll help you."

"You may not even need to," Tara says. "We got hours before our folks expect us home."

"Good thinking," Jett says, giving Tara's hair a tug. "A girl with brains."

"Did you ever doubt it, Jett Dupuis?" She starts talking in a southern drawl. "Ah do manage to get straight As on mah report cards, suh."

"Are we allowed to play at the city piers?" I ask, thinking about the nervous scarred girl and her dire warnings.

"We're not talking about *those* boring old docks, Shelby Allemond," Tara tells me, staring at me like she's giving me a dare. "We're going to a private pier — by the town cemetery."

CHAPTER EIGHT

AFTER WE LEAVE A NOTE TIED AROUND ONE OF THE CITY pilings where Mirage had docked that morning, a couple other boys join us, but I don't recognize them.

Crossing back over Main Street, we leave the neighborhood of the school. Soon we're walking down a dirt road lined with giant oaks and no sidewalks, the Bayou Teche running lazy and muddy alongside, our backpacks bumping against our shoulders. When I stare down the road it seems to go on and on, no end in sight. Sugarcane fields stretch on forever.

The edge of the narrow road slopes down to the water and a sweep of uneven grass leads straight to scraps of elephant ears hugging the bank.

"See that forest of oaks way over there?" Alyson says, pointing out a cluster of giant-limbed oaks on the far side of a low wooden fence that disappears into the surrounding brush. "That's the cemetery. It's real spooky at night."

Now I wonder why the scarred girl didn't warn me away from *that* place. A pier seems pretty innocent, but the graveyard looks terrifying. Dark and forbidding and gloomy, completely enclosed by bent and twisted trees that have probably been growing there for two hundred years.

Prickles of dread start in my toes and run right up to my eyebrows. I quit staring at the graveyard and catch up to Tara farther along on the road. "So who is that girl in our class with the scarred face?" I ask her, curiosity not letting go. Her warnings were so spooky, I gotta find out more about her story.

"Nobody. She was new last year. Don't know much about her."

"How'd she get those scars on her face?"

She shrugs. "Don't know. She came like that. Maybe a car accident?"

"Well, she has to have a name," I say, my voice dropping off so I don't look too weird asking over and over again.

Alyson comes up behind me. "Her name's Larissa, okay? Now can we talk about something else?"

Larissa. I know her name now, but for some reason I don't feel any better about her and what she told me about the cemetery pier and its danger.

Suddenly, Tara runs ahead, yelling, "Turn right here!"

The day is getting hot fast, muggy and sticky and suffocating. I'm sweating even in the shade.

The path to the water slopes down through tangles of brush, and I follow the group, counting three girls and three boys, Jett and two friends he introduces as Ambrose and T-Beau. I skirt an old tire hiding under a pile of leaves.

"It's so dang hot, I can't wait to jump in," Ambrose says.

A crawly feeling turns my stomach inside out. They aren't going skinny-dipping, are they? Boys and girls together? Maybe this was what that girl was warning me about. Everyone jumping in the water and then stealing your clothes? I shudder at the thought.

"Aren't there gators in that water?" I ask.

"Sometimes, but they won't hurt you," Jett says, pushing his blond hair out of his eyes. "Gators are so shy, they quick swim away when they hear us coming."

"Or they spy on us," Ambrose adds with an ominous hiss, coming closer to me. "Sittin' in that black water jest waitin' for their supper. You!" he adds loudly, his voice punching the air.

I jump, barely holding back a scream, but Tara and Alyson squeal as the boys thump Ambrose in the arm for scaring us.

When we get to the edge of the water, I finally see the pier. It's actually a bridge or a walkway, made of wooden planks and reaching out into the bayou like a long, straight arm.

Except the bridge ends right in the middle of the bayou. Just ends, like someone forgot to build the rest of it.

Across the water there's a little island. At least it looks like an island, but the land and trees curve around the bend in the Bayou Teche and I can't tell where it starts or stops.

Staring hard as I can through the far-off groves of cypresses and oaks, I see the shadow of a little house set way back in the darkness of the trees. Just a clapboard wall, part of a porch, and the top of a chimney. From across the water, it's like looking at a dollhouse.

"There's a house back there!" I say. "Who lives in it?"

"Nobody no more," Alyson answers. "It's called Deserted Island. Always has been."

"Who used to live there?"

"Some family long time ago."

"They just left their house?"

Alyson shrugs. "Guess so, not really sure."

"How'd they get off the island into town?"

"Boat, silly."

I feel stupid for asking the obvious question. I'm still not used to people getting around by boat everywhere.

Tara shades her eyes from the sun as it bursts from behind

a cloud. "The pier used to go all the way across the water so the family could walk across the bayou. So it's really a bridge. They built the pier so they didn't have to boat across all the time. Come on, I'll show you."

I follow her and Alyson, watching the boys as they run hollering straight down the pier like there's no tomorrow, stopping short of the end and peering into the water.

After just a few steps, I've left the shoreline. Suddenly, there's only water all around me. The long, snaky pier starts to quiver and sway. "Um, is it safe?"

"Don't be such a skeered-y cat, Shelby," Tara says, tugging at my arm. "That's part of the Truth or Dare game. We see who can go out the farthest before the bridge falls into the bayou another plank or two."

Truth or Dare game? The sound of that ain't good at all. *Isn't,* I correct myself inside my head. "So just how deep is it?"

"Probably ten feet or so. Sorta rises and falls with the rain. See the watermarks on the pilings?"

I take note of the dark line on the wood pilings indicating the potentially high water level. There's a seasick sensation in my stomach as the bridge sways with the rushing movement of the bayou as the river runs south and disappears around the next bend, leaving the town of Bayou Bridge behind.

When I look at Jett and Ambrose and T-Beau racing up and back, I can tell they've run this bridge many times. Even though it sways a lot, they're zigzagging back and forth and laughing like maniacs.

All at once, T-Beau pretends he's going to fall in, then Ambrose pulls on his sleeve to save him. I let out a gasp when they both nearly teeter over the edge and fall into the water. They just laugh and snort some more.

I'm sweaty and afraid just watching them. Chewing on the inside of my cheek, I ask, "So how did the pier cave in?"

"That's the most sad story of Bayou Bridge," Tara says dramatically. "There was a bad storm one year, don't know when exactly, but a long time ago. Lightning hit the pier and cracked it to smithereens. All the cypress planks splintered into a million pieces and floated down the bayou."

"Worst part was —" Alyson says, jumping in. "A *girl* died when the pier got hit by lightning and broke all to pieces."

I stop walking my tiny baby steps and hold out my arms for balance, fighting the dizzying urge to run back to shore. Or jump into the water like a crazy person. "That's awful. And nobody fixed the pier after that?"

"Nope, the whole family moved away after that, like to New Orleans or somewhere. The house is haunted by the girl who drowned and nobody wants to live out there."

T-Beau shoots past and I stand stock-still as the bridge bounces up and down.

Think I'm going to throw up right then and there. "Stop!" I cry. "Please!"

"Sorry!" T-Beau says, running backward again in the opposite direction to the shoreline.

"You guys are crazy," I tell Jett as the rest of the kids run back and forth past one another, creating a breeze on my face, their whoops and yells piercing the air.

"Mebbe. But it's fun. Now you gotta try it. Run all the way to the end and back without fallin' into the water."

"Can I just *walk* real fast?"

Jett considers this and gives me a little smile. "For today. But no tellin' 'bout tomorrow."

"Okay," I agree. "Just walk with me so I don't fall off the edge."

The pier feels like a mile long even though I know it's not. The closer I get to the middle of the bayou, and the farther away from the bank, the more unsteady I feel. My legs are shaking, my stomach flip-flopping like a fish, my steps slowing down, slower, slower.

Abruptly, I stop about ten feet away from the end where the planks have fallen in, half submerged under the chocolate-colored water. I gaze out across the wide bayou, the water practically rolling like ocean waves from the wind out here in the middle.

"What's wrong?" Jett asks me.

"I am most definitely nau-se-a-ted," I whisper.

"You just gotta get used to it. Tara and Alyson got a little green first time they walked out here, too, but they'd never admit it." He grins at me sideways when he says that, like it's our little secret.

When I look the rest of the way to the island, there's no bridge left at all. Just two narrow rows of pilings, empty between them where the planks used to be. I wonder how many gators are swimming back and forth between those pilings just waiting for supper. The pilings look like they're floating even though I know they're submerged into the muddy bottom below.

My eyes follow the pilings back to the pier where I'm standing. I can see the broken planks where they crashed into the water, nails and splinters rising up like monster's teeth.

"Creepy, huh?" Jett says, wiggling his eyebrows.

Ambrose and T-Beau are suddenly standing next to me and I get the crazy feeling they might just shove me right off the end.

"Lightning did all that? Just broke it all up?" My voice sounds really small so I pinch my arms to make myself stop.

I don't want them to throw me in just to scare the heck out of me so's they can laugh.

"Yep, it was a bad storm," T-Beau says. "My mamma and daddy talk about it sometimes. Worst storm ever, long as anybody can remember."

"Show her the *blood marks*," Ambrose says next, like we're in a spook alley or a haunted house.

"What blood?" I squeak, grabbing for Jett's arm and feeling only air. He's not as close as I'd hoped.

"The blood of the dead girl, 'course," T-Beau tells me. "The girl who got hit by lightning. Biggest goll dern lightning bolt ever seen on the Bayou Teche. Like it was looking jest for her. Like it *wanted* her."

I edge backward a few inches. Away from the scary, moldy planks and rusted nails. "Lightning don't go lookin' for someone to hit."

T-Beau just shrugs and pushes his hair off his face.

I swallow hard. "So what happened next? Did the lightning kill her right off?"

"All that blood means it got her good. Probably split her skull and then she fell into the water."

"She couldn't help falling in," Jett adds. "The lightning zapped this pier but good. Right where you're standing. Wood and stuff went flyin' sky-high into orbit." He pulls an apple from a pocket on the leg of his baggy pants and starts crunching, spraying juice with each mouthful.

Ambrose's been standing quiet, listening to the story he's probably heard — or told himself — his whole life. Now he says, "After all these years, all them wooden planks been falling into the bayou. One. By. One."

I am way too far out. The bank feels two miles out of reach, so far I'll never make it back because there are just too many steps, too much water whispering at me to jump in and get eaten by gators or get sucked down by the pier. I can practically see all those planks rotting away down below, full of rusted nails, waiting to tear up my toes.

Alyson and Tara are right behind me, hanging on T-Beau's every word, their eyes intense and bright.

"You can see the blood right down there," Alyson says, waving me closer.

"See those red spots," Jett points out. "About a dozen splatters. That mess of splintered planks is right where the lightning hit. Down she went. Must a hit her head going down, too. Never had a chance."

Sure enough, there are spots of red, like tiny sprays of paint, faded in the sun. I wonder why they'd still be here years later. Unless it *wasn't* that long ago.

"Are y'all allowed out here?" I suddenly ask. "Is it legal?"

They all look at one another and then back at me again, and then they laugh.

Tara shrugs her dainty shoulders and tugs at her pink and silver embroidered top. "Not really. Nobody's allowed on the pier. Used to be a sign warning people away, but it got torn down."

"Who's gonna stop us?" T-Beau adds. "Long as we're not here during a storm, we're okay."

"Now it's time for the Official Pier Games," Tara says importantly.

"What're those?" I ask.

"Just watch," she answers with a smile.

Jett and Ambrose and T-Beau grin at one another and slap hands. Then all three boys take a giant step forward and land on one of the round piling stumps, their arms stretched out for balance.

I let out another scream and cover my eyes with my hands, peeking through my fingers. "Those wood posts are only a few inches around!"

"Look at this, Shelby!" Ambrose says, grinning over his shoulder.

Jett spits his apple core into the water, where it bobs under the pier and floats away into the rushes nearer the banks.

Then he swings his arms, gets ready, and jumps onto the next piling a few feet away. The bayou laps at the edges of each piling.

I can't catch my breath. "Are they crazy?"

"Yep," Alyson says. "Totally crazy."

T-Beau and Ambrose follow suit on the opposite row of piling stumps.

"They're gonna fall in one a these days," Tara says, but she speaks with a certain fond admiration.

We watch the boys leap down the row of pilings until they get about twenty feet away from us.

"Look!" Jett cries out, stopping on the next stump and rocking his feet back and forth. The piling is loose and wiggly, but he manages to keep his balance.

"What a show-off," Alyson says, but she sounds impressed.

I'm impressed, too. They're idiots, but they're impressive idiots.

"Now it's your turn!" Ambrose yells back at us.

"Come on, scaredy-cat girls," T-Beau adds, balancing on one foot.

I realize that Tara and Alyson have inched forward to the end of the pier where the broken, jagged planks are staring up at me from the depths of the water.

Getting dizzy, I blink and glance away, but when I look at

the boys jumping to the next pilings, I feel my own feet wavering.

Don't look down, don't look down, I tell myself.

The next instant, Alyson has taken a huge step and is now standing on the first piling away from the pier. A breeze whips her hair around her shoulders and she gives a thumbs-up sign to Tara, who steps out to the piling directly opposite from Alyson.

Locking hands across the water, they stand there until they get their balance, and then a moment later, the two girls jump to the second pilings.

Alyson lets out a screech and Tara giggles.

"Me, that's as far as I'm goin' today!" Alyson declares. "Wind's gettin' too strong."

The three boys return to the bridge, jumping from piling to piling until they reach the girls. Then they all sit down on their individual stump and swing their legs, feet skimming the top of the water.

I shut my eyes because I just can't look, then pop my eyes open again. "Y'all are insane!" I yell at them. "Just teasing the gators to come and chomp on your toes!"

The boys just laugh at me and start joking that they can see alligators rising up out of the water. "Oh, look, there's a gator! He's comin' for us — watch out!"

Alyson starts giggling and can't stop.

"There's them red eyes!" Ambrose screams, and for a moment he looks like he's gonna fall in, but then he shakes his hair out of his eyes and grins at Alyson, who just keeps laughing like a girl who got bit by the love bug.

Jett leans way back on his piling, holding out his arms and legs so that he's practically lying straight out over the water.

"Hey, Shelby," Tara says. "Hand me that board over there behind you."

I'm shuddering at Jett's balancing act so I jump a little when Tara calls out to me. Then I spy the board she's talking about. I hadn't noticed it when I passed it earlier. Lifting the board, I'm surprised it isn't heavier, but I guess cypress wood is light and floats. It's about six feet long and I drag it along the pier, stopping at the broken-up end and trying not to look into all that water and the nails that look like rusted gator teeth.

The pier creaks under my feet as Tara says, "Hand it out to me and Alyson. We're gonna set it down across the pilings and then sit on it."

It takes me a minute to stretch my arms out with the board, hoping I won't fall in as Tara and Alyson each grasp an end and then place the board across two pilings behind them. Tara goes first and manages to crawl onto the board and keep it secure while Alyson steps across onto the end of it and sits down.

"Think there's room for three?" Alyson asks.

"'Course there is. Can't play Truth or Dare while she's back there staring at us, or running away to tattle."

"Why would I do that?" I feel insulted.

"Never know with new girls," Tara says, swinging her legs.

Jett and Ambrose hop back along the pilings and sit on the round stumps closest to Tara and Alyson on their make-shift seat.

Alyson dips the toes of her sandals into the bayou and flings some water up on T-Beau as he sits down.

"Shelby," Tara says, "you have to jump out here and sit with us. It's part of the rules."

"What rules?"

"Rules for the Bridge of Deserted Island."

I glance around, my gut zinging like I've got a Ping-Pong ball inside me. There's no way I can do it. I know I'll fall in.

"Actually, there's no piling for me to step on to get to you," I say, hiding my relief. "The boys are all sitting on them."

Ambrose yells, "Come on, you can do it! Just take a really big leap."

"And fall right in, and never come back up again," I mutter.

Ambrose and T-Beau laugh hysterically, holding their stomachs.

Jett calls out, "Jest sit on the edge right there where it's broken and then we can hear each other better."

Prickles of fear run straight up my nervous system. I don't want to sit and swing my legs over all those jagged, rotting, moldy boards and bent and ugly nails. Submerged like creatures lying in wait to rise up out of the bayou and pull me under.

I bite my cheek, wishing I was anywhere else but here. Wishing I had the guts to run back across the bridge and head for the town docks.

Tasting blood inside my mouth, I fold up my legs and sit crossways on the planks of the pier, several feet away from the edge so I don't have to look down into the water.

"Cheater," Ambrose calls out.

I ignore him, licking at my lips.

Jett is such a daredevil. He leans back again, holding out his legs and arms and teetering like he's going to fall into the bayou. Soon all three boys are doing it and Tara rolls her eyes, but I can tell they probably do this every day.

"So now we play Truth or Dare," Tara announces. "Everybody has to have a turn."

My heart crashes against my ribs. I hate slumber parties

where girls play that game. I always end up having to do something stupid with my eyes blindfolded.

The sun is beating hot as peppers on my head and my stomach growls. It's almost noon and those grits and toast for breakfast was hours and hours ago. "Isn't it time for lunch?" I ask, thinking about the sandwich in my backpack on the bank.

They ignore my request for food.

"Who's goin' first?" Ambrose asks.

"New kid always goes first," Tara says. "So, Shelby. Tell us something bad you've done. And you gotta make it good. I mean bad. Something real good bad." And then she and Alyson start giggling.

CHAPTER NINE

I TRY TO THINK OF SOMETHIN' THEY WANT. "YOU MEAN LIKE
the time I yelled at my grandmother when she made me
do the dishes for a month straight?"

"Why'd you have to do dishes for a whole month?"

"Talking back about chores and rules, stuff like that."

"Not *near* bad enough," Tara says. "That happens every
day in my family."

Alyson's forehead wrinkles. "Tell us about your swamp
witch mamma. Does she have a black cauldron in the
backyard?"

I snort. "No! That's just stupid."

"Hey, watch who you're calling stupid," Tara says.

"Didn't mean nothin' by it," I mutter. My heart is

pounding so hard the sound whooshes inside my ears, making me feel dizzy.

"I know," Tara says, snapping her finger. "Let's give her a Dare instead. She has to make a choice. Bring us back her Mamma's spell box — or jump off the end of the pier."

"Hey, Tara," T-Beau says. "We never made nobody else jump off the pier their first day."

Tara looks me up and down and gives me a sweetly sly smile. "But Shelby's real brave, don't you think?"

My hands close into fists and sweat breaks out on my forehead. No way I'm messing with Mirage's spell box, let alone taking it out of the house. I'd get in trouble for the rest of my life. And no way I'm jumping off that pier into deep water with gators.

"Seeing a witch's spell book would be great," Alyson says. "We could try a potion, turn Ambrose into a frog or somethin'."

Ambrose chortles with laughter, and his stomach jumps up and down. "I'll make you a toad, Alyson," he shoots back. "Or a cockroach."

"I won't settle for nothin' less than a frog princess, Ambrose Guidry," Alyson says, almost like she's flirting. I wonder if she secretly likes him.

I don't make a single peep, hoping they'll forget about the dare *and* the truth they're asking. The charms of the bracelet cluster against my fingers, as though trying to comfort me. I hold them tight against my palm, trying to figure out what to do. That girl Larissa was right. I shouldn't have come out here. My whole body feels tense, just waiting for something bad to happen.

"Oh, look," Tara says, pointing at me. "New girl's got a charm bracelet. Hey, let me see it."

The whopping in my ears goes a hundred miles an hour now. "It's my mamma's," I say weakly, holding my hand against my chest.

"Even better!" she exclaims, getting up from her wooden plank seat and jumping from the piling back to the bridge. I'm shocked at how easily she does that. Having long legs has advantages.

"Let me put it on." She grabs my hand and uncurls my fingers.

Instantly, Alyson leaps up and back onto the bridge to hold my other arm so I can't fight off either one of them. Her fingers curled tight around my arm hurt and leave red marks.

Tara is good. And fast. In two seconds, she unclasps the bracelet and holds it up, fingering each of the little charms, the silver chain dangling dangerously over the water. I think about that bracelet being passed through so many generations, almost two hundred years old, and feel sick through and through.

"Please give it back," I plead. "It's actually an heirloom."

"An heirloom? Don't you sound like a city girl?" Tara laughs and her pretty white teeth sparkle in the sunlight. She seems to take delight in my agony. She couldn't care less about making friends or my bracelet or me drowning right in front of her eyes.

Tara tosses the bracelet back and forth between her palms and any minute now I'm gonna hurl. "Please, please, *please* don't drop it in the water!"

I'd taken that bracelet and worn it against Mirage's orders. If I lost it, she was gonna hate me forever. 'Course, why'd I care about her feelings now? I'd been hating her all year long myself.

Standing there on that broken bridge, all them kids staring at me, it hits me hard that I like that old-fashioned bracelet. I want it to be mine for keeps next year on my twelfth birthday. I want to keep it forever and put my own charms on it someday.

"Here's the deal. You get your *heirloom* back as soon as you take the dare and jump in the water," Tara says. "We'll count to ten and T-Beau will fish you out. That's a better deal than anybody else ever had."

I think about Larissa and start really wondering what happened to her. Wonder about that awful scar. Wonder about the truth.

"Never took swimming lessons," I say, trying to keep my voice from shaking. "What if my head cracks on all them rotted planks?"

Then I glance down, trying to hide the tears, and make eye contact with Jett, who suddenly glances away.

"Aw, come on, Tara," Jett says, not looking at me. "That dumb bracelet might be worth some money. What if the police come and arrest us for stealin' the dern thing? Let's go back to shore and go wadin' instead."

Tara lays the charm bracelet across her legs, and I almost throw up as it slips and slides across her shorts, nearly falling right into the muddy water. Tara looks up at Jett, and the expression on her face wavers. Obviously, he has influence over her.

That's when it hits me. This is my chance.

Do it, do it, do it, my brain chants. Before I lose my nerve, I scoop the bracelet off Tara's lap, jump to my feet, and tear straight down the middle of the bridge, trying not to fall over the edge as the wooden planks shudder and shake.

Leaping over the steps to the soft muddy banks, I keep running. Straight up the slope, down the road, until I reach the cemetery wall. Hoping no one's following me, I race along the perimeter of the graveyard until I run smack into the gates. A graveyard's gotta be the perfect place to hide out for a while. Nobody'll think I've come here.

Quick as I can, I dart inside and fall to the ground, gasping like I'm gonna pass out for sure. Overhead, the clouds jump and whirl, my eyes go dark, and then clear again as I gulp in air.

Catching my breath, I lie there in the prickly grass listening, hoping nobody saw where I ran to, prayin' hard as I can that they'll never have the guts to actually go inside the cemetery. I stare up into the big old oaks and watch the flat green leaves whisper back and forth in the breeze. It's quiet and peaceful and my heart quits jumpin' so crazy. It's for certain that a cemetery, even an old scary one, is nowhere near as bad as getting pushed off that bridge.

Finally, I roll over and kneel at the old stone wall, dark green with moss. I peek over the edge and see that the road is clear. No voices or kids. Not even any cars in sight. Am I safe? Was Larissa tellin' the truth after all? Is the bridge where she got that terrible ugly scar?

I imagine her falling into the water, the long rusted nails

tearing at her face as she hits those slimy boards. I picture Larissa bleeding, rushed to the hospital.

The drops of blood on the pier. Maybe that blood is actually hers. Maybe that whole story of the girl who got struck by lightning is just something they made up to scare me. Scare all the new kids while they try to get you to jump in or fall in. Scare you forever just so they can keep a hold on you. Like they did to Larissa. She's still afraid of them, all this time later.

I lean against the rough stone wall and slowly unclench my fingers holding the charm bracelet tight in my fist. I count the charms, all eight of them. Safe, the silver clasps intact.

Can't help shuddering, thinking about how close I came to losing it. What would Mirage have done if her antique family bracelet had sunk to the bottom of the bayou? She'd send me away forever, maybe to an orphanage or somewhere horrible until my daddy got back. Maybe she'd pretend I never existed or tell Daddy I'd run away.

It could happen. She left me once already. I take a swipe at my eyes, thinking about how I may not be worth as much as a charm bracelet, especially an antique heirloom from the Civil War.

I hold the silver loops up to the sunlight and study the charms, thinking about how I should have left it at home like

127

I was supposed to. If Mirage knew I'd secretly worn it, she'd probably hide it away permanently. Keep it hers forever and I'd never get it.

The sunlight moves, catching the blue bottle just right. My heart does a handstand, backflip, and somersault all at the same time inside my chest.

The little blue bottle charm has something inside.

It takes a minute to get the miniature piece of cork out, but finally I do and lay it carefully on the stone wall so I don't lose it in the grass. The tiniest piece of paper has been rolled tight, tight, tight inside. Someone was very careful when they rolled it perfectly round, perfectly snug, so it would fit.

Carefully, I unroll the paper and suck in my breath. The black ink writing is intact, not even smudged. All my fears of being chased by the kids from school, of falling in the bayou, getting eaten by a gator, fly right out of my head.

The note is terrifying.

She's dead. She's dead! I'll never forgive myself long as I live.

CHAPTER TEN

Sure as heck my eyes are *not* playing tricks on me.

"She's dead?" I whisper, reading the words. My voice seems to echo over and over again in the silent graveyard.

Who wrote this? It sounded like *they* killed her.

I'll never forgive myself long as I live.

This charm bracelet belonged to Mirage. Did she put the note inside the tiny blue bottle? I can't picture her writing this. Maybe it was written by my swamp witch *grand-mère* and not by Mirage at all. If that was true, this spooky note would have been inside the blue bottle charm for decades.

No, that can't be right at all. Mirage told me that my

grand-mère put away her own charms when she gave Mirage the bracelet. All the charms on the bracelet right *now* belong to Mirage.

Plus the rolled-up piece of paper wasn't faded and falling apart like it was sixty years old. Maybe the blue bottle charm *came with the note*. Maybe it was put there by someone else.

The afternoon is so muggy it's like the air is sweating, but I feel cold.

Now I wonder . . . is the blue bottle *charm* note connected to the blue bottle *tree* notes? I'm pretty sure this tiny, rolled-up note is in the same handwriting as the second bottle note I found. I can't wait to get home to double-check. But why did someone put notes in the blue bottles in the first place? Is there a secret story behind them?

Guess I could ask Mirage . . . but she's not the kind of person who would put notes in a bottle. Besides, who'd she be writing to? Nobody else lives near Cypress Cove. All them notes were *meant* to be read by someone. They were heartfelt, like someone afraid or heartbroken. Mirage couldn't have written them since she didn't have many heartfelt feelings of her own. If she did, she wouldn't have left me and my daddy. She would have stayed in New Iberia with us. With me. She would have told Grandmother Phoebe that *she* was the mamma, and not let her run everything. She wouldn't have disappeared into her bedroom soon as she got home. She wouldn't have stopped talking to everyone, or acted like she was irritated and angry all the time.

All them months before Mirage ran away from home, she did it all wrong. Even if Grand-mère *was* sick. Kids ran away from home, not mammas.

My eyes feel hot and scratchy. When I glance up, all of a sudden I can't see too good.

Most of all, Mirage should have wanted me more than she did.

I take a gulp, trying to hold it all in. Maybe I'm thinking too much because my head hurts. My heart hurts. And now my whole body does, too.

Mirage should have taken Daddy and me with her. She could have asked us to run away with her. And my daddy should have gone after her and stopped her car from driving away instead of locking himself in his room for a week.

My chest gets a funny sharp pain, right under my ribs, and I press my fingers against the spot. I'm in a graveyard wanting to cry my eyes out, but I feel stupid. And I want my pillow.

Falling back to the grass, I press the little blue bottle charm note to my chest and hold the bracelet against my eyes, wondering who the *she* is that died, wondering where she's buried. Right here in this graveyard?

The grass tickles my neck and I roll over, spooked, as I look out over all them graves. Where are *her* bones — the *she* from the note? How long has she been underneath the earth in her coffin?

I lurch to my feet, feeling dizzy, and chew on the fat, hard blister inside my cheek that always hurts. Wiping the dew on my palms across my jeans, I glance around and try to get my bearings.

The cemetery sits inside a low stone wall, but there are rows and rows of headstones, angels, stone slabs, small markers, and big family granite plots with names engraved in fancy lettering.

Now that it's past noon, it's not so spooky. The trees rustle overhead like they're chattering back and forth with one another.

In the back of the graveyard, the cut grass slopes downward and I'm pretty sure there's a little creek inside the cypress cluster at the bottom of the cemetery. Somebody mowed recently.

I roll the small note up tight and slide it back into the blue bottle charm. After stuffing in the cork, I clasp

the bracelet around my wrist again. The charms make a tinkling sound as I walk up and down the rows, checking
out names.

Ten minutes later, I come on a newer grave. The grass is
growing back in clumps, and the marker is small and made of
wood, like somebody who don't have much money. Simple
block letters with the name ANNIE CHAISSON and a recent
death date.

A peculiar emotion rushes up to my heart and closes up
my throat. That's my *grand-mère*. Small and insignificant.
'Course she'd be buried in Bayou Bridge Cemetery. I'd missed
the funeral. Grandmother Phoebe wouldn't let me play hooky
from school for it. I wonder how much Mirage cried when
her mamma passed, after taking care of her all them months.
I wonder if she misses her. I wonder if she was mad I didn't
come to the funeral. Now I wonder if anybody came to it
besides Daddy and the priest.

I stand on the lumpy ground where the sod is pieced back
together and feel a little guilty. My stomach is hollow, but
maybe I'm just hungry.

I start walking again, glancing back at the little gravesite,
my conscience pricking me in the center of my chest.

When I reach the last row of headstones, I start to hear
music.

Someone is humming, but I can't tell where it's coming from. I head closer to the sound and suddenly a girl steps out from behind a white angel and leans against one of the angel's beautiful white wings. She stares at me with the darkest brown eyes I've ever seen.

All the air leaves my lungs and I have to stop fast so's I don't skid right into her.

"I didn't see you!" I stammer. "I'm sorry —"

"How you do?" she says, real friendly. Her blonde, wispy hair floats around her head even though there's no breeze down here under the last big oak tree. "Been waitin' for ya."

I gulp past my dry throat. "You have?"

"Saw you coming up the grass," she says. And then she smiles.

Her smile is like a sunbeam floating down from the sky. Her golden hair hovers on her shoulders, falling into place after a moment. Her smile is so different from Tara's bossy smile, or even from Alyson's smile that watches to see who's gonna do what so she can follow the most popular person at the moment.

"I — I was just walking," I say, wondering if she can tell I've been crying. "Actually, I was just leaving. Sorry to bother you."

"You ain't bothering me. It's real lonely out here. Not

many people live on the edge of Bayou Bridge. And there hasn't been a funeral in a few weeks."

"Really? You go to all the funerals? You must really be bored."

"I'm partial to the music, especially that song 'Goin' Up a-Yonder.' I keep waiting to see what it's like to go up a-yonder."

"Hey," I say. "That's the song LizAnn's mamma sings when she does the dishes. Practically tears out my heart. But why would you want to go to heaven? You're only a kid."

She lifts her shoulders. "I'd rather go to heaven than, you know, that other place." She stage-whispers, "H-E double toothpicks!"

"Ain't *that* the truth," I agree wholeheartedly, then kick myself when I hear Grandmother Phoebe correcting me inside my head. *Isn't, not ain't.*

The girl looks at me from under her wispy bangs. "Saw you up there, sittin' on the grass by the gates. You ain't happy, are you?"

I'm embarrassed she was watching me when I didn't know it. Then I wonder if she's truly being friendly — or if she's one of the Truth or Dare gang that just showed up late.

"Why you so sad?"

I'm chewing so hard, I can taste blood again. "Because I don't want to be here."

"In the cemetery? Me neither."

"No, I mean, Bayou Bridge."

"How long you lived here?"

"Just a couple weeks. My daddy brought me and left me while he went off to some country by Russia."

The girl's eyes widen and I can see tiny flecks of green inside the black of her irises. "He left you all alone?"

"No. I mean, I just got here — to live with my mamma. She's the *real* person who left me." I pause. "It's complicated."

She nods sympathetically. "Know all about that. It's hard to move someplace new when your heart is in your old home. That happened to me, too."

"Really? I never moved to a new place before. And the kids from school — well — they — you know." Since I have to go back to school tomorrow, I don't want to be known for tattling or gossiping so I stop talking.

The girl nods her head and I notice that her eyes look older than her face. Old, like she's full of knowledge or wisdom or something.

"Those kids're *always* there. Hanging around on that broken bridge, playing jokes, getting into trouble."

"I got that impression. Um. . . ." I break eye contact and stare at the angel statue instead. "Did you used to be one of them?"

She pauses, like she's wondering how much to tell me. Finally, she says, "Don't know those kids I saw you with today, but that pier is a terrible place. Wish they'd tear it down and throw all them rotten boards and pilings away for good."

I'm confused. "Why don't the town just fix it?"

She sort of glares at me. "Because that pier ain't no use no more! It's supposed to go out to the island, but it don't. All those broken planks and nails staring at you from under the water. Empty pilings rising out of the water like ghosts."

"That's exactly what I thought!"

"Never did like that bridge," she adds. "Going by boat is much better. I should know. That island is where I live."

"You *live* on the island?" I ask her. "Those kids said it was deserted."

"Not no more. My family left, but I'm back. Those kids should pay better attention."

My mouth lifts in a smile, thinking about Tara and Ambrose and T-Beau and their cruel games. "I guess they should, huh?"

Then we both burst into giggles and suddenly I'm bent over laughing. After a while I can't remember the last time I laughed so hard, it's been so long.

A hazy memory barges right into my brain. Me and Daddy and Mirage driving somewhere, just the three of us, laughing in the front seat of the Chevy. Daddy was telling a corny joke and Mirage was teasing him. Me, I was curled up under the crook of her arm. Where was Grandmother Phoebe? A strange feeling comes over me as I realize part of the reason the joke was so funny. We'd escaped Grandmother Phoebe's house and were off on an adventure, our own family, just us.

Up until now, I never remembered doing anything that didn't include Grandmother Phoebe.

I shake my head and realize that the girl is watching me, her head turned to study my face. She's wearing yellow shorts that match her yellow hair. Her smile is the prettiest thing I've ever seen.

Without thinking, I reach out and touch a finger to her hair. The golden strands feel like spring sunshine, warm and soft.

Words pop out of my mouth. "Are you real?"

She pats her arms, laughing softly. "I think I'm real."

"I was just thinking about a girl I saw a few nights ago in

the moonlight. By the edge of the swamp near our house. That wasn't you, was it?" Even as I say it, I know it's crazy. Who'd be out so late at night?

"Might a been me. I like to paddle my boat. Not much else to do. Other side of my island is the deep swamp. The Bayou Teche and the inlets and coves all curve around together and sometimes it all connects. I know all the shortcuts."

"I figured you were a trick of the moon, maybe just a shadow from the tree bottles."

"You have a bottle tree?" she asks.

"Hundreds of blue bottles. It's gigantic."

"I do know where you live! And yeah," she says, glancing off toward the bayou, "probably me on my way back home. I love that tree, that house. Makes me not so lonely to go visit that swamp house."

"Why would you be lonely?"

She puts a finger to her lips and her eyes dart around the cemetery, but the only sign of life is the oak tree branches swaying in the breeze. "My parents disappeared a while back. But don't tell nobody! I could get in trouble. Kids aren't supposed to live by themselves."

My eyes feel like they're bugging right out of my head. "Your parents disappeared?"

"I'm sure I'll find 'em soon," she says. "But the house with the blue bottle tree is comforting. My best friend used to live there."

She keeps surprising me with practically everything she says. I didn't figure nobody else had ever lived in Mirage's swamp house.

"Why are *you* livin' there?" she asks.

I roll my eyes. "My mamma lives there and I gotta live with her."

"Well, my friend lived there a *long* time ago." Swinging her arms, she starts walking up the hill toward the road.

A big shiver snakes down my arms, curling all the way to my toes.

The girl looks back over her shoulder. "You wanna come on to my house? My boat is over there at the bank."

I can't stop a grin from spreading over my face. "Yeah, I do. Even if I do gotta cross that bayou again."

She waves a hand at my concerns. "Long as you don't use that broken pier you'll be okay. And don't cross when it's raining. That's all I gotta say." She reaches back and takes my hand in hers. Her palm is cool and soft and I wonder if six months in Bayou Bridge won't be so bad after all. Meeting this new girl who's so easy to talk to and knows what it's like to be lonely means I don't have to spend much time with Mirage, either.

"What's your name?"

"Shelby. What's yours? Besides Graveyard Angel Girl?"

She laughs at the nickname. "Gwen," she answers simply. "Just Gwen."

She squeezes my hand as we zoom back up the slope, then dart past the silent gravestones and tombs and plaques and pillars. Once we leave the cemetery gates, we climb through a hole in a hedge of prickly bushes and head for the bayou banks. Hidden among a cluster of cypress knees and elephant ears, there's a pirogue tied to a tree trunk.

I glance down the water toward the bridge, wondering if Tara and Alyson and Jett are still around. They must have left while I was in the cemetery because there's no sign of them now. Not even on the road. I'm so relieved I could spit with happiness.

Gwen steadies the boat while I slide onto the seat without making it tip too bad. Think I'm gettin' better at climbing in and out of boats now. She unties the knot and picks up the paddles, handing one to me. "Jest head straight for that little cove on the left. My daddy named it Gwen's Cove just for me. That's where we'll dock."

"You sure it's okay without a grown-up?"

"Sure I'm sure," Gwen says. "My daddy made me this boat and I been boating my whole life. Takin' a boat is safer than walking that pier, let me tell you!"

I laugh because her statement is so obvious when the bridge is half gone.

It only takes about fifteen minutes to cross the bayou and as we pass the halfway point, I can see the broken end of the long pier, water lapping at the pilings. Remembering what it looks like makes me feel like I got spiders crawling up my shirt.

Thrushes and whip-poor-wills flit through the trees as we tie up, using a cypress knee for our dock, then we jump onto the damp, squishy bank.

A strange feeling of joy spills over the afternoon as Gwen leads me through a maze of secret, weaving paths, like she owns her very own forest. Guess she actually does!

The ground grows firmer when we get to the clearing. The house sitting in the center of the meadow is almost like Mirage's house, high up on stilts, rickety porch and all, with a tire swing hanging from one of the oak trees.

It's all as real as the dirt under my feet, as real as the hot sunshine buzzing with mosquitoes and gnats.

A sprinkler waters the lawn, and a hose left running in the flower bed threatens to drown the marigolds. Gwen shuts off the spigot. "I'm starved, how about you?"

"Starved times two," I tell her.

The house is small and cluttered. Old and musty.

Handmade doilies lie on the curved sofa and the armrests of the easy chairs, reminding me of Grandmother Phoebe.

"Up here is my room," Gwen says, leading me up the stairs and down a dim hallway. When she opens the door, light pours through the dormer window. Her room faces the bayou and I can see the busted pier dangling like a broken arm across the murky water. I don't like looking at it, and just then Gwen darts across the floor and pulls the curtains across the window as if she's feeling the same thing.

A yellow quilt sits crookedly on the unmade bed and there's an assortment of rocks and shells and Spanish moss on her dresser. A fishing pole leans inside a corner, and clothes and shoes spill out of the closet.

The next instant, I freeze right in the middle of the room, staring under the window.

"What is it?" Gwen asks, watching my face.

"Your bookcase," I say softly. "I can't believe it."

In the center of Gwen's bookcase sits the porcelain doll from the antique store. The very same one. I recognize the rose-colored lace gown and the pink ribbons on the bonnet perched on top of her long golden curls.

I crouch down in front of the case and just stare and stare at the doll. The blue eyes gaze back at me serenely. There's even the same tiny chip on her chin.

"Isn't she beautiful?" Gwen says. "Her name's Anna Marie and I got her when I was eight. She used to be my mamma's doll. I dropped her the very day I got her. That's why she has that chip on her chin. It was terrible, but jest an accident. I wish she was perfect and not damaged because of me."

"She *is* perfect," I tell Gwen. "No matter what."

"Well, almost, I guess," Gwen says.

"Anna Marie," I whisper. The doll looks perfect here in Gwen's bedroom, not dusty and fading like she was at Bayou Bridge Antique Store. Questions crowd my mind, mixing up inside my brain.

"She's the kind of doll you keep for your whole life," Gwen says.

"I would keep her forever, too," I agree, my mind going crazy trying to figure out how the doll got from the store to here in just a couple of weeks. Was Gwen lying when she said that she'd had the doll for years already?

"I plan to keep her my whole life until I die," Gwen says, flipping her buttercup-yellow hair over one shoulder.

I hold my breath as I reach out to touch the lace swirls on the edge of the rose dress.

All of a sudden, Gwen grabs my arm and shakes my wrist so that the charm bracelet jiggles loose from my sleeve.

"What's wrong?" I ask, so alarmed I practically fall over.

Gwen stares at my arm. "You're wearing a charm bracelet!"

I clutch my hand to my chest, afraid she's going to take it like Tara did. "What's wrong with that?"

"Nothin'! But it looks jest like *my charm bracelet*."

"You have a charm bracelet, too?" It's astonishing how much alike we are.

"My bracelet is one of my most prized possessions. Besides Anna Marie, of course."

I hold up the bracelet so Gwen can see the individual charms. "Mir — my mamma used to have this bracelet. This one is our birthstone, a ruby for July, and here's an owl. She actually has a pet owl, if you can believe it. And there's this little carved box — and a locket without pictures. But who would have a locket without pictures?"

Gwen sits up. "And there's a key. It looks jest like my key —" She goes to her dresser and pulls out a jewelry box, then gives me a meaningful look.

"Do you really think it will fit?" I ask, unclasping the bracelet and holding out the key separate from the rest of the charms.

Gwen inserts the key into the jewelry box lock and instantly the lid pops open.

The room tilts and whirls like a ride at a carnival. "How can *my* key open *your* jewelry box?"

From the depths of the jewelry box, Gwen pulls out her own charm bracelet. Without a word, she lays it across her yellow bedspread.

"See, Shelby?" she says. "My bracelet has a carved box and a French fleur-de-lis and an owl and a key and a locket —"

"And," I add, my throat dry as dust, *"we both have a blue bottle charm."*

CHAPTER ELEVEN

MY VOICE PRACTICALLY GASPS OUT THE NEXT WORDS, "DO you have a birthstone charm, too?"

Gwen picks out a charm and holds it apart so I can see the sparkly gold-colored stone. "Topaz for November. I'll be twelve in a couple of months."

"What's inside your little carved box?"

Gwen cracks it open with a fingernail and shows me a few dark bits of green leaf flakes. "Herbs. My mamma is a *traiteur*. She gave me the bracelet and a couple charms to start and I get to add to it every now and then."

Goose bumps rise like braille on my arms. "Your mamma is a *traiteur*? *My* mamma is a *traiteur*! *Look*," I whisper, holding out my arm so she can see the goose bumps on my skin.

Gwen holds out her own arms to show me the goose bumps she has, too. "We're twins!"

"Are you thinking what I'm thinking?"

"What are you thinking?"

I shake my head. "I'm not sure, but I got the strangest feeling. Something really weird is going on."

"That is *for sure*," Gwen says, and her voice is low and spooked.

The next instant, I grab at her hand again. "We both have a baby gator charm! Your gator has black eyes, mine has red eyes. Almost just alike."

Gwen counts the charms dangling from both bracelets. "We have exactly eight charms each."

I study the two bracelets side by side. "I wonder what that means." It'd be impossible to believe if I didn't see it with my own eyes. Then I think of something else. "Gwen, do you have any pictures inside your locket?"

"'Course, I do. Me and my best friend in the whole world." She snaps open the locket and shows me the tiny cut-out photos of herself and a dark-haired girl.

Gwen and her friend are complete opposites, one golden blond and the other girl with long dark hair and a solemn expression. Her chin is sort of down like she's shy, but her big black eyes are looking upward, like she suddenly got curious and stared right into the camera.

"My locket is exactly the same," I say, digging into the edge of the gold oval and snapping it open. "But I only have plain pieces of yellowish paper where the photos should be."

"Probably these charms were bought at the very same charm store right here in Bayou Bridge." Gwen lies back against the bed and gazes at the ceiling. "Strangest day I ever had in my whole life."

"What time is it?" I ask, still studying the nearly identical twin charm bracelets. I feel like I'm inside a snow globe and someone shook the world so hard I'm floating upside down.

"'Bout three o'clock."

"Can you take me home? I mean, back across the bayou? I need to get to the town docks."

"'Course I can."

I can tell we're both thinking lots of strange thoughts as we head toward the bedroom door. I take one last look at Anna Marie, the porcelain doll sitting with her serene smile in the glass cabinet case, then we climb down the stairs, down the porch, and get into the pirogue to paddle back across.

The sun is pounding hot now and by the time we hit the opposite shore I'm sweating bullets. In New Iberia, summer never really ends until sometime in October. Guess not in Bayou Bridge, either.

I climb out of the boat and jump onto the mushy bank,

standing in the elephant ears while Gwen turns the boat around. "See you tomorrow," I tell her reluctantly.

"'Bye, Shelby," she says, and her eyes are sad and dark again. "Wish you didn't have to leave."

"Me neither." I watch her paddle away until she reaches the swamp island safely. Then we wave to each other far across the water, she a tiny blonde dot, one arm in the air, before disappearing into the cypress trees.

I bite my lips, worried about Gwen out there all by herself. Maybe I should have invited her to stay with me and Mirage until her parents return.

But I'm embarrassed by Mirage and the pet birds and my ugly room.

I get the most peculiar feeling Gwen's parents have been gone a long time, maybe weeks already. And I get an even more peculiar feeling that they're not coming back.

I guess kids like Gwen would get put into a foster home. That would be worse for her than living by herself. At least she could stay in her own house. Wish I coulda done that while Daddy was gone.

Gwen's days are probably numbered. She can't live out there forever by herself. One day someone is going to go out there with a big boat and take her away. She's probably got a relative, an aunt or uncle, who will take her to live with them.

What will happen to that little house? Her clothes and books and bed — and the porcelain doll? How did that doll end up at Bayou Bridge Antique Store? Maybe my eyes were playing tricks on me or my memory is all wrong.

I rub the back of my hand against my nose as I pass the end of the pier anchored into the bank just off the road.

Sinister images fill up my brain.

No wonder Gwen prefers her boat to walking across the bridge.

Suddenly, this road is too quiet, too lonely, too deserted.

My heart starts to chatter inside my chest as I search around the bushes and trees for my backpack. For a moment, I'm certain that Tara stole it, but then I finally find it peeking under a large elephant ear.

I take off for Main Street fast as I can, looking for Sweet Ellen's Bakery on the corner, even as the late afternoon sun starts to slant across the sky.

All the kids from school have long disappeared and there are only a few houses set back off the road, quiet and sedate like old ladies. As I glance over, some of the houses are dark under the oak trees, and the black empty windows stare at me like haunted eyes.

I start running toward town so fast, I'm sucking in air like I'm drowning by the time I reach the docks. An ache in my side makes me bend over in pain. Then I see Mirage.

She's sitting on a tree stump, waiting for me, studying some papers and frowning. She's taken off those ugly boots and her bare toes rub against the dirt while she reads.

"Hey," I say, and she looks up, startled.

"Well, hey, back, Shelby Jayne," she says. "Where you been? Heard school had a fire drill."

"Yeah." I figure it's better not to elaborate on the details.

Mirage folds up the papers, tucks them into an envelope, and then stuffs it into her backpack. "And?" she asks. "Found your note, but it was skimpy on the details. So where you been all this time?"

"Just up that road. Playing some games with kids in my class. Then I explored the cemetery for a while."

"You did?" Her eyes go big and she jumps up from her tree stump to pace the ground.

I cross my fingers behind my back and play dumb. "Did the school call you? They was supposed to."

"Promise you won't go down that road no more," Mirage tells me, ignoring my question. "Nobody I know lives down there. That part of town is too lonely and dangerous — and cemeteries ain't for playin'. It's disrespectful to the dead."

She's bossing me and I can feel the hairs rise on my neck. I want to revolt against her stupid rules. Besides, if I obey her, I'll never see Gwen again. "I'm fine. You can see that I'm perfectly and totally *fine*!"

She swings her arms around, throwing her pack into the boat, acting all agitated and growling under her breath like I just did the worst thing in the whole world. "Promise me, Shelby Jayne. Never go down there again. Never."

I fold my arms across my chest. "No, I ain't gonna promise you."

The rope for the boat drops at her feet and she looks up, stunned. "You ain't goin' to promise even though I jest asked you to?"

"You're tellin' me to do somethin' with no good reason."

"Oh, lorda mighty, I got my reasons. And dern good ones. That bayou down there is dangerous. Water's deep, could pull you under, and there's gators — and — all kind a things. You don't know all my reasons. Heck, you don't *want* to know my reasons —"

All of a sudden, she spins around so I can't see her face and there's red splotches along her neck like she's about to cry. To pretend she's busy, Mirage picks up the boat line and checks the knots.

My throat is dry and scratchy and I wish I had a drink of water. "A bunch of kids from school were down there playing games but nobody got hurt."

She stares at me, and this time there's a different kind of look in her eyes. More than worry. More than anxiety. It's close to terror. "What kind a games?" she asks slowly.

I shrug. "They call it Truth or Dare. And they're just dyin' to push somebody in the water. But it's all supposed to be just for fun."

Her face gets a pained expression and she wipes at her eyes real quick. "Yeah, I've heard 'bout that. That game's been around a lotta years in this town. If I was their mamma and knew they were down there playing on that broken pier, I'd —" She stops, and her lips are trembling. "Well, they'd be in big trouble, that is for sure."

I've noticed that when she gets excited or upset, her accent gets thicker, too.

I'm sort of noticing that I've been doing the same thing. Grandmother Phoebe's training the past year is fast becoming extinct, all the words and phrases from when I was younger jumping right off my tongue again.

"What would *you* do?" I ask, a funny feeling rising in my stomach. When I think about those kids playing tricks on me, trying to get me to fall into the bayou — or *jump* in — I get mad all over again. I coulda drowned and that makes me go cold all over.

Then I'm afraid. I don't want to go back to school tomorrow. I want to go back to my real home, and I want my daddy so bad I could spit and cry at the same time. A rush of sadness comes over me so strong, it's all I can do not to start bawling right there on the docks. It's the most unfair thing in the whole world that I have to be here.

"Well, back in the old days, kids'd get a good lickin'," Mirage tells me, her eyes locking on to mine. "Might have to stay home and do chores for a month. Get their boat taken away. No supper. Stuff like that." She pauses and glances at me. "So what should I do to you?"

She's going to punish *me* for all those stupid kids scaring me? I take a shaky breath so I don't start crying with the injustice of it. "You aren't Grandmother Phoebe and this isn't my house so you don't get to give me all these rules."

Mirage blinks like she can't believe I actually said what I just did. "No, I ain't your grandmother Phoebe. I'm your mamma. And mammas can give any orders they want to. And expect their children to obey."

She picks up her boots, sticks her feet into them, then plops herself into the boat. She's such an expert, the craft hardly moves.

There's a long, stretched-out silence while we don't look at each other.

I sniff, my nose running again even though my eyes are dry. Then I glance down at the water and think about Gwen in that house all alone, without her family or anyone at all.

In the distance there's the sound of cars on Main Street. Cicadas and gnats start buzzing the air like they want their supper.

Mirage finally clears her throat. "If you don't want to stay out here all night you better get in."

I purposely don't answer, just slowly, slowly, slowly get in the boat and sit on my plank.

"Once I get us off the bank, dig left," Mirage adds.

I don't answer, but once we're away from the pier piling, I dig left. And keep digging and digging as we head the opposite direction of the broken pier and Gwen and her little island house.

It's the longest ride ever, and we don't say a single word.

"Supper's in half an hour," she says as the boat bumps the bank of the swamp house at last.

Mirage ties up the rope and I carefully get out, stiff and achy after sitting and digging that oar for so long. I swear I won't be able to move my arms tomorrow. They've been sore ever since I got here.

"Didn't think I was getting any supper," I muttered.

"Shelby, I was sayin' what I'd do if you purposely disobeyed. But you didn't know about that old broken-down pier and that stupid game of Truth or Dare. So you're not being punished. Not yet."

Now she's trying to be nice to me, and I'm not ready for that after our fight. She keeps acting all sweet, but then something happens and she gets agitated and gloomy like living out here is my fault. Like she hates it and loves it, always contradicting herself.

I want something from her that I can't even figure out myself.

I run up the rickety steps of the porch and go straight to my room — after I throw my backpack on the floor and bang the door.

Flinging myself on the bed, I bury my face in my pillow. All the hurt and aching and sadness is so full up inside me I can't stand it. But ten minutes go by and the tears still don't come. I squeeze my eyes tighter. Hardly even any watering.

Rolling on my back, I hold up my arm and touch every single charm on the bracelet, studying them for clues. Or information. Or something.

I think about the pier, the cemetery, the porcelain doll, and the identical charm bracelets and feel the hair rise on the back of my neck like I'm inside a scary movie.

Meeting Gwen felt almost like a dream, and now that I'm back with Mirage in the swamp house, I wonder if it was all real.

I shake my head, trying to get rid of the fuzzy feeling in

my brain. I know I saw Gwen. We'd talked and laughed and rowed across the bayou. Just fine, too! We'd been perfectly safe. There weren't any undercurrents. Never even saw any gators lounging on the banks sunning themselves.

That broken-up bridge fell apart because of lightning. Long as I didn't go out there during a storm I'd be just fine. Mirage was just being bossy. Trying to keep me chained here for six months because she wants to get back at Grandmother Phoebe.

I stick my chin over the edge of the bed and stare at the rug on the floor, the rainbow colors of the threads mixing up until I go cross-eyed.

I can still remember when the big fight happened. The biggest fight ever between Grandmother Phoebe and Daddy and Mirage. The night Mirage threw her stuff into a suitcase and stomped out.

"Feel like I been chained here for years, Phoebe," I remember Mirage saying as my grandmother stood in the door of my parents' bedroom. "You're always comin' up with one excuse after the other."

"I have no idea what you are talking about, missy," Grandmother Phoebe had retorted, holding herself up tight and rigid.

"You're always sick. Or you sprained your ankle. Or the heater stopped working and you'll freeze to death." Mirage was on a tear, working herself up into a dither. "Then you got no money, the cars are at the shop so we gotta share yours so we can get to work or school. Everything we have goes into this here house so we never got all the rent and deposits or down payment to get our own place. We're thirty years old now and we want our own house, our own family."

"You have a family," my grandmother had said coldly.

"Now, Mirage," my daddy had said soothingly, "you don't mean those things. You're hurting Mamma's feelings. We can work this out; we always have."

I remember standing in the bedroom doorway, too. Watching Mirage throw clothes and stuff into a suitcase, all helter-skelter.

"Yes, Philip, I do mean them," Mirage had said, her voice breaking, eyes spilling over as she searched his face. She took a shaky breath. "I'm sick and tired of always workin' things out. I'm done. She's held us down for years with all her guilt and excuses and stupid reasons. And you are always sticking up for her. Never me." And that's when she really started to sob, tears streaming down her face. "Never me, always *her*. I'm your wife and I got nothin' to show for it."

"Mirage —" Daddy had started, but Grandmother Phoebe cut him off.

"After all I've done for you!" she said stiffly. "Helping you out with school and rent. This is how you treat me?"

Mirage looked at her, shaking her head back and forth and almost laughing now through her tears. "You jest don't get it and I don't think you ever will, Phoebe Allemond. And now my own mamma is bad sick, probably dyin', and I have to go help her. I'll be back in a few weeks."

But a few weeks passed and she never came back.

I remember it was pouring buckets as she ran to the taxi sitting by the curb. I guess she took that taxi all the way out here to Bayou Bridge. Now I almost can't imagine Mirage sitting in a taxi like a regular person.

As soon as the taxi pulled away, Daddy yelled a bunch of stuff and curse words I don't want to remember, banging doors, throwing shoes. He even smashed a glass into the kitchen sink, sharp splinters flying everywhere. Then he stormed out of the house and didn't come home until the next day.

I slept with Grandmother Phoebe that night in her big, soft, king-size bed with all the fluffy down pillows. I cuddled up against her and cried into her shoulder.

"You'll always be safe with me, Shelby, honey," she'd whispered as I fell asleep. "No worries, my darling girl. You can always come to me. And I can be your mamma."

The words were soothing and comforting, the bed warm and cozy as the rain drummed on the roof, washing down the tiles and pounding in the gutters. But I remember thinking that I didn't want Grandmother Phoebe to be my mamma. I wanted my real mamma. But in all her yelling and packing and crying, my own mamma had forgotten to take me with her. Had even forgot to say good-bye.

Getting up on my elbows, I run my finger along the silver chain of the bracelet while a tear I didn't know I had drips off the end of my nose.

I squeeze my eyes shut and swing my legs around, my stomach sick and empty with all the bad memories. The night I watched my family break apart for good.

It takes me a while to figure out why the things I'd told Mirage on the ride home in the boat made her so angry. I guess I pretty much told her that Grandmother Phoebe was the only one who could make the rules. Like my own parents didn't count.

But what'd she expect? I've lived with Grandmother Phoebe practically my whole life. And so had Mirage until a year ago. Since it's Grandmother Phoebe's house she's entitled to make the rules and tell everybody what to do. We have the Rule Chart on the fridge. The Schedule. The Chores. She's president of the Garden Club and on the hospital board and a volunteer at the old folks' community center. That's just how life is.

But sometimes I don't like being bossed around by Grandmother Phoebe.

And now I realize that maybe Mirage doesn't like it, either.

The dirty rice and biscuits and honey for supper is better than I expect, but me and Mirage hardly speak. Except to be all polite and say, "Please pass the salt."

I just stare at my plate and lick the honey off my fingers, thinking about those first telephone calls from Mirage. When I begged her to come back home. And she said she couldn't. That Grandmother Phoebe told her she wasn't welcome no more. And that her own mamma, my *grand-mère*, was getting worse sick.

Mirage also said that she wouldn't come back home until Philip, my daddy, got us our own house. That it was time we had our own home and could be our own family.

But that never happened neither. Daddy just started traveling more and more. And I kept going to school and doing homework at LizAnn's house and wishing LizAnn's mamma was my mamma because she sang while she dusted and gave us huge wedges of her famous buttermilk pie and told us stories about her brother who got into trouble for pulling pranks on folks when they were kids.

Thinking about LizAnn makes me sigh with homesickness as I finish drinking my milk and wipe my mouth with a napkin. I'd like to call her again, but for the first time in my life I'm not sure she'd understand what I'm feeling.

We're still not really talking when we finish supper and Mirage asks me to help with the dishes.

I pull out a dish towel and dry while she washes, biting my cheek and staring at the blue bottle tree through the window while I'm doing the forks and spoons, wishing I could go out there and search for more notes. I want to find a note that's been signed with someone's *name*. I want to find out who *wrote* those notes.

If it was Mirage, then who was she writing notes to? Was she pretending to talk to her own mamma? The one who'd died three months ago? Is that what that note meant: "She's dead"?

What did she mean by, "I'll never forgive myself long as I live"?

Mirage unplugs the water in the sink and lays the rag across the counter. She takes a hair tie from the windowsill and pulls her thick hair up in a ponytail to get it off her sweaty face. She clears her throat. "Got something on the back porch to look at with you, Shelby."

Miss Silla Wheezy and Mister Possum Boudreaux are lying in the lounge chairs and Mirage says, "Scoot! You two're lazies all the day long. Now it's me and Shelby's turn to sit and do nothin'."

The blue bottles are shivering in the evening breeze, tinkling together like they're making music.

"Those bottles sound just like that charm bracelet, don't they?" Mirage says, leaning back in her chair like we hadn't argued earlier. She's still barefoot, her toes brown, the edge of her skirt sweeping the unpainted porch slats.

"Yeah," I say as Miss Silla Wheezy wraps herself around my ankles, purring to beat the band. "I mean, yes, ma'am."

I feel Mirage give me a sudden, surprised look when I correct my grammar, but she don't say anything.

Miss Silla Wheezy's sandpaper tongue scrapes against my skin. "That tickles!"

Then that silly, funny cat flies down the porch steps like she's seen a mouse and hasn't eaten in a week.

"You know, I got all them charms when I was a girl 'bout your age," Mirage says out of the blue. "Well, probably started about ten or eleven. My mamma had the bracelet first, of course, but she had her own special charms and her own special memories. After she took off her own charms and gave me the bracelet like I told you the other day, my mamma did leave one of them on the chain."

I glance up at her, curious, but I don't let on that I'm *too* interested.

"She gave me the carved *traiteur* box. Like a replica of my big box when sick folks come out here. All the rest of the charms I got when I was 'bout your age, charms that meant things to me. Like that little gator. Did you know I caught me a baby gator once? Tried to make a pet out of him, until my daddy found out and let him loose in Alligator Cove on the other side of town. And did you know that Mister Lenny is the offspring of my first owl?"

"You had an owl before Mister Lenny?"

"Yep, got him when I was fourteen. He was a baby and some animal got him and hurt his leg. My mamma helped me heal him up. That's when she started teaching me about being a *traiteur*. My mamma said I had a special touch, the gift."

"A gift? Like somebody giving you a present? Who gave it to you?"

"God Himself, Shelby Jayne. All our gifts come from Him. All our talents and abilities. That's why we gotta use them wisely. So when I healed Mister Lenny, my mamma celebrated by giving me an owl charm. Every charm has a story, and stories can have power in our lives to help us."

"You mean like a healing spell?"

"Well, almost. You see, the things that happen to us, the things we go through — sometimes they hurt us real bad, sometimes they can help heal us — and sometimes we just gotta find the strength inside to keep moving forward. Stories and charms can help us figure all those things out."

She stops talking and when I glance at her out of the corner of my eye, she's looking off at the blue bottle tree. Then I realize that she's actually looking *past* the blue bottle tree into the deep blue-black of the dusk and swallowing an awful lot. Her fingers clench the armrests of her chair. I wonder what's wrong with her.

When she speaks again, her voice is real quiet, almost like she's talking to herself. "Easier said than done, that is for sure. It's too easy to keep looking back at all the sadness in your life. You jest want to give up, but there are some things that can't be undone, even when you feel bad about yourself. And even though it might not be your fault, the sadness is still tearin' your heart into little pieces of sharpness that keeps cuttin' and bleedin'."

As I listen to her, I feel a knot building in my stomach. I wonder what she's talking about. Leaving me was her fault. Or is she even talking about me? I'm not sure anymore.

"Some stories jest get shut down. When I turned sixteen I put my charm bracelet away and stopped wearing it."

"Why?" I ask. I can't see Mirage's face very clearly any longer, mostly just the outline of her shoulders and her knees under the long skirt.

"Partly I thought it was babyish, but mostly I had a sorrow and a melancholy I couldn't seem to get past. My last charm didn't give me the strength to move forward. Jest kept me back in time for years. Like that blue bottle tree. I love it and I hate it."

"How could you hate it? It's — it's enormous! There must be hundreds and hundreds of bottles."

"Yep, and they were all supposed to keep the bad spirits away, but it don't work right. Never did." Mirage glances away, pretending to look for Mister Possum Boudreaux. I'd swear she's trying to hide an eyeful of tears.

And that's when I *know*, for certain sure, that the last charm she's talking about — the last charm she ever got — is the little blue bottle charm. I wonder where she got it and why it never healed her. She's talking in peculiar riddles, but I know she's not going to tell me the story. Least not right now.

"All right, *shar*, I didn't bring you out here to talk about those dratted blue bottles," Mirage says, getting up from her chair. "I brought you out here to show you the photo albums I stole right out from under your grandmother Phoebe's nose."

She gets up and flips on the outdoor light, turning the porch a hazy yellow.

My stomach takes a leap into my throat. "You stole photo albums from Grandmother Phoebe? Nobody does that to Grandmother Phoebe."

"Then I guess I'm the first." Mirage pulls an album out of the box and onto her lap, her voice turning razor-sharp around the edges. "She don't own these. *I* took these pictures of you myself. With my own camera that I bought and paid for myself. She didn't have the right to take them away and hide them in her cabinets."

Her words are confusing and my head feels like a jumble of mixed-up thoughts. I don't like her talking about Grandmother Phoebe that way. It just seems wrong. I re-member the fight that night — I remember it all — but Grandmother Phoebe is the one who took care of me after Mirage left so I can't help defending her. She cared about me when Mirage didn't. My own anger deep inside my gut starts to boil all over again, like a pot that don't have a lid to hold it all in. "If Grandmother Phoebe's so bad, why don't you use your *traiteur* magic and make her stop then? Why don't you just fix *all* of us with a spell and make us just the way you want us? You could make us the perfect daughter, the perfect daddy — then you wouldn't have to run away and leave us behind and become some kind of embarrassing swamp witch!"

"Shelby Jayne!" she cries, her voice cracking now. "I never wanted to leave you behind. I didn't want to take you away from your home — or away from Daddy. That night was terrible. There was so much going on — so much I couldn't fix or do anymore —"

When she reaches out a hand to grab me, I shrink away, backing over my chair with a loud ruckus. Miss Silla Wheezy, who'd been sitting underneath purring against my ankles, lets out a high-pitched yreowl and darts down the porch steps. She claws her way up the trunk of the blue bottle tree like a shotgun just went off.

All the tears I wanted to come earlier are now spilling over my eyelids and running down my cheeks. I fling open the back door, run through the kitchen, and straight to my room.

CHAPTER TWELVE

I SLAM THE BEDROOM DOOR SO HARD THE WALLS SHAKE.

I hate myself for what I just said, but I hate Mirage for what she did, too. I hate everything about the past year. I hate feeling like if I'd done something different she wouldn't have left. And yet, I don't have any idea what I'm supposed to do different.

Launching myself across the bed again, I bury my face in the pillow, choking on too many stupid tears. I want Mirage to feel what I feel and make it better — without me having to ask. She should already *know*.

I want *her* to apologize for leaving. I want her to fix our family. Even with all of Grandmother Phoebe's faults and the mean things she says and does, Mirage is the one who has to fix us. She broke us up, and I want her to glue us back together. She could make us a family again, but she don't ever talk about it, and she never came back to get me. Just stayed away forever. And it's probably too late now.

I rub my face with my arm in the dimness of the bedroom. I can see shadows on the wall from the outside porch light, the outline of the oak tree in the faint glow.

As I stare at the shadows, I know what I want. More than anything else. Most of all, I want Mirage to love me more than she did. Thinking about it makes my heart hurt, but I can't remember the last time she told me she loves me.

Right then, the bedroom door clicks open and I freeze. I try to look like a sleeping statue. Footsteps cross the room and then the edge of the bed creaks as Mirage perches beside me.

I suck in all the tears and go quiet as a mouse.

"Shelby Jayne. *Shar*," Mirage says, and I hear a funny catch in her throat.

I hold my breath waiting to see what she's gonna do.

"You know, your daddy always calls you Sweetie Pie. And every time he does, it reminds me of sweet potato pie, my favorite in the whole world."

My face is against the wall, but I can't breathe right. I'm not going to look at her. I don't want her to think I'm crying over her. I'll bet she never cried over me. She just cries over

Mister Lenny or that stupid blue bottle tree like it's got more feelings than I do.

"I'm doin' everything wrong, ain't I?" she goes on. Her hand reaches out and she starts to stroke my hair. "I jest want you to know that I'd give anything to redo the whole last year. It was all such a terrible mistake. I wish't I'd done everything different."

I hear her sniffling and her voice is shaky and weepy, but she keeps talking, slow and quiet.

"Your grandmother Phoebe is a good woman and I know you love her, but she and I couldn't live in the same house no more. Your daddy and I got married right outta high school, had you fast, he was goin' to school, I was goin' to school, we was broke. Good Lord, jest a hard, hard situation all 'round. The tension'd been buildin' for years. Exploded when your daddy had to start working so much around the country and then overseas. Wish he could find a different job . . . but that's neither here nor there. We all made mistakes, me most of all."

"So fix 'em," I finally say with a gulp, still staring at the wall.

Her breath catches when I speak, like she's surprised I'm talking to her. "I'm tryin' to, Shelby, I am. But it's gonna take time. I jest want you to give me a chance, okay? Please?"

"Aren't I givin' you a chance by coming here in the first place?"

"Yeah, you are, *bébé*, and I'm glad you're here, more than I can ever tell you. I also know I can't stay out here much longer. I grew up in this house, but there are too many painful memories — and they all came back a year ago, stronger than ever. It jest — hurts. I can't explain it any better than that. Stuff from a long time ago, some of the worst pain of my life. Staying here ain't workin'. Feel like the guilt is goin' to eat me alive some days."

Before I can wonder what she means by all her guilt, there's a fluttering of wings and I peek out from under my hair to see Mister Lenny perching on the ledge of the bedroom door.

"Did you know that when you were young and we'd come out here to visit your *grand-mère*, you and the first Mister Lenny would have a staring match every morning," Mirage says. "You'd eat your grits and he'd perch across from you on the edge of a chair. You and he could sit there for thirty minutes straight. Then you'd share your bacon with him."

"I think I might remember a little." I didn't want to admit it, but old memories were stirring up inside my brain.

"I have pictures if you want to look at them albums. Also

used to have a swing in the oak tree. You loved me to push you for hours. My arms used to get so sore, but I remember your soft baby hair flying in the wind and you giggling so hard until you practically fell out and I'd catch you up in my arms."

I remember that, too, but I don't say nothing.

Mirage keeps brushing my hair with her hands and the room gets darker and darker as night comes on. The bed creaks as she lies down next to me and she twists the ends of my hair around her fingers. Wonder if she remembers how much I used to love that. Still do.

I'm starting to fall asleep when she says, "Don't know if I can even sell this old place, but I'm gonna talk to a realtor. Figure I better move back to New Iberia if I want to see you more regular."

My eyes fly open, but I don't roll over. I'm stuck facing the wall and I can't unfreeze myself because I'm so surprised. I try to imagine Mirage getting an apartment in New Iberia and me going up in an elevator to visit her.

I can't picture her going to college, living in the city, or even grocery shopping anymore. After being here these last weeks, I'm starting to think maybe she really does belong out here with her animals and crawfish traps and healing people.

"My biggest problem, Shelby Jayne?" she says with a strangled little laugh. "Don't know *what* I'm gonna do with all those blue bottles when I get outta here."

I stiffen when she says that, thinking about all those pretty bottles packed up or thrown away. She couldn't move the whole tree; it's way too gigantic. And there'd be no yard in an apartment. I can't imagine that tree disappearing forever, getting junked. And what if there are more notes I haven't found yet, higher up in the branches? The thought of finding more secret messages makes my heart race.

"Maybe the new owners will want the tree, but I may not even be able to sell at all. Not many folks want to live so far out. And" — she pauses — "even after all the sad and terrible things that have happened out here, it would be strange to never come back."

Once again, I wonder what she's talking about. Such terrible things that she wants to move away forever?

"Well," Mirage says, finally rising from the bed, "good night, Shelby Jayne. Have some of those sweet potato pie dreams for me."

She closes the door and I lay in the dark as a forgotten memory floods my brain, poking at my heart like I have a pincushion inside my chest.

"You forgot something," I blurt out to the empty wall. Hot tears roll down my face, stinging my nose and making my eyes swell up.

Back before she left, Mirage used to kiss me good night, tell me to have sweet potato pie dreams — and whisper in my ear how much she loved me.

Tonight, she left that last part out. The part I want the most.

How am I supposed to know that she *really* loves me if she don't say it?

I use the quilt to wipe my eyes and nose, wide awake now. Knowing I should get up and get my nightgown on, brush my teeth, but I don't feel like doing all that boring stuff.

Instead, I think about Mirage putting the house up for sale. What if it actually does sell right away? I may never get another chance to look for blue bottle notes, and I'm too curious to stop. If I find more of the notes, maybe I can solve the mystery of who wrote them and why. Are they messages from a bad imp or fairy spirit trapped inside like I been thinking — or something else entirely? If an evil spirit is writing those notes they seem to know English pretty good. And why would they be talking to me anyway? That don't make much sense. It's more likely a ghoul would play mean tricks on me or haunt my bedroom.

Somebody wrote those notes. *Two* somebodies. With school paper and an ink pen. Somebody alive? Or somebody dead? If it's somebody who's dead, that means it *is* a ghost or a spirit come back from the beyond. But a good ghost or an evil ghost? That's what I have to find out.

Rolling off the bed, I tiptoe into the kitchen, glad I'm still wearing my sneakers. I snatch the flashlight and slip out the back door quiet as I can, heading for the blue bottle tree.

Grabbing a stepladder from the side of the house, I open it up under the tree and make sure it's steady. Then I flick on the flashlight and shine it up into the branches, checking out every bottle I can.

Miss Silla Wheezy jumps up on the first rung of the ladder while I'm standing there, rubbing against my legs and making me feel like I'm gonna fall. "Hey, cut it out!" I tell her softly. "I'll pet you when I get down."

The cat leaps onto the trunk and claws her way up to one of the bigger branches. She sits and meows at me, cocking her head like she's asking a question.

"What are you sayin', Miss Silla?"

She keeps meowing and then climbs out onto one of the limbs, a whole spray of bottles stuck on little branches. She sniffs the bottles and rubs her head against them, then pokes a paw at the whole row.

"You are a mighty peculiar cat," I tell her, trying not to laugh in case I fall and break a leg.

I shine the light on the limb she's poking at and suck in my breath. There are notes in the bottles Miss Silla Wheezy is pawing at! How did she know that?

Since I gotta reach so far out along the branches to get to the bottles, it takes a while to slip them off and set them on the ground without breaking the glass. I have to get up and down off the ladder over and over again.

Finally, I get to press my eye against the mouth of the bottles — and *three* of them have notes! Setting the flashlight down, I shake the notes out and stick them in the pocket of my jeans. My stomach is jumping around like beans in a skillet as I replace the bottles on their branches, stash the ladder against the house, and tiptoe back inside, being sure to hook the flashlight on the wall.

The center of the wooden floorboards creak under the rugs and I halt quick, hoping Mirage doesn't hear me. A minute later the house is still quiet, so I hug the wall and dart back into my bedroom, making sure the latch on the door doesn't make any clicking noises.

After I take off my shoes and stash them under the bed, I'm panting from holding my breath so much and hurrying.

I open up the new notes, and my hands are shaking as I spread them out and smooth over the fold lines.

It's the same school notebook paper as the very first note I found. And the same handwriting. Slanted letters and a scrawly hand.

I have a plan. Come to the pier and all will be revealed.

My mamma says we're going into Lafayette today. I'm sorry!

Do you think you have the gift? What if we mess up?

"Wow." My heart pings in a hundred different directions, like a pinball machine where the ball zings off the levers and bounces off the holes.

The blue bottle notes are like a story. A mystery story and I gotta be the detective and figure out the clues. I keep thinking Mirage must have written the messages since it's her blue bottle tree, but I'm not so sure anymore. I gotta match the handwriting somehow. I stare at the notes; the messages about the pier and some kind of gift. But who is the sender and who is the receiver? It's almost like a conversation.

My breath stops. I pull open the top drawer of the bureau and snatch the first two bottle notes and the rolled-up one from the blue bottle charm, then spread them across the bed to compare.

There are six notes now, including these three new ones. All the notes have the same handwriting, except for two. I stare at the one that makes my skin crawl. An eerie feeling creeps down my legs and zaps at my bare toes.

She's dead. She's dead! I'll never forgive myself long as I live.

And then I have one of them lightbulb moments, like out of a cartoon.

Clutching the death note, I return to the kitchen. First I check the back door to make sure I really did lock it, and then whirl around the room, looking, looking, looking. A clock ticks on a shelf, but Mister Lenny is nowhere to be seen. He's usually awake at night and floating around the house. Maybe Mirage let him outside tonight because I haven't seen him and he hasn't been following me.

"Where is Mirage's spell box?" I whisper to the dark kitchen. Then I spy it, up high on the cabinets next to the stove. I'm afraid to drag a chair over and try to lift it down. Just my luck I'd drop it. "Hallelujah," I whisper, finding the next best thing to her spell box. Maybe even better.

Underneath a stack of old newspapers and cookbooks and a bird-watching book sits Mirage's recipe book for healing remedies.

Carefully, I get the book out from under the stack of stuff and set it on the table. I try not to mess up the loose papers, or the leaves and flowers tucked into some of the pages.

Turning the pages I see a *Recipe for Cough Syrup*, *Recipe for Liniment*, and recipes for warts, sunstroke, stomachaches, joints, sprains, you name it. There's even one called *Recipe for a Healing Spell*. I wonder how it's different than the others, but the handwriting is really old-fashioned like it's been handed down from a hundred years ago.

But *all* the other recipe pages are done in the same handwriting. I spread the blue bottle note next to one of the pages and get the flashlight again.

I knew it. *I knew it!*

The death note *was* written by Mirage. Even though the lettering looks sort of like a kid wrote it, the style is the same as the handwriting in Mirage's recipe book. The same up-and-down letters, the big exclamation points with the dots slightly off center.

The other four, which include the very first one I found plus these three new ones, are definitely *not* written by Mirage. I'm positive of that. So they must be written by my *grand-mère*? Is she the *she* who died?

181

Then I look at the note that says:

My mamma says we're going into Lafayette today. I'm sorry!

That don't sound like my *grand-mère* wrote it. Sounds like a kid getting dragged on a trip. Who was the other person who had written these notes? Someone who was young. Or maybe my *grand-mère* turned senile?

The whole thing is very odd and confusing.

Another lightbulb pops like a spark in my head and since I'm already out in the kitchen, I go out to the backyard one last time. I can't stop now.

All the notes I've found so far have been on the left side of the tree.

When I get back outside, Miss Silla Wheezy's eyes are glowing in the dark. She's perched on a limb that stretches long and gnarly — to the right of the blue bottles where I just found the other notes.

I scratch the top of her head and stare straight into her green eyes. "You are one spooky cat. I swear you are readin' my mind."

It takes a few minutes of searching, but then I find another cluster of bottles — with folded notes inside. "I knew it!" I whisper and Miss Silla Wheezy yowls at me like she knew it all along.

My legs are trembling now as I climb down the ladder, dump out the notes, and run back inside.

I double-check the lock, replace the spell book under its bed of papers, and let out one of those big sighs of relief when I make it back to my bedroom.

The thrill in my stomach is exhilarating.

"Dern!" I mutter as my fingers fumble on the tightly folded notes.

Finally, I lay them out and just stare and stare.

Yeah, Mamma says I do. Don't believe her. Annoying!

My boat sprung a leak, dad gummit! In town gettin' it fixed. Don't start without me!

Got my baby alligator charm today when Daddy took me to town. But he says if he ever catches me with a baby gator he'll give me a whippin'. Gotta be more careful. . . .

My mind is worked up like crazy.

My hands are shaking as I pull on my nightgown. I decide to skip the teeth brushing because Mirage will hear the water running. Just as I yank the curtains closed — a figure peeks out from behind the blue bottle tree.

It's the girl again! My heart leaps into my throat as I cup my eyes against the glass. Is it really Gwen? The girl looks up at my window, staring, staring, staring.

I wave back, flapping my hands at her, but she doesn't seem to see me.

A moment later, she buries her face in her hands like she's crying.

And runs away into the swirly fog rising off the swamp water as it gently laps against the banks.

CHAPTER THIRTEEN

THE NEXT MORNING, MIRAGE KNOCKS SEVERAL TIMES before I hear her.

I'm dreaming that I'm dancing with Gwen under the blue bottle tree in the moonlight. We leap and float in our nightgowns, our faces pale and ghostly. Gwen and I hold hands and run along the bank, jumping over the elephant ears and splashing in the water. When we get tired, we sit under the tree and write notes to each other on crisp, lined paper. An angel floats down from the sky and taps our heads with a magic wand.

The next instant, I'm standing on the broken pier, alone and sobbing.

Gwen has disappeared.

Rotting wooden planks like jagged teeth fence me in so I can't escape back to dry land. I can see the blue bottle tree, but I can't get to it. My hands are full of notes to stick inside the bottles, but I'm stuck. I want to go home so bad my bones ache.

"Shelby Jayne!" Mirage calls through the door and I hear her voice through the dream fog.

"Yeah," I finally croak and slit open my eyes. My lids are crusty and I'm sweating. My heart is racing like I've been running a marathon.

"It was just a dream," I whisper aloud, but the dream world and Gwen were so real, my mind is still caught up in it all.

I glance around and the bedroom looks cheerless in the hazy morning light. I remember that I wanted to go home real bad. But where's home? With Daddy in the Ukraine? Or New Iberia with Grandmother Phoebe? Or right here in the spooky swamp with Mirage, my mamma who ran away and doesn't tell me she loves me?

I woke up sweaty, but now I get a peculiar shiver. Soon as I'm dressed, I head out to the porch. It's warm and muggy and foggy. The feeling of the dream is so strong; I head down to the banks behind the blue bottle tree and look for footprints.

Strands of wispy fog rise from the flat surface of the bayou. Cypress knees and a forest of trees stretch as far as I can see like there's no end ever in the whole world.

It's damp and muddy, but I can't find no footprints at all.

Maybe I'm just tired after all those trips up and down the ladder last night.

I wish I'd taken Miss Silla Wheezy in my room with me last night. Would she have seen the girl in the fog? If Miss Silla had looked out the window when I saw the girl and meowed, then I'd know for sure I wasn't seein' things.

"Breakfast, Shelby," Mirage calls.

I scoot back up to the porch, passing under the blue bottle tree. Drips of dew plop onto my head.

"Can I eat out here?" I ask, pointing to the card table on the porch. Maybe it's dumb, but I want to be here if Gwen suddenly shows up in her pirogue. I hold no real hope. Gwen is ethereal and dreamy and just a teensy bit strange. Like she belongs in the moonlight and hiding in graveyards.

Mirage clears off the tools and sets down some scrambled eggs, grits, biscuits, and fried tomatoes. "Gettin' close to the last of the summer tomatoes. I'll be canning all day while you're at school."

Miss Silla Wheezy sits on a chair next to me and stares at my eggs.

"I do believe you've made a friend," Mirage says as the telephone starts to ring its loud, throaty ring like it's fifty years old.

"How old is she anyway?" I ask Mirage.

"Oh, she's old," Mirage says, her hand on the screen door. "She was jest a tiny kitten when I was a bit older than you are now. So she's 'bout eighteen now. I do believe she's been using them nine lives of hers wisely."

"The word *peculiar* describes you perfectly," I tell Miss Silla Wheezy after Mirage runs inside and grabs up the phone.

"Mreow!"

"Is that all you can say for yourself?"

"Mreow!" She licks her mouth and keeps staring at my food.

"This is people food, not cat food."

Suddenly, Miss Silla Wheezy jumps down from her chair and runs around the table like she's chasing an invisible mouse. She darts in and out from under my feet, circles the table twice more, then finally slows down.

A second later, she hops back up in her chair, flicking her tail neatly around herself. Slowly, she blinks, almost like she's thinking, "I know I just did a crazy thing, but I'll pretend it didn't really happen."

Her feline eyes seem full of secrets. My arms prickle. "I'm thinkin' you know the mystery story and just don't want to tell me."

My answer is a pair of solemn, unblinking green eyes.

"On second thought, maybe you *are* trying to tell me the story. If you been living here all these years, then you probably *saw* who put those notes in the blue bottles. You've seen Gwen in her boat down there by the water when you're sneakin' around in the dark catching mice."

Miss Silla Wheezy yawns, stretches her legs out, then curls up in the chair next to me, laying her chin on her front paws and slitting her eyes. She ain't gonna tell me a single thing.

The photo albums are still on the table from last night.

I stuff a forkful of eggs into my mouth and turn the pages, then almost choke on my breakfast.

Me and Mirage are at a park and I'm sitting on a swing, soaring so high my mouth is wide open with laughter as she pushes me. Then there's me and Mirage curled up on the couch at Grandmother Phoebe's house reading a stack of books. Me in the bathtub full of bubbles. Mirage letting me pour a cup a sugar into a big bowl of cookie dough.

Daddy must have taken these pictures. I can suddenly see him in my mind sneaking up on us and snapping shots.

The next instant, I hear Grandmother Phoebe tsking her tongue and telling Daddy that they are spoiling me rotten as well as messing up the house.

I remember all those nights Mirage or Grandmother Phoebe stomped off to their rooms after dinner, Daddy and me pulled between them like a tug-a-war rope.

"Shelby Jayne," Mirage says in my ear.

My head's so far into the photo albums that when she speaks I practically jump out of my skin. "What?"

She looks at me with a peculiar-like expression. "You gone a million miles away, *shar*. You're actin' so funny the past couple a days. Could hardly wake you up this morning neither."

"I'm not funny," I tell her, indignantly.

She glances down at the photographs and runs a finger along the empty plastic sheets at the back of the album. I'd already looked through to the very last page. "You like 'em?" she asks.

I bite my cheek and flick my eyes away. "Yeah," I tell her, but my voice is so quiet I can hardly hear it myself. "I mean, yes, ma'am. Guess I forgot we did all this stuff together. And Daddy, too."

She looks at me with her dark brown eyes and touches my arm. This time I don't jump. "Once upon a time, we used to be a real family."

My ears are buzzing like I got cicadas stuck inside my eardrums. My eyes burn a little bit, too, but that's probably due to finding all them blue bottle notes last night at midnight.

"I know we can be a family again, Shelby Jayne. I mean, I'm hopin' real bad we can. I'm prayin' for that every single day."

"What about Daddy? Didn't you get a — a divorce?" The word tastes bad in my mouth, like bitter beets and burnt onions, but I've been wondering about that and Daddy's never told me for sure.

Now Mirage bites at her lips, and my curiosity radar is on high alert. "We been separated this last year, but nothing else is official. We never done no paperwork or lawyers or nothing. Don't got no money. And neither one of us got the heart. Least not yet."

I look down at my lap and then I look at the photos again because I'm having a hard time looking at her. But I want those pictures to be true. I wish I could remember it all better. "You ever wish you could go back in time and start all over again?"

"All the time, *shar*, all the time." Mirage gives a start. "Oh, lordy, your grandmother Phoebe's been waitin' on the phone for you! Told her you were eatin' your grits. Hurry inside!" She motions to the kitchen table and I scrape my chair back and run.

My grandmother is calling from the hospital. "My goodness, did Mirage forget to relay my message? I'm a patient woman, but not that patient." She's huffy and perturbed.

"I'm sorry, Grandmother Phoebe. I was kinda busy," I tell her, pretending I was in the powder room.

She harrumphs, but changes the subject. "So how are you, my darling girl?"

"I'm okay," I say, stifling a yawn. Maybe Miss Silla Wheezy's yawns are rubbing off on me. I heard once that yawns are contagious. Didn't know I could catch it from a cat.

"Are you surviving that swamp house?"

"Yeah." That's a funny word. Surviving. "I'm still alive," I add, trying for a joke.

"Very funny, Shelby Jayne Allemond. And please use the word *yes*, not *yeah*."

"Yes, ma'am."

"I called because I am finally coherent after that horrible anesthesia. I've been so groggy and nauseated. But the doctors say the surgery was successful and I should be my normal self in a few months."

"You mean you can't walk for months?"

"I can get around with a walker, but it's going to be very slow and I am required to do detailed lists of exercise and therapy. Being away from my own home and bed is going to be the death of me."

"Don't sound very fun."

"Not much is 'fun' anymore, Shelby. I just wish my darling girl were here with me. You could read to me and we could listen to music and you would be such a big help fetching things for me. You could be my hands and feet and eyes for me while I'm forced to recuperate."

"Yeah. I mean, yes, ma'am." Sitting around a hospital, fetching magazines and ice water sounds sort of awful, actually.

Grandmother Phoebe lowers her voice. "Does she still have that smelly owl?"

I glance up at Mirage, feeling guilty that we're talking about her, but she's busy scouring the frying pan and not looking at me.

"Yes, ma'am."

"Well, I hope she's feeding you something besides crawfish and wild mushrooms. And I hope you have a decent mattress. If you bring home bedbugs that will be the death of me! You're attending school, correct?"

"Yes, ma'am."

"Good. I must go now. The nurse just walked in. They're forcing me to get up and roam the halls every two hours. The people I must put up with are quite taxing, my darling Shelby."

I give a little laugh thinking about the nurses and orderlies in the hospital trying to get my grandmother to do what *they* want instead of what *she* wants. "I'm sorry you have to go through all this hospital stuff, Grandmother Phoebe. I'll bet it hurts, too."

"Yes, it does, but my will is stronger and I will survive." She gives a long, drawn-out sigh. "We will get through this, darling Shelby. And be reunited soon. The hardest part is being apart from each other and our own routine."

"Yes, ma'am," I say, but secretly I'm thinking about what it'd be like going back to our too-quiet house in New Iberia without Daddy. Grandmother Phoebe's particular ways. The Schedule Is Everything. No cats. No sleeping in. Dressing up for meetings. Some things about home I'm not missin' at all.

When I arrive at school, everything is almost back to normal. The kids bring packed lunches instead of money for the cafeteria, but other than that it's almost like there wasn't a fire at all. Except for that charred smoky smell permeating the halls. The teachers have fans on to keep the air circulating and push the burned smell out the open windows.

I see Tara and Alyson talking with Jett and T-Beau and Ambrose on the other side of the playground and my stomach twists. I want to go home and crawl under the sheets again. I wonder if I can change my schedule, but I don't have the guts to go to the office and ask.

I get through my classes, pretending those kids don't exist. They pretend I don't exist, either, and we're just fine. At least I tell myself that.

I catch a glimpse of Larissa with her skinny legs and arms full of books turning a corner of the hallway during lunch, but I don't see her eating nowhere. I wonder where she goes. I wonder if she has any friends.

Don't have much time to think about her because I get real busy avoiding the Truth or Dare group, dodging them in hallways and around corners, or ducking into the bathroom. They seem to multiply like a math problem gone wrong. When I see them eating lunch in a big circle on the lawn across from the gym, I notice that a couple other girls have joined the group.

Soon as the last bell rings, I race out of class and dart down the road, hiding behind the huge oak tree trunks and then bursting into sprints in between. After I pass the long pier walkway across the bayou, I'm at the cemetery again.

I wait a full thirty minutes, but there's no sign of Gwen. The place is silent as a tomb. I try to laugh when I think about silent tombs since I'm sitting right smack-dab in a graveyard. But I'm terribly, horribly disappointed. I've been waiting to see Gwen all day, especially after spying her last night through the window. And those spooky, ghostly dreams.

I give up finally and slowly walk back through the grave-yard, crossing the narrow dirt road and bounding down to the water's edge. Her boat isn't here, either. I stare out across the water at the little island. Can't even catch a glimpse of Gwen's house from here. Like it doesn't even exist. I didn't dream her up, did I? My stomach starts to hurt when I wonder if I'm going crazy. I saw her. I talked with her. We rowed across the water, spent the afternoon at her house. I've seen her twice through my bedroom window. *I know it.*

I scratch my arm as a mosquito tries to drink my blood, and glance down the bayou. The pier is deserted, too, and I breathe a big sigh of relief. Guess there aren't any other new kids to torment with Truth or Dare today.

Then I remember that Mirage is waiting for me back at the town docks and I run as fast as I can back the way I came.

Even if I'd seen Gwen, I would have only had the chance to say hello and good-bye. Can't let Mirage see me come down this road neither.

Twisting the charm bracelet around my wrist, I touch the cute little gator, the pretty ruby birthstone, the mysterious carved spell box, the empty locket, and the blue bottle, which holds such meaning. I want to look at those notes again. I want to figure out the story.

I need a different plan.

The next day there's a test in math I forgot to study for and a group project starting in social studies. I'm assigned with Tara and Alyson and some girl named Mabel.

I excuse myself to go to the restroom and try not to cry as I stare at my splotched face in the mirror. I blow my nose ten times, take a hundred deep breaths, get a drink of water, and finally go back. Tara and Alyson ignore me, talking only to Mabel about their plans and excluding me. I'm pretty sure they'll help me flunk the project. And throw a party afterward.

Every day gets more miserable. I want to see Gwen, but I don't know how to reach her. I don't even know her telephone number.

Then I realize that she probably doesn't have a phone no more out on that island.

I wonder what she's doing. I wonder why she doesn't come to school. Is she out looking for her parents every day? What would I do if my parents were missing? I sort of know what that feels like. Practically lost my mamma for a year.

A few days later after Mirage drops me off, I get as far as the school fences and stop. Gripping the chain-link fence, I stare through to where kids are kicking balls and playing tag or having races on the field.

My heart begins to thump.

I don't want to go face those kids and the teachers and the schoolwork.

I don't even want to see Larissa, that scarred girl in my class. I feel guilty that I haven't made any effort to get to know her. She doesn't seem to have any friends and the other kids ignore her like she's invisible. Almost how I'm starting to feel, except I have Gwen now.

I just know in my heart that Larissa went to the pier and played Truth or Dare. Did she fall? Did she get pushed into the bayou? Did a gator take a bite out of her face?

I shiver as a cloud crosses the sun.

Larissa tried to warn me. She knew what was going to happen.

But if I hadn't come, I would never have met Gwen.

I worry something fierce that if I don't get to the graveyard every day, Gwen will disappear on me. She might find her parents and not have a chance to tell me. She might take a bus into a different town to look for them. What if I never see her again?

Pretending I'm an invisible person myself, I start walking down the street again, turning left when I get to the dirt road and the oak trees. I don't look back even when I'm sorely tempted and my neck is just plain itchin' to turn around and see if someone's following me.

But no footsteps, no voices calling after me, nothing. ·

When I get to the cemetery, I can hear a girl's voice singing again, humming and la, la, la-ing like she's trying out for the New Orleans Opera.

I start running, my heart leaping inside my chest. When I get to the bottom of the slope, Gwen and her flyaway hair and dark eyes peeks out from behind the angel.

"You're here," I breathe.

"*You're* here," Gwen says, and then we both just stand there trying not to giggle with happiness.

Without saying a single word, we run to the banks and jump into her pirogue. Like we can read each other's minds.

"I know a place where there are baby alligators," Gwen says. "Other side of this here island."

"Is it safe?" My brain keeps hearing Mirage's warnings and threats about being out here on this side a town. Near the pier. Taking a boat out on the water without permission. She'd ground me but good if she knew I'd left school, but I had to come. Gwen is for sure the absolute best thing about Bayou Bridge.

We row around Deserted Island and come across a small inlet under a stand of cypress, dark and shadowy and secretive.

"This here is Alligator Cove," Gwen tells me.

An egret swoops out of the branches of a stand of tupelos and Gwen points upward. "He's got a nest up there. See it?"

I squint upward and sure enough, there's a nest made of moss and twigs perched high on some interlocking branches.

"Now look over there on that patch of mud and twigs," Gwen whispers. Her voice is muted by dead leaves and duckweed and the murky water that surrounds us. Here in the swamp it feels like I'm in another world altogether.

"Baby gators!" I hiss.

"Ssh! Don't want to startle 'em."

We paddle closer, then ease up on our oars and set them in the bottom of the boat.

Sure enough, baby alligators are crawling all over a half-submerged log, stumbling over branches and mounds of leaves and elephant ears. Patches of sun filter through the leaves. The light falls on their backs, and the babies' heads are up and alert lookin' out on the big, wide world.

I count at least twelve gators, their skinny bodies and tails decorated with bands of dark black and blue and yellow. Eyes like spilled ink, and unblinking.

When they sense that we're close, the baby gators freeze on the log, as though they think we won't notice them if they stop moving.

"They got tiny teeth, don't they?" I ask. "Will they bite?"

"Sure they'll bite! Like the sharpest needles you ever felt in your life. My daddy used to get a net when they're first born and scoop 'em up so's I could pet 'em. These here are bigger than just hatched newborns, though."

"Is the mamma gator close by?"

"Nah. These gators are old enough to be on their own now. Adults nest and then move on." Gwen puts a hand flat on top of the water, skimming the surface. Before I can even blink, she scoops up one of the babies and cups her hands around it.

"You did it!" I cry real soft so I don't startle the rest of the baby gators squirming around on the log.

Pulling the reptile close, Gwen clamps her fingers around his snout so he won't snap at her while she strokes his head to keep him calm.

I'm holding my breath from pure astonishment. "Can I touch him?" I ask, and then wonder where those words came from. I've never been this close to a gator in all my life. Except in a zoo or a library book. Holding a gator seems crazy. And kinda wonderful.

If Grandmother Phoebe could see me now, she'd die of shock and never let me serve lemonade and cookies again.

Gwen moves the boat closer to shore with her paddle, and then transfers the gator to my lap. His skin is smooth and yet ridged, and he sits, head up, staring straight forward while I stroke my fingers along his back and tail. "I can't *believe* I'm doin' this! For real!"

"Doin' good, Shelby. He's real calm with you."

I glance up at Gwen. "Or maybe he's just waitin' for his chance to escape over the edge and dive back in. Did you ever want a baby gator for a pet?"

"Yeah, I used to, but my daddy says that it don't take long before they're big and start snapping. I could lose a finger before I ever had a chance to get outta the way."

"They are pretty cute, though."

I hand the baby gator back over to Gwen as a breeze rustles the leaves, soft and gentle-like. Yet it's so quiet, too. Quieter than I've ever heard the world in my whole life. Feels like Bayou Bridge don't even exist no more. School seems like just a dream.

"You cutting school, too?" I ask Gwen, realizing that I've never skipped school before in my life. Can't help wondering if Principal Trahan will call Mirage and tell her. She don't get many phone calls. None really, except for Daddy's and Grandmother Phoebe's calls.

Gwen lies back in the boat, her hair floating like strands of gold ribbon over the bow. "School? Haven't been in the longest time. S'pose you could say I'm homeschooled now. Need some books, I guess, and I keep meaning to go to the library but never seem to get my legs movin' that direction."

"Where do you think your folks have gone?"

"Not sure. Can't even remember how long they've been gone. Then I remembered them talkin' about moving away. To a different city."

I'm shocked, pure and simple. "They forgot you!" I bite my lips and hope I haven't hurt her feelings now.

She doesn't look at me, just keeps stroking the baby gator. "Used to cry a lot. I remember that I had a lot of pain. My body hurt, but it finally stopped. Then my heart hurt like it was breaking into a million pieces, but that's starting to go away, too. I'm not sure what that means. Do you think I'm heartless, Shelby?"

"'Course not. You can't spend every moment crying, I guess, but — but — all your stuff is still in the house."

"That's the strangest part, isn't it? But the house hasn't

been cleaned in forever. It's dusty and musty-smelling with crud everywhere. The yard's got piles of moldy leaves and junk the storms bring in and dump all over the place."

"That's so peculiar, Gwen," I tell her. I'm gonna say more, but I stop myself. Sure seems like something happened to her parents, all right. Like maybe they had an accident or something. But wouldn't the police come and tell her?

She sits up. "Guess it's time to join your brothers and sisters again." As Gwen sets the gator down on the log, the other babies scatter, startled. Our baby gator opens his mouth big and wide, showing off his little razor teeth.

"Look, he's smiling, Shelby."

"Smiling real wicked, I'd say." We paddle out of the cove and I call back, "Good-bye, babies, be good while we're gone."

As we keep going 'round the island, a field of purple water hyacinth spreads out like a meadow. I stop paddling to stare. "It's like a fairytale woods."

"Yeah, it's the last before autumn sets in. Them yellow swamp flowers are budding now and the purple hyacinth will start dyin' off soon as it starts coolin'."

We finally pull up at the island dock and tie up the boat. As we hike up to the house, darting around patches of water and shrubs, all kinds a birds flit through the trees. Robins and doves and bobwhites talking up a storm, oak leaves chattering back, like I've just landed on a whole different world.

Guess I can see why Mirage likes it out here so much. I never knew the swamp could be beautiful.

Which makes it even stranger why she'd want to leave. She grew up here. Her animals are here and her *traiteur* life. Why'd she want to go back to New Iberia and stuff herself into an apartment or some rented room? That don't make much sense. Why couldn't Daddy come live with us in the swamp house?

He could when he gets back from that country by Russia.

I realize for the first time that he really could. What if all I had to do was just ask him?

My stomach makes a queer, jumpy feeling — and I know I'm not hungry.

While Grandmother Phoebe's having rehabilitation therapy, our house is being taken care of by a once-a-week gardener and housekeeper. It don't get dirty much when Mirage and Daddy are gone. But I know my grandmother'd be happier if nobody had shoes and homework and books and jackets lying around.

Grandmother Phoebe's always kept a tight grip on us, but now I'm wondering if she'd be better off with us in our own house. And only certain visiting hours. Posted on the front door.

I hold my stomach with one hand and put my other hand on my heart. I'm thinking thoughts I've never thought before. Picturing a life I've never imagined.

"Gwen," I say, hopping over a root in the path, "do you ever get the feeling that you could change your own life if you wanted to?"

"We're only eleven. We have to do what grown-ups tell us. But most days, I know I lost the life I used to have. Memories are slippin' out of my head, disappearin' into the air, sinkin' into the bayou. I can't hardly remember what my mamma looked like, or my baby sister, Maddie. I have to look at the photo albums to bring it all back."

I glance over at her, the pale white of her skin, the black and green of her eyes. She's so different from anybody I've ever known. LizAnn and I talk about homework and piano lessons and curfews and shopping. Gwen never talks about any of those things.

Her words make me sad. I wonder if she's really a runaway. Or if she broke out of juvenile detention. But she doesn't seem like either of those kinds a people. Just lost. Lonely. Not a part of Bayou Bridge, not a part of school. Just floating on the edge of life.

"I'm trying to get my family back together, too," I suddenly confide to Gwen. "My mamma left a year ago. My daddy's halfway across the world, and my grandmother's in the hospital."

"We really are almost just alike, ain't we?" Gwen says,

gazing into my face. She reaches out to grasp my hand and hangs on tight, like she's trying to hold on to a lifeline. Like she might bust into a million pieces if I wasn't here.

"I want my daddy to try living here for a while. But I don't think he'll come unless my mamma does the asking. I'm finally figuring out that it's *both* of their fault, not just my mamma's."

Soon as I say the words, it's like the whole world shifts, and the telescope I'm looking through grows about ten feet across.

CHAPTER FOURTEEN

I WANT TO SHOW YOU SOMETHING," GWEN SAYS A FEW weeks later as she walks over to her bedroom closet. She shoots me a mysterious smile like she's practicing to be a movie star. "I made a secret chamber, but nobody else knows nothin' about it. Actually, one other person does, my best friend."

"Your best friend?" I say, and my voice goes faint.

"Yeah, we've known each other since we were babies, but she disappeared long time ago. Don't know where she is, and I can't help bein' mad at her. Best friends shouldn't just move away without telling you."

"I agree," I say, thinking about LizAnn and how hurt I would feel if she stopped being my friend or just up and disappeared.

I think about Larissa at school and wonder if she's ever had a best friend. Maybe in her old town. Don't think she has *any* friends here in Bayou Bridge, though. Little pings of guilt start up again, stabbing at my conscience. I'm lucky to find Gwen, even if it means cutting school.

Gwen turns to look at me. "Maybe we can be best friends."

A lovely warmth spreads from my toes all the way up to my heart. "Forever," I tell her. I guess it isn't a very nice thought, but I can't help being glad Gwen's best friend isn't around no more. If she was, Gwen would never have been hiding behind the angel statue.

"Now, look at this secret chamber. I made it myself."

I peer over her shoulder as she reaches deep into the closet. She makes a fist, pounds on the frame, and a little door pops open. It's even got a cute brass doorknob.

"I've been making a scrapbook. Not a single person of the human race ever laid eyes on it before now." The scrapbook is also a photo album, the cover a stiff cardboard and covered with blue material. "I made the cover, too, but I'm not a very good artist. It's kinda sloppy. See the corners where the glue doesn't hold together right?"

"I think it's beautiful," I tell her, admiring the little cut-out hearts and stars and the purple hyacinth climbing along the edges of each page.

"Oh! Got an idea!" Gwen cries. "Gonna get my camera. Be right back."

She runs downstairs and while she's gone I sit on the bed and slowly turn the pages of the beautiful little book. My ears start to buzz and my throat goes dry as an empty lake. Gwen's handwriting is all over the pages. Titles and picture captions and little jokes.

I run my finger over the caption that says, *Me and Daddy and Mamma in New Orleans for Mardi Gras.*

I've seen those same fat letters before. The circles dotting the *i*'s on the blue bottle notes. Gwen's handwriting *is the very same handwriting as those messages in the bottles*!

My heart thuds and I keep blinking and staring at those scrapbook pages, wondering if I'm dreaming it all up.

I study the pictures of Gwen on trips with her parents, a school play, hanging upside down on the jungle gym at school. There's also a little girl with red curls and a grin with missing front teeth.

Then I see photos of Gwen with her best friend. The girl with the dark hair from the locket — which is so tiny. Some of the pictures were taken far under the oak trees in the shadows so their faces are hard to make out.

Suddenly, Gwen is back, out of breath from running up and down the stairs. She's holding a black old-fashioned-looking camera. "This is my daddy's. I want to take a picture of this day so we won't forget it. Let's go out on the porch. This camera needs lots of light. Here, you take mine first and then I'll take yours. I'll frame them in the album after Daddy gets the film developed, okay?"

"Is this your little sister?" I ask, pointing to the girl with reddish hair and the same pretty smile Gwen has.

"Yep, that's Maddie. She's nine and in fourth grade — I mean, if she was here. She's pretty cute for a little sister." Gwen pauses. "I think I miss her the most."

We run downstairs to the front porch and I take the camera and aim it at Gwen, who stands on the top step, smiling her sad, faraway smile.

"Press the button on top when you've got it focused," Gwen calls.

I wiggle the focus control and the odd buzzing in my ears returns. Through the tiny camera window I can see Gwen, one arm clutching the post of the porch. When I press the button, the camera clicks done.

Gwen trots over. "Now I'll take yours. Stand over there where I was."

I get into position and Gwen groans. "Oh, no, that was the last picture on this roll!" She glares at the camera as if it has purposely betrayed her.

"That's okay," I tell her. "We can get more film and take my picture another day."

"It won't be the same, because it won't be today, will it?"

I nod my head, agreeing with her, but my mind is whirling about so many other things besides taking pictures. I know now for sure the two people who wrote the notes in the blue bottles. Mirage and Gwen.

Questions burn on my tongue, but I don't even know where to start. And I'm afraid of the answers. Swallowing hard, I say, "Gwen, you ever go out to the swamp house with that big blue bottle tree?"

She stops fiddling with the camera and her body stiffens. "Yeah, I know that house. Everybody does. The other *traiteur* lives there."

"Do you ever — did you ever — write notes and put them in the bottles?"

Gwen frowns at me. "How you know about that? You been spyin' on me?"

"No! I just — I mean, I think I've seen you out there some nights."

Gwen glances away, staring into the dark forest of cypresses surrounding the house. "Supposed to be a secret."

So Mirage and Gwen have been writing notes to each other? I'm so shocked I can't hardly swallow. That means they know each other, because the handwriting matches both of them.

Maybe Mirage did a healing spell for Gwen. Maybe more than one. And maybe they started becoming friends. What if Gwen has sat in the very same chair where I eat my supper by the stove? What if she's petted Mister Lenny? I wonder if Mirage ever prayed over her or stroked her hair.

Now I know what an evil imp is because it's sittin' on my shoulder making me jealous like I never felt before.

Does that mean that all this last year while I was in New Iberia, Mirage made friends with Gwen and they spent time together? Went places together? Talked to each other through secret, fun notes in the blue bottle tree?

That must be why I'd seen Gwen down by the banks. Times when she'd paddled up the bayou and hidden her notes. Their own secret, private game. Like Gwen was Mirage's daughter, not me.

My nauseated stomach comes back with a vengeance and I feel sorta green. My face gets hot. I think I need to sit down. "Why do you write notes to each other in the blue bottles?" I finally choke out.

She gives me a small smile. "Mostly for some spooky fun. Especially when the power is down in the swamp during a storm and the phones go out. We sneak out and write notes to plan stuff we're gonna do. Or where we're gonna meet."

I was right then. The messages *were* like two friends secretly passing notes during class. My mamma — I mean Mirage — and my new best friend, Gwen. I don't know whether to stomp off and never speak to them again or just cry my eyes out.

A year ago, there were times I thought I hated Mirage. I wouldn't a cared a single little bit what she was doing or who she was friends with.

My legs stumble across the yard to the oak tree, my mind a cyclone of peculiar thoughts. I chew on my cheek and it hurts worse than ever. Mirage was supposed to love me. And she was supposed to love me *best*. And now I find out she's secret-note friends with Gwen and treats her like her very own daughter. Maybe that's why she didn't come visit more often — because she never missed me all that much.

Gwen saunters over. "I got this plan to have a note in every single bottle by the time I get to high school."

I take a big, hard gulp. "That's a lotta notes."

"Only problem is if my best friend really did move away. Like my family. Like everybody I know just up and disappearing on me. But I still go out there some nights when I'm not too scared of the dark. To look for new notes."

She's not making any sense again. She's talking like Mirage is the best friend she hasn't seen for a while, the friend that disappeared. But Mirage still lives at her house. Is Gwen just a little bit crazy in the head?

Gwen reaches for my hand. "You gonna disappear on me, too?"

"Where would I go?" I say, but inside I'm thinking that maybe she's right. I really will leave. Me staying here is supposed to be temporary. And if I had my way, my daddy would come get me tomorrow. In a small voice, I ask, "Do you still find some notes then? How long has it been since the last message in the blue bottles?"

Her shoulders shake, like she's holding back tears. "Nothing new for longer than I can remember. She never answered my last note."

"And you didn't ever see her again?"

"Nope, never again. Sometimes I'm afraid she got sick or died. But I don't know! I don't know nothing! She jest disappeared into thin air."

Gwen is mixed up, that is for certain. Mirage isn't sick or dead. And she's still living at the swamp house, although not for long probably.

None of it makes a lick of sense.

Except the fact that Mirage and Gwen have a secret friendship and left me out.

I'm still puzzling over all of Gwen's mixed-up stories and the blue bottle notes when I get back home later that afternoon.

I also try to figure out the homework I missed, avoiding Mirage's eyes because I feel guilty about skipping school and lying to her. Used to be I didn't care much about what she thought, but now I do. And it hurts all over again.

Mirage is quiet, puttering around the house, cleaning some fresh-picked moss, doing dishes. Mister Lenny gets his bandages off for good, too.

"Now he can practice his flying again." Mirage makes those cooing noises, encouraging him to spread his wings and lift off. Finally, he does, in fits and starts across the kitchen.

After I finish up my homework and rummage in the cupboards for an after-dinner snack, I see her sitting on the front porch in the dusk. The *front* porch that's so rickety. "Why you sitting out here and not on the back porch where the tree is?"

She gives me a wistful smile. "Sometimes I jest don't want to be reminded of sad and terrible things. I don't want to think about the bad things I done and that blue bottle tree is the biggest reminder in the world."

I blink at her, thinking about her and Gwen writing notes to each other through the bottles and I try to push the envy deep down in my gut. Sometimes she don't make any sense, either. Just like Gwen. "But it's so pretty."

"Pretty is sometimes ugly dependin' on your point of view."

I stand there, hanging on to the railing, not sure what I want, but not leaving.

"Sorry I'm bad company, Shelby. This is a bad day for me."

I glance over at her, at the way she's bent over like her stomach hurts, at the sudden lines along her mouth, the puffiness around her eyes. "Why's it so bad?"

"Somebody I loved very much died on this day many years ago."

I wasn't expecting her to say that at all. "I'm sorry."

"Me too, Shelby Jayne, me too, more'n you could know. Because I could have prevented it and I didn't."

I'm shocked. "Someone dying can't be your fault."

"Oh, yes, it can," she says tightly. "I wasn't there when she needed me."

I watch her rub at her eyes, then fold her arms against herself like she's cold even though it's been one of those steamy hot days. "But what can you do about it now?"

"I'd give anything in this world to do that day all

over again. Jest about anything. Wish I could have a chance to redeem myself and get rid of the guilt, but I gotta live with it and it gets me down. Too bad the Good Lord don't give us do-over days, huh? Got a few of 'em I'd like to do over. Like the day I left Grandmother Phoebe's house."

I get up my courage to speak, wanting to know what she'll say, but dreading the answer, too. "What would you do over that day? Would you have stayed?"

She shakes her head. "No, I'd still leave because I had to get out of there. Plus my mamma needed me. But if I got a do-over I'd take you with me, *shar*. In a heartbeat."

I breathe a sudden sigh of relief as the porch goes quiet. I can hear owls hooting as they skim above the trees, the hum of a bat zipping over the house. Water laps at the dock down by the elephant ears, but mostly it's tranquil and calm except for the summer crickets in the bushes. "That why you want to move away? Because of today. What happened, I mean? The person who died."

"Yeah, Shelby Jayne, that's why it's so hard to be out here again. Didn't like New Iberia much because it was too much city. But out here there's just so many sad memories."

"Where would you go?"

"Don't know. Guess I better get a plan together, eh?" She

looks out at the water where dusk is turning the swamp black, then leans forward in her chair. She gazes at me full and deep, and I try not to squirm. "Wherever I go, Shelby Jayne," she asks softly, "will you come with me?"

My stomach turns upside down. I don't know what to say. All the hurt I've been thinking in my head about her and me and Gwen starts shifting again. All the plans between her and me and Daddy shift, too. Me thinking I could get him to live out here with us.

"You don't gotta answer right now," Mirage adds. "But will you think about it?"

Silently, I nod, not sure what I'm going to do, not sure how I feel. Moving is grown-up stuff. Parents are supposed to stay together and tell everyone in the family where they're going to live. And make it all good and right.

After we say good night, I slip into bed, putting my hand under my pillow to pull the charm bracelet out from where I place it each night for safekeeping.

The bracelet isn't there.

I switch on the light, flip over the pillow, and stare at the empty space underneath. Where'd it go? Didn't I put it there when I got my nightgown on?

Now I can't remember for sure. Maybe I left it on the bureau. Maybe it's in my pockets. Quickly, I jump up and search all the spaces in my jeans and backpack. Nothing. And it's not in any of the dresser drawers or sitting on top.

I've lost Mirage's bracelet! She'll never forgive me, never. She'll change her mind about taking me with her wherever she ends up going. I came so close to losing the charm bracelet that day at the bridge during Truth or Dare and now I've lost it right here at the swamp house.

It might have fallen out somewhere else. It could be anywhere. School. The graveyard, the road, the swamp, the boat.

How can I tell Mirage that all her charms and the antique bracelet from her great-grandmother is gone? Just when I start thinking maybe I want to move away with her. When she finally asked me for the first time.

Clutching my stomach, I head to the bathroom, flush the toilet, then go into the kitchen for a drink. Before I give up, I'll search the house and the yard, the boat, the dock, everywhere I can think of.

There are so many places to look I feel knocked over. I fill a glass of water at the sink, my mind running a dozen different directions. Maybe I should make a list of places to look.

Mirage's conversation on the porch earlier interrupts my brain, too. Today is the day someone died. Someone real important. Someone special. Grand-mère only died a few months ago so it's not her. What did Mirage do that caused the "her" to die? How was it her fault?

Mirage wrote that note:

She's dead. She's dead! I'll never forgive myself long as I live.

Mirage has secrets I'd never dreamed of.

Gwen has secrets, too.

I guess, I do, as well. Cutting school. Lying. Wearing the bracelet when I'm not supposed to. Going to the cemetery and bridge pier when Mirage told me not to. Hiding the blue bottle notes. Notes that don't belong to me.

After I drink my water, I push the curtain back and stare through the window at the blue bottle tree. Silver beams of moonlight catch the glass. Gwen said that she and her friend wanted to fill up all the bottles with notes, so there had to be more of those notes out there, right?

I'd have to plan a time to find them.

Just as I let the curtain fall back into place, the moonlight catches the glint of something overhead. Jerking my chin up, I stare at Mister Lenny blinking at me from his perch on the mossy branch.

"You scared me!" I whisper at him, just as I see the charm

bracelet hanging from the end of his branch. "You took the bracelet! You little thief!"

I reach up to grab it, but Mister Lenny curls his claws around the chain and flies away, ducking through the doorway and heading for the front room.

"Give it back to me," I cry as soft as I can under my breath, chasing after him.

He flits through the house, the bracelet dangling from his feet.

"I guess your broken wing is all better," I hiss at him.

Mister Lenny zips back to the kitchen as I jump up, trying to get him to drop it. My fingers grasp at the charms and he nearly crashes into the refrigerator, finally dropping the bracelet on the stack of papers and junk by the stove.

The bracelet slips off the teetering stack of papers and disappears behind the stove, but I dive for it, snatching it just in time.

Relief floods through me as I clutch the bracelet to my heart, realizing for the first time just how much I love the charm bracelet. Catching my breath, I count up the charms, making sure all eight are still there.

The heirloom bracelet from the Civil War is different from Gwen's chain, but the charms are exactly alike.

Matching charms. Matching handwriting on the blue bottle notes. The handwriting of Gwen and Mirage. Did Gwen copy Mirage's bracelet? Or did Mirage give Gwen matching charms as a sign of their friendship and love?

I wish I hadn't thought of that because those sorry imps are back at it. Eating into my head, making me crazy with jealousy.

The photo albums Mirage took from Grandmother Phoebe's house are still sitting on the kitchen counter. All the good feelings I had when I was looking at them seem to be falling apart. I know it's stupid, but Mirage is *my* mamma, not Gwen's.

I guess I'm not a very generous person. Here Gwen lost her whole family, can't find them nowhere, and I can't even share Mirage with her — the mamma that, for more than a year, I've told everybody I hate.

Suddenly, I pull one of the photograph albums closer. The one that has the pictures from when I was a baby. The years Mirage was younger, just out of high school, just married.

Quiet as I can, I flip on the kitchen light and bend over the pages, studying Mirage in the photographs in a whole new light.

Every piece a my body starts to feel weak, like I'm gonna faint. I'm hot and cold at the same time. My thoughts go wild as I realize that Mirage is the girl in the tiny photo in Gwen's locket. Eleven years ago when she had me she looks so young. Still like a teenager. Now I see the similarities in the hair and her nose. The look in the girl's eyes is so much like Mirage's eyes are now. I wasn't looking for it before, but it's there. It's there!

All this time I've been thinking that Mirage and Gwen are currently friends, slipping secret notes into the blue bottles, having fun together without me. Mirage not actually missing me at all.

But if Mirage is the best friend in Gwen's locket — the girl in the photo with the dark hair and shy eyes — that makes everything all crazy again!

Because the picture of Mirage in the locket is when she's only eleven years old.

But Mirage grew up, got married, and had a baby. Me.

But Gwen is still only eleven.

When I get to school the next day, I know I'm gonna ditch again, but I have to go to the bathroom first. I sneak in the back door of the first hall and hit the restroom before the bell rings. The sound of lockers slamming comes through the open outer door and the smell of Lysol makes my nose hurt.

I cover my face with my hands, thinking about Gwen, thinking about Mirage. The charms and the pictures swirl in my gut. Nothing makes sense. Does Gwen have some sort of disease that makes her never grow up? Is she a time traveler?

Suddenly, someone pummels the stall door, shaking the hinges. "Hey, who's in there? You stuck or somethin'? It's been ten minutes."

My stomach jumps into my throat. Those voices sound familiar.

"I can see her feet," someone else giggles.

"Yeah, there's a backpack on the floor."

"Looks fresh brand-new," the first one speaks again. *"Hey,"* she cries with sudden meaning. "I bet it's that new girl, Shelby, the one with the frizzy hair."

My stomach sinks like a rock to the floor.

I blow my nose, then flush the toilet and brace myself. When I push the stall door open, I pretend not to care if it hits the girls on the other side.

Alyson and Tara are standing there rolling on lipstick in front of the mirror.

I brush past, swinging my pack over my shoulder. "Excuse me," I murmur, but the sound of my voice is deafening.

"Excusez-moi?" Tara says, fake sugar dripping from her lips.

As if on cue Alyson casually moves in front of my path, blocking the door to the corridor.

Tara folds her arms in front of her chest. "You can't go anywhere unless we give our permission. From now on you'll take orders from us."

"What are you talking about?" I say, cursing the way my voice shakes so bad.

"You never finished our game on the pier. We can't release you until the game has been declared over."

Alyson turns to Tara. "How will we do that? We can't watch her all the time."

"Won't be that hard. We're in the same class. And there's only one lunch hour for sixth graders."

"We can give her assignments with deadlines!"

I watch their excitement grow as they get caught up in their plans to make my life miserable. The bathroom is stuffy and warm. I can feel my pulse in my throat.

"What'll we make her do first?" Alyson asks, sounding more curious than vindictive.

Tara taps her foot, and I notice that her gold sandals are beaded and sparkly like they cost a lot of money. "Your first assignment," she drawls, building suspense, pretending to think real hard. "Your first assignment is to cut your hair!"

Alyson squeals like she can hardly believe her best friend actually suggested such a horrible idea.

Tara goes on, "Cut it off above your ears by Friday. That gives you two days."

I break into a sweat. "You're crazy."

"Don't talk back," she orders. "Since you won't play Truth or Dare like every other new kid who comes to this school, you won't be allowed to speak unless we give you permission. Or a teacher asks you a direct question."

"You're brilliant, Tara," Alyson tells her.

Panic rises like I'm havin' a heart attack. If I do even one of their ugly requests, they'll make me their slave for the whole year. But how do I get outta here alive?

Sweat drips down my neck. I'm picturing hair pulling and scratching and my backpack dumped in the bayou if I try to fight them. I gotta come up with some way to catch them off guard. Do something so I can get outta here.

Tara surveys the dirty floor where gum is stuck between the tiles and toilet paper litters the corners. "Before first period starts you can clean up this bathroom. Scrub it good because this is where we always meet in the mornings. I'm the leader here and I want this place to look real fine."

I cross my fingers behind my back and put on a fake smile. "Yeah, that's because you're the queen, right?"

Tara smiles, obviously pleased at the title I just gave her. She turns to Alyson. "She's catching on."

I brace myself, hoping my sudden plan works. "I understand perfectly. You're the Queen of the Latrine, and you, Alyson, are Princess of the Potties!"

The girls drop their jaws. The next instant, squeals of outrage echo off the tile ceiling. Before they can do anything else, I hold tight to my backpack and plow through them both, racing into the corridor and almost colliding into a group of kids on their way to class.

"Get her!" I hear Tara cry out behind me.

I keep running. Flying past homeroom and pushing my way through the double doors at the end of the hall.

After the dingy school restroom, the sun glares so bright I don't see the person walking toward me and crash right into her, banging my elbow.

We both cry "Ouch!" and then I'm staring straight into the face of the scarred girl.

Neither of us says a word, but I take note of the grubby jeans, the plain brown hair, and the girl's shy, hesitant look.

She's alone, and I'm suddenly sorry I don't have time to talk to her. But it's urgent I get off the school grounds.

"Sorry I ran into you," she apologizes, her hair hanging in her face like she's trying to cover up what she looks like.

"No, I ran into you. But I — I gotta go. Sorry!"

I keep running, praying the girl won't say anything to Mrs. Daigle about me leaving school.

In less than a minute, I'm running down the dirt road to the bayou. After a few hundred yards I get a stitch in my side. My pack is heavy, too, the math textbook jabbing me between the shoulder blades.

The second bell rings and I know that class has just started.

I'm late.

I'm more than late.

I'm going to be absent again.

CHAPTER FIFTEEN

A TRUCK HAULING THE FIRST OF THE CUT SUGARCANE ZOOMS past, kicking up dust. A flock of migrating birds skims over the trees and their wings look dark pink against the sky. The road feels lonelier today. I wipe my nose with the back of my hand. My throat is parched and scratchy and the sun is beating down so hard, feels like my hair's burning up.

Turning back the way I came, I run down the fence line, crossing the street for Pete's Gas-Up Station. If I get marked absent again today, the school will call Mirage. In the phone book at the gas station, I search for the number in the crumpled, dirty pages. When I find the school's number, I deposit the coins I have in my pocket and punch the buttons.

Taking a deep breath, I try to make my voice sound like a grown-up's. "This is Miz Allemond. Please excuse my daughter, Shelby, from classes today. She's been absent due to the flu."

School noise and chaos hovers in the background as Mrs. Benoit says, "When she returns, have her bring a note."

I replace the receiver, my head buzzing with the lie, but for now I breathe a sigh of relief. I'm free the rest of the day.

Pumping my legs, I run all the way down the long dirt road until I reach the gates of the cemetery. I smell grass and sugarcane and wet fur like a dog's passed through here recently.

Dust motes float through pillars of yellow sunshine. Shining down like columns on the headstones.

I keep running, gulping in air, as I race across the grave-yard, jumping around headstones. Then I hear Gwen's melancholy humming, and an instant later she drifts out from behind the angel. She's not smiling today. Her eyes seem even darker and sadder than ever.

We hug each other, but her gloom seems to infect the day as though a curtain of dreary clouds hangs over it.

"I think I've been waiting for you for a long time," Gwen tells me. "Maybe years. I'm not sure. Time is strange, like it speeds up and slows down. Like my whole life keeps

231

happening over and over again. That probably sounds like crazy talk."

"No, it doesn't. I know some crazy things, too," I tell her, thinking about the picture of Gwen and Mirage when they were girls. I want to ask all the questions multiplying in my brain, but I'm also afraid. Instead I ask, "What do you mean that you've been waiting for me for a long time? How did you know I'd be coming here to Bayou Bridge?"

"I knew someone would come. I just had to wait long enough."

She makes the strangest statements.

"I'm so thirsty I think I'm going to pass out," I tell her, feeling jumpy and nervous. "Want to go back into town and get a drink?" I wonder how to tell her about the things I've discovered. I'm not sure how to ask the questions I need to ask.

Cicadas buzz in the trees overhead, making such a racket we can hardly talk. Sunlight swirls in lazy yellow patches across the bayou, and mosquitoes and dragonflies skim across the shallow water along the banks like they're swimming.

"Okay," Gwen finally says. "Let's go to Verret's Café."

The café sits behind the post office, a little place with picture windows and a bell above the door that jangles when we walk in.

A college-aged girl seats us at a wrought-iron table by the window and takes our order.

I have a little bit of pocket money from my daddy so I treat us to root beer floats with extra ice cream.

After the waitress leaves, we watch a couple gazing at each other over a milk shake with two striped straws.

"You can almost see the cupid hearts circling their heads," I whisper to Gwen.

The waitress deposits two root beers in great glass mugs on our little table, whipped cream brimming over the tops. She lays down napkins and straws and skinny spoons with a flair — like we're young ladies instead of two almost-twelve-year-olds.

The root beer is ice cold. I take a long drink while Gwen spoons up a big heap of vanilla ice cream.

Suddenly, Gwen puts down her spoon. "Have to go. Been here too long."

"What do you mean? It's not even noon yet. I gotta lot of time before school's over."

Gwen scrapes her chair against the floor. "I have to get back."

I gulp down my root beer. There's so much I need to talk to her about and she's running off already.

I hurry to catch up to her outside on the sidewalk. She's walking fast, fast, fast.

"What's wrong, Gwen?"

"I just can't stay away from the graveyard very long."

We dart down the sidewalks, cross the street, and head down the road back to the cemetery. She's real hard to keep up with and her golden hair flies straight out behind her like a flag. I dodge rocks, panting like I need an oxygen tank. Once she sees the stone wall and the gates of Bayou Bridge Cemetery, we finally slow down.

I sprawl on the cool grass, exhausted, and stare up at the sky while she circles the headstones and tramps up and down the rows. She looks upset and more lost than ever.

"Tell me what's wrong, Gwen. Why did we have to leave town so suddenly?"

Gwen stops pacing, but her eyes look wild. "I think maybe my best friend might have died. There is this terrible ache in my chest that never goes away."

I know who her best friend is, but I can't say anything yet. I'm afraid of what she might do. Afraid the shock will kill her. That she's sick in her body — or her head — and don't even know it. "Wouldn't you remember something so awful? How she died — or the funeral?"

She gets more agitated. "It's like that part of my memory is gone. Like somebody picked it right outta my head. I can't seem to leave my house or the cemetery for very long, either. They're the safest places. If I go too far from here, I find myself disappearing. Like I'm nothing. Like I don't exist anymore. There's something I have to do, but I don't know what it is!"

I chew my lips, getting sorta creeped out. And I'm losing my nerve. She keeps looking off across the water like she's searching for answers — or searching for someone.

"I gotta leave Bayou Bridge, I gotta leave the cemetery, but I don't know how! I want to find my family, but I'm stuck here, stuck on the water. Sometimes I make it to Cypress Cove and the blue bottle tree, but I can't never stay very long."

She's starting to panic. "I keep thinking about her, that I have to help her, but I don't know how to do that neither!"

"Who's her? Who you talking about?"

She stares at me like she's finally figuring it out. "My best friend. She needs me. I made her go that night! I shouldn't have, but I did! I been looking for her ever since."

I nod my head like I understand, take a deep breath, and plow ahead. "You mean Mirage?"

She steps back like I just shoved her away. "How do you know her name?"

I chew on my cheek, afraid that if I say anything else, she'll go off the deep end, run away, or tell me never to come back. I realize how fragile she is, and I know it's more than just her family disappearing. "Let's go wading. My toes are ready to burn up my shoes."

She doesn't look too sure, but follows me back to the water anyway.

"I should have stolen a picnic lunch from home," I joke, rolling up the bottoms of my jeans and testing out the water temperature.

Gwen sits on the edge, hugging her knees to her chest.

"We'll pretend we have our own private river beach."

She gives me a hesitant smile. "I'll pretend I'm eating chocolate cake. Been a long time since I had my mamma's chocolate cake."

I hold out my little finger and flounce my imaginary skirts. "Lady Gwen, do you see that mansion behind them big ole trees? My daddy gave it to me for my birthday. Wonder if the maid has finished making the beds."

Gwen's smile grows bigger.

I offer her an imaginary plate and fork like we really do have a picnic. "Would you like seconds on the cake?"

"I'm stuffed," Gwen says, patting her stomach.

"You mean you don't want another piece of this delicious feather-light chocolate fudge cake? It only has two calories a slice and vitamins just like broccoli."

She finally giggles as I find a log to sit on and dip my feet into the cool water. Then I get braver and squish the mud between my toes. "See any gators?"

"Nope, no gators out this way for a long time," Gwen says, adding her shoes and socks to my pile. "Mostly on the other side of the island."

The water's only a few inches deep, but when she finally takes the plunge to join me, she squeals and rolls her pants even higher.

I walk out farther, my feet sinking into the cool, slimy mud. Hot sun blisters my back and dragonflies dart past my nose. The air is absolutely motionless.

Seconds later, Gwen screams and grabs my arm, a horrified expression on her face.

"What is it?"

"Look!"

Water is lapping over her ankles. The water level is starting to rise and she's panicking. In a few more minutes, the water is almost to our knees. It's the most peculiar thing. And getting more frightening. Good thing we aren't too far from the shore.

"I gotta get out of here! The water's gonna get me!" She starts breathing like she's going to hyperventilate, then lurches back to the bank, slipping and sliding and splashing muddy water everywhere.

After Gwen grabs her shoes and socks, I watch her race all the way back to the cemetery, not even looking behind her.

It all happens so fast I'm still standing in the bayou, about ten feet from shore. The low places are now covered and every second I watch, the water level rises higher. My head feels muddled with heat and sun, but somewhere along the Teche it's storming and sending water this direction.

Fear finally gets me moving, but in just minutes the water is moving faster and deeper, past my knees, and the mud is so slimy I keep slipping and staggering around, trying not to fall over.

The water level sucks at my ankles, drags like hands on my legs. Finally, I reach the shoreline, pick my way around the cypress knees, grab my shoes, and run for safety.

Gwen is sitting on one of the granite headstones, her shoulders shaking.

"You okay?" I ask, cleaning off the mud between my toes with damp grass.

She buries her face in her knees. "You saved my life."

"I didn't save your life, silly. You ran out of the bayou yourself. The water was barely to your knees."

Sometimes I wonder if she really is a teensy bit crazy.

"I could have drowned, Shelby. I think I'd rather die any other way than by drowning."

Her words make me shiver even though it's so hot. "Don't talk like that. I don't want to die any way at all. Maybe old age in my sleep. Painless."

"I think drowning is supposed to be really painful, right?"

"I don't know," I tell her, searching for a way to change the subject.

Gwen keeps talking, her voice ominous. "I keep dreaming about drowning every night. I think it is. Very painful."

The hair on my neck rises like fingers are tugging on the strands.

"When you drown, there's only muddy water all around. You can't see nothin'. Your throat and lungs fill up with cold, slimy water until you think you're gonna burst. All of a sudden, you start breathing water until you swell up like a balloon. And then you're dead."

"Gwen, stop it. That's so creepy. You're not going to die like that. Anyway, how does anyone know what it's like? Everybody who's ever drowned can't come back and tell people about it."

"You think that's what happened to my parents? To Maddie? And nobody knows? What if the whole town thinks they moved, but they really drowned? And maybe my best friend drowned, too."

"No, Gwen, no," I tell her, squeezing her hands between

mine. She feels icy cold, like a draft of freezing air. "I'm sure that's not true. You gotta stop thinkin' such awful thoughts. Make you go crazy thinkin' that stuff."

We look at each other for a long, peculiar moment. I know I need to tell her. Ask her my questions. Figure all this out. Even if I don't want to.

"Gwen," I say softly, "I know who the girl in your locket is."

Her eyes fix on to mine. "My best friend. But I already told you that."

My hands are shaking. "I know her name. It's Mirage, right?"

She stands as still as the angel statue at the bottom of the cemetery. "You said that before, but how do you know that?"

"I figured it out in my family photo albums. I know because, well, because Mirage is my mother."

CHAPTER SIXTEEN

A BREEZE RUSTLES THE LEAVES OF THE CYPRESS AND GOBS OF hanging moss sways like it's dancing to its own silent music.

"That's impossible," Gwen whispers.

My heart pounds in my ears. "Gwen, I have to show you something."

I pull out the very first note I found in the blue bottle tree and unfold it.

Gwen looks at the note and then looks at me, her face going red, her eyes looking hurt. She starts tearing up clumps of grass, breathing hard.

When I set the paper down, the black ink looks stark, even as the sky overhead turns darker with clouds I hadn't even noticed until now.

"Where did you get that note?" Gwen whispers.

"From the blue bottle tree," I whisper back.

Her eyes get so big I think they're going to pop right out of her skull. "But it's mine. That note is *mine*."

"I know it's yours. I recognize the handwriting from your scrapbook."

"You're snooping in our blue bottle tree!"

"The first one was an accident," I tell her quickly. "Then I found more. I wanted to see what they said. Wanted to find out who wrote them."

"You should have left them there! You shouldn't have taken them out! Now I'll never find her! Never! I'll be lost forever!"

"You're not lost, Gwen! You're right here with me."

I move closer to her and try to take her hands, but she flings me away, and her breath comes in little whimpering gasps.

She shakes her head so hard her hair whips against my face. "But everybody left, they're gone. They don't want me. They forgot about me."

"That's not true! Your house is still here; you're still here. I'm here." I'm trying to reassure her, but I'm doing a terrible job.

She starts to cry, tears falling like rain down her cheeks.

"But I haven't seen them in so long. They must not love me to leave like that."

"You mean your parents? When did they leave, Gwen? How long's it really been?"

"My parents left the night of the storm. The big storm. Biggest storm ever in my life." I can tell her brain is zooming ahead as memories come back to her. "They had to go to New Orleans to do the house paperwork." Gwen jerks her head up like she just remembered. "They bought a house there. My daddy's job moved him. Can't remember what his job was, though. Sort of remember my mamma packing boxes."

"It don't matter," I tell her. "Why didn't you go with 'em?"

"It was a school night and I had play practice — and some other stuff," she adds vaguely. "And they said they'd probably be late. They took Maddie and never came back."

Her eyes are so stricken, my heart wrenches inside my chest. I thought Mirage abandoned me, but I think I'd go crazy if my whole family just up and left one day. What if I never saw my daddy again? Or Grandmother Phoebe? Or even Mirage. And Miss Silla Wheezy and that Mister Lenny flitting around the house? I'd miss 'em. I know I would. And that makes me happy and sad all at the same time.

I wish I was wearing the charm bracelet, and that it truly

did have magical powers and could give me the answers I need. Ever since Mister Lenny stole it, I'd been leaving it at home so Mirage didn't catch me wearing it. It's too boiling hot to wear long-sleeve shirts every day to hide it. "Then what happened?"

"After I ate the supper my mamma left me in the fridge, I met my friends on the bridge. We'd jump off and swim and have races from one end a the pier to the other." She looks up at me and almost smiles. "I always won. Even beat the boys." Then she pauses and glances away. "We weren't supposed to be on the bridge at night though. Especially not when my folks were gone. It was gonna be the biggest dare of all. We'd planned it for weeks."

A disturbing prickle rises along my arms. Gwen was talking about the time when the bridge was still whole. Before it cracked apart and broke. Before the empty pilings and the sharp, rusty nails. A group of kids who met on the bridge. Played games. Before the blood.

"Was your best friend — Mirage — there?" I ask, taking a gulp because it's hard to even say her name to Gwen.

Gwen thinks for a minute. "She was busy after school with her mamma so I couldn't find her right off. Nobody answerin' their phone neither. So I rowed real quick and left her a note in the blue bottles to meet me at the pier."

"Then what happened?"

"I knew she didn't want to go that night. That she was scared. But I kept pushing her. And I left her a message in the blue bottle," she repeats and then glances down at my cupped hands at the note I'd just showed her. *"That note."*

All at once, Gwen snatches up the scrawled-on note and runs for the riverbanks.

"Aah!" The sound rips from my throat as I stare at my empty hands.

Jumping up from the grass, I race after her, pumping my arms hard as I can, but she runs faster. While I watch, Gwen jumps into the boat and begins to paddle toward her house.

"Gwen!" I shout. "Stop! Let me go with you!" The wind snatches my words and throws them away.

I keep shouting, but she doesn't turn around. The way her head is bowed, I can tell she's still crying, but she rows and rows and rows without looking back.

There's no way to get to her without a boat.

But Mirage has a boat.

Do I have time to get to the town docks, row out to the island and back, before Mirage arrives? I think she's in town today running errands, but I can't remember. If she is, then the boat is sitting at the docks. I hope.

I run past the cemetery and the broken-down pier and down the long, lonely road until I reach Main Street and head to the Bayou Bridge docks.

When I pass the school, I notice that it's empty and deserted. Everyone is gone. What time is it? I have no idea.

My mouth is so dry by the time I get to the dock pilings, I can't even swallow. I stop short and chew on my lips.

Mirage is there, sitting on the dock reading a book and tapping her foot like she's impatient. I must be late and I wonder just how late I am.

Gwen has the blue bottle note and I feel an emptiness, a nagging worry, like I'll never see her or the note again.

Mirage looks up as I stand there, panting, and I realize that I left my backpack somewhere. The cemetery? The café? The bayou bank when the water started rising?

I can't remember.

"You missed going to the library with me," Mirage says.

"Bayou Bridge has a library?"

She nods, frowning at me. "Startin' to wonder what happened to you. You're missin' your school pack, too. Where's it at?"

"Um, I'm not sure . . . maybe school? Gym?"

"You got homework?"

I don't know how to answer her because I have absolutely no idea. I haven't been in school for at least two days. Mrs. Daigle and Tara and Alyson feel very far away and not quite real.

"Shelby Jayne?"

I get into the boat, pretending everything is okay. "No, I don't got any homework." I cross my fingers and plan to work really hard to make it up tomorrow. Assignments and grades don't seem very important, not when Gwen is upset and has disappeared. Not when everything about her is turning upside down. I don't want to think about it. She's real, she's real, I keep telling myself. If she's not then maybe *I'm* the one who's gone crazy.

Maybe Mirage just gave Gwen a picture of herself when she was eleven years old so the pictures in the two sides of the locket matched. Maybe that's the simplest explanation. They met somehow and became friends. Bayou Bridge is a tiny town. Everybody knows everybody else. Nothin' to be jealous about.

I want to pull out all the blue bottle notes and look at them and piece them together, but I have to be patient and wait until we get home.

I listen to the water shushing against the sides of the boat as the wind rises, blowing moss through the trees and bending the cypresses. I sneak a glance backward and Mirage has a pained look on her face.

"Storm's comin'," she says as we turn the last bend in the bayou and see the swamp house up ahead. "Thought it was just some rain blowin' through, but it's gonna be bigger. Watch out for snakes and gators; they tend to be on the move when it's gonna storm. Jest gettin' to their favorite hiding places so they're safe."

I chew on my cheek and just nod, then jump out as soon as we touch land and throw the rope around the piling.

I want to steal the boat and go find Gwen, but now I can't. With every second, I'm getting more and more worried about her taking off like that. I wonder when the coast might be clear to leave and go out to Gwen's island. Probably just enough daylight if I leave in the next hour.

While Mirage gathers her pack from the bottom of the boat, I run up to the porch. At the front door, I look back. She's not following very fast.

She doesn't even glance at me as she throws her stuff on a patch of scraggly grass, then turns back to the boat again. From under a piece of canvas, she hauls out a wooden stake.

Next I see a square, red-lettered sign from Bayou Bridge Realtors. HOUSE FOR SALE.

I stand at the top of the porch and watch Mirage pound the sign into the front yard. She trudges the rest of the way up the slope of yard, gusts of wind throwing old cans and nets and traps around the place. Mirage chases after them, but I think she's tired because she gives up easily and then stomps up the porch.

I don't know what to say to her. Seeing that HOUSE FOR SALE sign makes my stomach feel out of sorts, my heart heavy in my chest. Mirage is serious. She's really going to sell the house and leave the swamp.

I perch on the edge of my bed, toes digging into the rug. Isn't that what I'd wanted? For her to move back to New Iberia and show that she really loves me? I can't imagine her living with Grandmother Phoebe again. In some ways I can't imagine *me* living with Grandmother Phoebe again.

Mirage doesn't fit there. She never did.

Only took me this long to figure it out.

After a whole year away from Mirage, now I can't picture her being anywhere else. It's like she's a part of the swamp with its deep water and purple hyacinth and the stillness and birds.

I throw myself backward on the bed and squeeze my eyes shut, worried about Gwen, worried about Mirage, worried about me. Wondering how we all fit together.

The phone rings and I freeze.

Through the door, I hear Mirage answer it and her voice is murmuring, murmuring, murmuring.

I wait for her to call me to come to the phone, since Daddy often calls before dinner, but she doesn't and I wonder why he wouldn't ask to talk to me.

Finally, I get up, open the bedroom door, and stand in the hallway to listen.

Mirage says, "Thank you for calling, Mrs. Daigle. Yes, I will. Appreciate your help."

Mrs. Daigle, my teacher.

Mirage says good-bye and hangs up.

And I know that I'm in deep, deep trouble.

Quickly, I run back to my room and shut the door again. I think about hiding in the wardrobe, but she'll find me crouching inside that wardrobe in three seconds flat.

But Mirage doesn't come hunting me down.

Because the telephone rings again. I'm saved for the moment.

While I wait for all heck to break loose, I pull the blue bottle notes out of my pocket and lay them across the quilt.

The blue bottle notes tell a story. I just need to figure out what the story is, despite all the missing pieces.

I lay the papers out one by one, trying to put them in order of questions and answers. Half the notes were written by Gwen. The other half by Mirage.

Now that I really study them, I see that the first notes were written by Gwen and the other notes are from Mirage. Mirage's notes are sort of like answers to Gwen.

But then there's that first, urgent note I've looked at a hundred times by now. The note Gwen stole from me at the cemetery. I wish I had it in my hands right now. I close my eyes and picture the words in my mind.

Don't forget! Tonight's the night! Come to the bridge – and hurry!

Why? What was happening on the bridge? That's the note that makes my palms sweat.

Then I place the very last blue bottle message on my bedspread and freeze right to the floor. A deathly chill rushes over me.

There are two of the very same note! Why did I never realize that before? What bottle did this second one come from? I remember finding the first one, but I have no memory of seeing this second, identical one before.

The first one is the message written in Mirage's handwriting:

I can't find you! Are you lost?

And now there's this second note that reads exactly the same:

I can't find you! ARE you lost?

Like an echo. It's definitely written by Gwen, but her handwriting has changed a little bit from the other notes she wrote. The writing has become shaky and spidery. Just like a ghost. I shake my head, not wanting to think about that. *Refusing* to think about that. There has to be a logical explanation for all the peculiar-ness about her and Mirage. Of course, there ain't no reason why a grown-up *traiteur* can't be friends with a girl from the other side of the bayou. Gwen told me that *her* mamma is a *traiteur*, too. The families are friends. Nothin' strange about that.

So why can't Mirage find Gwen? Or why can't Gwen find Mirage? Why write the messages? Why doesn't Gwen just come to the door and knock? Why did they write the same words to each other? Most of all, why write notes in a blue bottle tree like Mirage is a girl again? That's the part that don't make sense. And that's the part I hate thinking about.

Maybe the bridge is some kind a mysterious time-travel portal? But that idea's like something out of a movie. And it still doesn't explain away all my questions.

And what about that very creepy death note rolled up inside the tiny blue bottle charm, the one that says, *She's dead*? *That* note was written by Mirage and put on her charm bracelet. *My* charm bracelet now. I retrieve the bracelet from under my pillow and smooth my finger against the various tinkling charms. The exact same charms as Gwen's bracelet. Spooky. Like it was planned. Two friends buying charms together.

I snap open the locket, wishing there were pictures inside. Wishing for more *clues*. I rub my finger across the plain yellowing paper inside, remembering the photographs inside Gwen's locket.

As I sit cross-legged on my bed, staring at the blank paper, I realize that it's not just any regular paper — it's got a glossy finish. Just like photograph paper!

Sticking my fingernail underneath one of the edges, I find the paper is wedged in tight and starting to crumple. Finally, it starts to come up around the inside where it's been tamped into place for so long.

I flip the tiny paper circle over in my palm.

And there's the picture of Gwen on the other side.

I feel myself go still and quiet. Hold my breath and count to ten.

Carefully, I lift up the edge of the opposite side of the locket.

And there's the tiny photo of the dark-haired girl with long curls and piercing eyes staring into the camera. Mirage.

The very same pictures that are in Gwen's locket. But *this* locket, the one in my hands, belonged to Mirage. And now it belongs to me.

Holding the bracelet around my wrist, I snap the clasp in place.

Just as quick, I take it off again and hide it deep in the empty pocket of my jeans so Mirage doesn't see it.

CHAPTER SEVENTEEN

I CAN'T THINK STRAIGHT. THE COINCIDENCES ARE TOO GREAT, too bizarre.

There is something seriously wrong with Gwen and that Deserted Island.

Mirage is still talking on the telephone, and if it's my daddy, I can't figure out why they just keep talking and talking and talking.

Scooping up the notes, I cram them into my jeans where I know they'll be safe. After I creep out of my bedroom again, I slide down the walls until I'm crouching like a mouse in the shadows.

I hear Mirage say my name in a low, tense voice along with a shuffling sound I can't identify. Then I realize Mirage is pacing back and forth across the kitchen floor.

I crane my neck around the corner and see her twisting the telephone cord between her fingers.

"Yeah, I gotta sell, Philip," she says in a choked voice. "Can't stay here no longer. It's jest too much. I can't discuss the house no more. Right now we gotta talk about Shelby —"

There's a pause while she listens.

"Yeah, Philip. Like I told you the other day, she's actin' real funny. Jest heard from the school. She's been cuttin' class. Playin' hooky or whatever they call it nowadays. No, I don't know where she's goin' all them hours." Pause. "No. Yes. No." Pause.

Dern, I wish there was another extension I could listen on.

"Didn't think it was this bad. Got a disturbing phone call this morning. Seems like someone on Main Street saw her talking to herself. Yeah, like Shelby Jayne's goin' senile, like an old crazy lady. You didn't believe me the other day when I said she's been acting peculiar, but it's true. I got witnesses now."

What is she talking about? I don't talk to myself! I'm not crazy! And I had a good reason to cut school today. Those girls in the bathroom drove me out of there. They're the crazy, mean ones. I'm just trying to survive.

"Philip, we gotta do something . . . what? Already? You are?"

Long, long, long pause . . .

I'm about ready to wet my pants.

"Yeah, is what I got here right?" Mirage repeats a series of ten numbers, like my daddy got a new cell phone number.

She pauses again and this time she listens so long I can't imagine what my daddy is saying to her, but I can hear her scribbling down a bunch of stuff with a scratchy pencil.

I feel the heat rise in my face, feel my gut twist into a big fat knot. I hold my hands against my thighs to keep them from trembling. I'm nervous, scared, and I wonder if I'm going to get detention. Do they have a jail for kids who skip school over and over again?

If Mirage sells the house and leaves, what will happen to me? What if she can't take me with her? I don't want to go back to New Iberia alone and live there by myself. Not anymore.

Mirage's soft way of talking starts up again. I listen to the pretty melody of the up and down way she says her words, even if she is talking about me.

"I think Shelby's lyin' to me, and you know how I feel 'bout that. I think she's disobeying me about goin' down to that old pier —"

257

I put my hands to my face and double over, feeling my stomach churn like never before. Is that all she cares about, her rules? And she's selling the house *while I'm here,* and moving away. Going away again. Just when I get here.

"Never knew we'd have such troubles with her," Mirage adds. "Think I'm gonna call a doctor, get an appointment for her. Mebbe the school has a recommendation —"

I can't stand them whispering about me anymore. I jump up from the floor and charge into the kitchen, even if it means I'll be in worse trouble for eavesdropping. I want to find out who's been saying all this stuff about me.

"I ain't sick!" I yell at Mirage. "I don't need no doctor! I don't talk to myself. Whoever said that is lying!"

Mirage drops the phone to the floor with a crash, then reaches down to pick it up. "What're you talkin' about, Shelby Jayne? You shouldn't be listening in on a private conversation."

"Why didn't you let me talk to Daddy? He don't belong to you anymore. *You* left. *You* didn't want us." I'm chewing on my cheek so hard my mouth feels like raw meat.

Mirage holds her hand over the receiver. "I didn't let you talk to him because me and him are talkin' first." She moves her hand away. "Philip, I'll let Shelby call you back in a bit, okay?"

I watch her hang up and I'm shaking I'm so angry. "How much do you and Daddy talk like that? Talk about *me*?"

"Couple times a week after you go to bed. Sometimes he calls during the day while you're at school." She arches an eyebrow. "Or mebbe I should say, while you *pretend* to go to school."

"You don't know what that school is like! You have *no* idea. You have *no* heart!"

"And you have a lot of explainin' to do, young lady. Lyin' on the phone, lyin' to your teachers, running away to who knows where. You're goin' to be grounded for a long, long time, believe you me. Although skipping school for a few days isn't going to permanently stunt your growth." Mirage lets out a big sigh. "And we don't always talk about you," she adds, folding up a note card and stuffing it into her skirt pocket.

My parents talk to each other that often? I had no idea and the knowledge makes me feel like I don't even know my own parents. "What's that?" I ask, pointing to her hand slipping into the pocket of her skirt. "Is that a secret message to put into one of those blue bottles?"

Mirage looks startled. "Blue bottles? What are you talkin' about, *shar*? You're makin' no sense."

"I know all about the secret notes! I know all about Gwen!"

259

Mirage steps back as though I've just hit her. Her face drains white. "How do you know about Gwen?"

I hold myself rigid as I try to keep back the wall of tears behind my own eyes. "I want to talk to my daddy."

"Me, too," she whispers, still staring at me like she don't know me, either. "But how could you know anything about Gwen? She's — I can't make head or tail of this conversation."

"She's in the locket! I turned the pictures over in my room just now. And she's in the cemetery. And the island. And inside the blue bottles. All them notes. I saw 'em. I have them."

Mirage stands still as a statue. The expression on her face scares me. "Show me," she demands, and then adds, "please."

I edge toward the kitchen door, tugging a couple notes out of my jeans. I want to go find Gwen. It's been almost an hour. I have just enough daylight to get there. She was so upset when she ran from the graveyard. I'm worried she's not safe on that island by herself. I'm worried about who she really is and why she's stuck here in Bayou Bridge all alone. All the pieces are clicking into place, the notes, the clues, the friendship between Gwen and Mirage. I think I know who she is. I don't like it. The thought makes me want to bawl my eyes out, but I gotta find out for sure.

I'm afraid the stories Mirage told me about blue bottles that keep away imps and ghouls and phantoms and haunting spirits were right. The evil phantoms might not come inside the house. They might stay on the edge of the bayou, but Miss Silla Wheezy knew they were there. That peculiar cat knew about the notes. And when I opened up the very first message I'd let loose a haunting spirit. I'd released the secrets that keep circling Mirage's swamp house and the blue bottle tree.

I think I'm the only one that can help Gwen. Even if I have no idea what to do.

I stare down at the notes in my cupped hands, afraid Mirage will take them away from me. I need them to find Gwen. "The notes summoned her from the graveyard," I whisper to myself, realizing for the first time how the notes and the bottles and Gwen all work together, but Mirage hears me.

She takes a step forward, sees the handwriting on the notes, and chokes out, "Oh, Shelby Jayne." Then she starts crying like I've just said the worst thing in the world.

"I gotta find her," I say, urgency hitting me like a brick in the head. "I gotta go."

Stuffing the messages back into the pocket that doesn't have the hidden charm bracelet, I race through the front room, past Mister Lenny perched on the lamp shade, and slam through the front door, taking the porch steps two at a time and running straight for the dock.

"Shelby Jayne!" Mirage screams behind me.

I don't look back, just jump into the boat, unloose the rope, pick up a paddle, and plunge the oar into the muddy water, rowing like crazy.

The wind whips my hair, stinging my eyes, but I dig that paddle into the water, even though the swamp is getting choppy and frothy, the water higher than I've ever seen it.

Storm clouds loom in the distance, but rain never hurt nobody. I don't care about getting wet.

"Shelby!" Mirage screams again.

I finally glance back and see her standing in the middle of the elephant ears, shirt whipping against her body, hair flying straight in the air, and up to her ankles in water. Like she's going to swim out to me. But I'm too far away to swim to. I'm almost around the first bend headed to town.

"Come back!" she yells, and I can hear fear in her voice. "It's not safe!"

"I'll be back!" I yell back. "I'm okay."

Mirage is shaking her head and still screaming. "No, no, *no!*"

And then she's gone. I face forward and keep my mind on Gwen.

Rowing by myself is harder than I ever dreamed. The boat keeps veering right, then left, bangs up against the cypress knees, then starts heading straight for the deep water in the middle.

"Dang it!" I yell. I'm not sure I'll make it back. Probably have to spend the night at Gwen's house. I'll telephone and tell Mirage where I am. Spending the night on the island is better than rowing back in the dark, right?

Besides, Mirage thinks I've gone loony. She wants to take me to a doctor, maybe put me in the mental hospital. She thinks I'm a crazy lady who talks to herself on the streets.

I glance behind me, half fearing and half hoping I'll see Mirage in a second boat, but there's only empty water and a sky full of black clouds and a forest of cypresses, moss whipping the branches with a fury.

If Gwen's on the water somewhere, I can only imagine how scared she is because I'm more terrified by the minute. Alone on the bayou, night coming on, is spooky. I think about gators, their red eyes following me. Or snakes slithering through the water, ready to crawl up the sides of the boat.

Instead of the left turn that heads to town and the docks along Main, I head right at the T, which loops around a different way and comes out along the south side of

Bayou Bridge. Right where the cemetery is across from Gwen's island house. I figure it'll save me time, but I hope I made the correct turns because it starts to drizzle and it's getting darker. Light raindrops hit my forehead and neck and shoulders.

"Stupid, stupid, stupid," I mutter. Why didn't I grab a jacket?

Getting wet doesn't affect my rowing, but I start slowing down because my arms are getting tired real fast.

The swamp finally becomes Bayou Teche proper and the last curve of the waterway opens up along the road. I can see the bridge and the little island, its forest of trees dark and dense in the storm.

Blisters form along my thumbs and I stick one in my mouth, feeling the scars and tender skin along the inside of my cheek where I've been chomping the past year.

Wish I had a drink of water.

Wish I knew what was written on that note Mirage stuck in her pocket. I know that there are numbers. A whole bunch of them that my daddy gave her. I wonder what they mean. Phone numbers to a doctor or a hospital for me?

I pull up closer to the island and see right away that there's no boat tied up along the cypresses. Where'd Gwen go? Is she trying to find me — or is she hiding out at the graveyard where she feels safer?

My shoulders ache like my arms are gonna fall off. My palms are so red and sore they're burning. I stick them in the water to cool them off, but I wish I had a pair of gloves.

Cold rain shoots down like pellets from the sky. My boat's gonna fill with water if I don't get to shore soon. Then I spot a boat tied up to a tree just a little ways down from the broken pier. A tree right across from the cemetery. Gwen's boat.

But she's nowhere in sight.

I think about the dark circles under Mirage's eyes, wanting to sell the house, her all-the-time sadness, the secret she's hiding about someone who's dead — and the secret guilt she has that she caused the death. And I think about those pictures in both them lockets. Mirage and Gwen being friends when they were *both* eleven.

Queer prickles race along my spine. Gwen has been lurking in the graveyard not just for a few weeks or a few months but for *years*.

I'm drenched by the time I pull up to the banks. Wrapping my boat line to one of the bigger cypress knees, I jump out, making sure I don't fall into the water when the boat wobbles.

The ground is real mushy and the rain is a steady downpour now.

"Gwen!" I call, but there's no sign of her. "It's me, Shelby!"

I run past the cemetery gates and head straight down the sloping lawn. Rain thumps the headstones, filling in the etched names with little dribbles. Puddles are forming along the low spots, creating mud pockets and hollow lakes in the grass.

"Gwen!" I whirl in circles, trying to catch sight of her. No golden hair, no pink shorts or beaded shirts. No humming or giggles as she pops out from behind the angel.

Maybe that's not Gwen's boat on the bank at all. Maybe she's somewhere safe and warm — and I'm the silly one who's not. Maybe I'm actually making up weird stories in my head. I might be wrong about everything. Am I crazy like Mirage thinks?

"Gwen, come on, where are you?" I whisper, rain coming down harder, darkness wrapping like cold fingers around my neck. "I should have brought you home with me long time ago. I have a feeling you'd like Mister Lenny and Miss Silla Wheezy."

I have a feeling I'm talking to myself. Like a certified crazy lady. What other kind of person would be creeping around a graveyard in the rain, in the dark, trying to find the ghost of a blue bottle tree?

All at once, I get the feeling someone is watching me.

When I reach the bottom slope of the grass, I know for positive certain that I really do *not* want to be here. The murky oaks and cypresses crowding around the graves are like lurking monsters. Wind whistles around the tombstones, scattering leaves across gloomy headstones and family crypts.

I peek around the angel statue, but, just like I thought, Gwen isn't sitting on the ground waiting for me like I'd been hoping.

A tear slips out of my eye, but maybe it's just the rain. Now I gotta row all the way home by myself. I'm so tired, I'm not sure I can lift my arms for more than ten strokes.

Nobody knows I'm here, either.

School's closed down for the day and I have no idea where anybody else lives.

Most of the shops are closed up now, too. It's getting really late, and really dark.

I want my parents, my daddy, someone to help me get back home.

"I want Mirage — I want my mamma," I whisper to the angel, surprise prickling down my body. I'd just called her Mamma for the first time in more'n a year. The name feels strange on my tongue. It also feels strangely good.

I crouch down at the stone base of the angel statue memorial, knowing why I'm there. Knowing I have to look. Afraid of what I'm gonna find.

Raindrops slip down my eyelashes. I wipe at my face so I can see better to read the inscription carved into the stone.

When I trace my finger across the fancy lettering underneath the angel's bare feet, that's when I know for the first time in my life, for shootin' certain — that ghosts are real.

GWEN RENAE DUMONDE
REST WITH THE ANGELS, CHERISHED DAUGHTER
BORN IN BAYOU BRIDGE
DIED IN THE BAYOU TECHE

CHAPTER EIGHTEEN

THE WORDS SINK IN WITH THE WEIGHT OF TWO TONS OF bricks.

"Gwen," I whisper, blinking over and over again to make sure I'm not seeing things. "No, no, *no*. All this time you've really been a ghost."

All my fears, all those eerie suspicions that Gwen is actually a ghost smack me right in the face. I feel dizzy, like I'm gonna fall right over on to the grass, the whole world veering left and right and upside down.

I'd seen Gwen, played with her, talked to her, drank root beer floats with her, seen her house, held her hand.

How was all that possible?

And where was she now, this ghost girl? The girl from the moonlight. The girl who'd left notes in the blue bottle tree . . .

I grab the locket from the charm bracelet and snap it open, shielding the photos from the rain with my other hand.

Gwen and her pretty friend with the intense black eyes. It's written right into the pictures and I've known it for a while; I just didn't want to believe it was really true.

Gwen and Mirage were best friends. All them years ago, they were best friends right here in Bayou Bridge. When Miss Silla Wheezy was a kitten — and Miss Silla saw the notes being hidden inside the blue bottles.

Gwen's best friend disappeared.

Because she grew up.

Leaving Gwen eleven years old, almost twelve.

Which means Gwen's dead.

She's dead. She's dead! I'll never forgive myself long as I live.

I press my forehead to the carved stone angel girl, and see the curved smile of the statue grinning back at me.

Gwen is out there somewhere. Hovering between death and heaven. Or is it life and death? How did she die? Why is she still here? And why can I see her — why only *me*?

Instantly, the answer flits through my mind. I'm the one that released the notes from the blue bottle. The bottles that trapped ghosts and spirits and long-ago messages.

My skin crawls with icy tingles as it all fits together.

I'm searching for a ghost I can see and hear and touch. Does that make me for real crazy? Or is it because I'm the one that can save her? Can I really save Gwen from dying? What an incredible idea!

Maybe it isn't too late at all. Maybe that's why I'd found her, because I can do something to stop the tragedy of her death. And if I can stop it, that means I'll be helping Mirage erase all her sadness and guilt. Might even erase that FOR SALE sign in the front yard.

I feel hot and frantic as I jump to my feet and race back to the entrance gates.

Gwen's ghost is still in this world because she *wants* something. Or maybe she needs to *do* something.

Seems like for-sure craziness, but why else would Gwen haunt the graveyard, talk to me like she was still alive, or dance under the blue bottle tree in the moonlight?

Lightning cracks like a whip over my head. Boiling black clouds burst. Rain stings my legs, and it's impossible to see more than two feet in front of me.

The slippery grass and thick, sloppy mud make running almost impossible. Cypress trees thrash overhead, the Spanish moss brushing against my face like nettles.

The night is scary and fear clutches at me like hands on

my throat. I'm having trouble running and breathing right at the same time.

When I reach the road, I see Gwen and my heart leaps into my mouth.

I watch her jump up onto the bridge pier, which is strange because I saw her boat tied up at the bank before I headed into the cemetery. As I get down the road, I see her boat, but it's not moving. The water is so choppy and it's so windy, it should be bobbing up and down, but it doesn't do a thing.

Then I realize that Gwen's boat is slowly lowering in the water. At first I can't figure out why, and then I realize it's sinking. The boat must have sprung a leak and is filling with water. Soon it'll sink to the bottom of the bayou.

Running like crazy down the muddy road, I hope I can get to the pier so I can grab Gwen and get to the island safely before it's too late.

When I reach the steps up to the pier, the wind is so strong, I almost fall over.

Alongside me, foamy brown bayou water rushes between the pilings, making the wooden pier shiver and quake. The bayou is like a nightmare. The water that started rising earlier that day is so many feet higher now. How can it rise so fast? It's almost as high as the bridge and ready to spill across the wooden planks. The water is like a force of its own, with a mind and a will, not caring who's in its path.

"Gwen!" I scream, running toward her.

She turns and sees me, just as the wind knocks me over and I fall with a hard thump, skinning both my knees on the cypress planks.

And then I see other people, nope — *other kids*, whooping and hollering and running up and down the pier.

I freeze where I'm kneeling, shocked all to pieces.

Is it Tara and Alyson and Jett and Ambrose? Are they playing Truth or Dare at night? During a storm?

A couple of 'em have flashlights. Beams of white are waving all over the place, up into the clouds, over the water, along the bridge.

"Chase the light!" someone yells, and I don't recognize the boy's voice. It's not T-Beau or any of the other boys I know from school. "You gotta take the dare if you ain't gonna tell the truth!"

A couple of figures line up, their toes on the edge of one of the cypress planks. Kids I don't recognize. Kids I've never seen before.

A moment later, I know exactly who they are: Bayou Bridge kids from the past.

I got stones for a stomach, rocks in my gut, as I hover between my time and their time. Almost twenty years ago.

Somebody screams, "On your mark, get set — go!!!"

The whole world is whirling as I rise to my feet and watch them take off toward the island like a shot. Other kids stand along the edge as they pass, in danger of getting knocked into the bayou if someone flails their arms two inches too close as they race by.

From the distance, I hear, "I win! I win!" It's a girl's voice, and I know the voice belongs to Gwen. She'd said she could beat anybody running, and that included the boys.

I wrap my arms around myself, the rain sopping my clothes, melting into my skin right down to the bone. How can they stand it? My jeans are heavy against my thighs, my shirt dripping under my collar.

There are giggles and shouts and nonstop chatter as they cluster together, deciding what to do next.

"This is a night to remember!" a boy says loudly. "The night we faced the elements together in one great dare — and won."

"Against all odds," another girl says, picking up on his triumphant tone. "We've faced alligators and deadly waters. Truths that made us squirm. Nobody can ever say we're afraid of anything."

"Whoo hoo!" the group shouts together and slaps hands, proud of themselves.

"So who's gonna go swimming tonight?"

"You is crazy for sure!"

"Nah, them alligators are hiding during a storm. Deep down on the banks over the other side."

"Nobody can swim in that water. It'll sweep ya right out to sea."

"Maybe the Gulf, but not the sea."

"Same thing, you idiot."

"How about Mirage? She ain't gone swimming yet."

"Yeah, Mirage!"

The rest of the kids pick up the chant and start pushing a girl to the edge of the bridge. "Don't be a chicken. We'll pull ya right up."

My blood runs cold through my veins. I feel myself swaying on my feet.

"Hey, I see a gator! Over there! Look at them red eyes!"

"You liar!" a girl screams, terror lacing her voice.

"Jest jokin', Mirage."

The whole group is behind her, not letting her back out of the dare. I squint through the rain and try to find Gwen. She's at one end, silent, biting her lips. Trembling as the rain pummels her head and drips off the ends of her hair. I can see

Gwen getting ready to charge the group, but she's afraid of accidentally knocking Mirage into the water, that's how close she is to the ledge. It's like Mirage is being forced to walk the plank on a pirate ship.

"Ten seconds in the water, that's all. Come on, just do it and get it over with."

"You gotta do it," another voice adds firmly, "or you're out of the group."

Mirage stares down at the churning water. I want her to push them all away, tell them to go to heck, grab Gwen and run like mad for the safety of the island.

Water starts lapping over the edge of the bridge, making me seasick to the extreme.

Mirage suddenly turns, flails her arms like a windmill, then dives through a hole in the group, hitting and kicking her way through. Her action reminds me of when I pushed past Tara and Alyson holding me hostage in the bathroom. I didn't want to face them or fight them. I just wanted to run away. There are shouts and screams of indignation, then taunts and yells. Next thing I know Mirage is flying toward me, her feet pounding the planks, running like an alligator is chasing her all the way home.

Her long dark hair is plastered to her skin, her eyes black and sunken. She's breathing hard as she flies by and I can feel the wind she sets off as she whips past and disappears into the darkness. A moment later, I can't even feel her feet pounding the boards anymore. She's jumped off the end and disappeared.

The other kids have no mercy.

"Mirage is just a stupid girl. She's got no guts."

"Aw, let her go. Forget about her."

"Okay, Gwen is next!"

My moment of relief turns to fear.

Gwen's face is pale, her eyes terrified as she screams at her friends.

Some friends. They're idiots. Tonight ain't a night for jumping in the bayou — and getting back out alive.

"We got flashlights! We won't lose ya!"

"Yeah, right!" Gwen is arguing, fighting back, not letting them bully her. "Y'all are idiots. Nobody could climb back up out of that rough water tonight. And I don't trust a single one a you to pull me up, either."

If she was smart, she'd leave, too. But she's tougher than I ever knew, not letting them order her around, standing her ground. But sometimes standing your ground isn't the smartest thing to do.

My limbs ache like I have a fever. The driving rain is so bad now, I can hardly see.

And the bridge is starting to move. It's swaying back and forth as the force of the churning, rising water pounds against the pilings. The whole pier shudders from the power of the river.

Through strands of plastered hair, I watch the kids slip and slide on the wet bridge as they try to set up another game.

We're farther out than I realize, and when I look over my shoulder the bank seems a mile away. If we don't leave now, none of us might make it back before the water knocks us clean off the bridge.

An instant later, there's a flash of lightning overhead.

A series of yelps and screams come from the kids and suddenly the entire bridge is jolting up and down and side to side as the group runs for the bank. I turn to run, too, but it's too slippery and I go crashing to my knees, banging my elbows.

Three seconds later, the kids have run past me and are gone. Every last one a them. Disappeared into the night like the ghosts they are. Even the sound of their voices is gone.

Still on my knees, I crawl my way down the bridge, trying not to throw up every time a wave of water comes over the walkway and attempts to wash me away.

Where's Gwen? I saw her earlier. In my time. As a ghost. But I can't leave her behind now. There's gotta be a reason I see her now, a reason she came to me. *Me.* Is it only because

I opened the blue bottle notes? Or is there something more, something bigger?

I'm the only one who knows how much Gwen fears drowning. How she dreams about the terror of drowning. How she is paralyzed by the thought of it. Because years ago she'd drowned once before.

Gwen is the girl from the story. The girl who drowned right here. The lightning. The blood . . . *no.*

I get to my feet and head back toward the middle of the bridge. Back toward Gwen. Where is she? I realize that she never ran by me with the rest of the kids.

They left her out here, alone. Then I see her, crouched on the pier, holding her arm like she's hurt.

"Gwen!" I scream as loud as I can.

She turns toward me and I'm so glad she can hear me I almost bust out crying.

I try to run toward her as fast as I can and keep my balance, careful to stay in the middle so I don't get swept off the pier. But I hate, hate, hate running away from the safety of the bank and back toward the middle of the bayou. It's terrifying.

Gwen peers through the slanting rain and starts moving toward me. Will I really be able to save her? If I can get her back to the banks, we can sit tight in the cemetery until help arrives.

I start to smile as I get closer, and I can see the smile of relief on her face, too — just as the biggest, ugliest bolt of lightning I've ever seen in my whole life cracks the sky right down the middle, splitting it in half. The lightning is fat and blinding and enormous and lights up the whole bayou. I can even see the trees illuminated in a flash of white on Gwen's island on the far shore, the bridge like a straight road tying the banks together.

I can also see the figure of Gwen outlined in that bright, incredible, dizzying light. A shock of surprise on her face. Her hands reaching out to me.

And then the world goes dark again as Gwen suddenly vanishes, disappeared like she never existed, the pier empty.

I'm desperate to chase after her but the bolt of lightning is so violent I'm knocked flat on my back. My body buzzes in the most peculiar way. First I'm hot, and then I'm cold, shivering like I got the flu.

My head hurts, my joints hurt, but I roll over and try to look for Gwen again. I hope she managed to get away, but it seems Gwen is truly gone. And so is the bridge directly in front of me. Splintered planks and pilings break apart into jagged pieces. They fall, crashing into the bayou like dominoes. The cypress planks give way, sprays of water thrown into the air as they drop into the bayou one by one.

There's a distinct, terrible smell of burning wood and I know that the lightning struck the bridge. That bolt was so violent, there's no way it would have missed, heading straight out of the clouds for the water like it did.

Wobbling and dizzy, I finally get to my knees, grab the splintery wood of the broken pier with one hand, and search the water for Gwen.

I know I saw her right here two minutes ago on the pier, right where the lightning hit. Most likely, she would have gone down with the bridge, but I don't see her now at all.

I rub the rain out of my eyes, and search the darkness. No sign of her golden hair. No screams or cries, just silence. It's suddenly quiet, peaceful, even as the rain continues to pound the surface of the water.

My heart slows its thumping inside my ribcage.

I think I just watched Gwen's ghost, her spirit, finally cross over to heaven.

Before I can take it all in the pier begins to groan.

Several more wooden planks drop away like toothpicks, disappearing into the swirling whirlpool of muddy water. The pier shudders, and as I try to stand and run back to shore, the board I'm standing on splinters and breaks clean away from the piling.

I plunge into the cold water, screaming as I hit the surface, then gurgling as I sink below into the deep darkness of the bayou.

The water is thick and murky, but I manage to grab hold of one of the pilings before I'm sucked away by the vicious current. My hands claw at the wood and my head breaks the surface. I'm coughing and spluttering, terrified to be in the water. Right along with a torn-up bridge whipping past me, cypress boards full of nails tearing at my skin.

Out of the rushing blackness, something grabs at my legs. I kick at it, thinking it's a snake or a gator, and scream at the top of my lungs.

Taking in gulps of air and water, I flail my hands, searching the current rushing past me, treading water to stay afloat.

Something bumps into me and I grab hold of it, sobbing with relief at a branch being swept downstream.

The branch is thicker than I first realize and wedges itself between two of the broken planks. I hold on, even though the water is roaring so fast I can hardly keep my grip.

I'm tired and sore and bruised. It hurts so bad to hang on and the muscles in my arms scream at me to just let go and float away.

Rain pounds the surface of the dark water relentlessly, brown whirling water foaming over and over on itself.

I wonder if I can climb back up to the bridge, but as soon

as I try to lift myself higher on the piling, I can't hardly keep myself from going under. The water is too strong, too fast.

The tiny sliver of hope that Gwen is still out there somewhere dies inside my chest.

I lower my head to the knotty branch and sob. Gwen is truly dead, and now, even her ghost is gone. I miss her already, and it don't make much sense to miss a ghost, but it's true. I can't get her face and that floating golden hair out of my mind.

Knowing I'll never see her again feels unbearable, and I know why my mamma agreed to leave the swamp and live in New Iberia with my daddy all those years. And why she wants to sell the swamp house now.

She's dead. She's dead! I'll never forgive myself long as I live.

Gwen has been haunting the blue bottle tree and the graveyard, waiting for her friend who never showed up. She wrote the message:

I can't find you! Are you lost?

Written in that spidery, ghostlike handwriting. Written *after* she died.

Those blue bottles really did capture a ghost.

My breath catches at my throat as I realize that Mirage never saw Gwen's note calling out to her, looking for her. Because Mirage won't go near that tree no more. I think about how she always stays on the porch. How she skirts the tree to do her chores or tend to the cats. That tree is filled with sad memories and real ghosts, *Mirage's* ghosts, so she tries to ignore it.

Rushing, dank water pours into my mouth and I start choking. It's pitch-black now and the awfulness of my predicament hits me like a hammer between the eyes. I don't have the strength to climb up out of the water. The slimy planks are slippery and too high to get a grip on.

Cold water pounds at my arms and my legs.

And nobody knows where I am.

That thought scares me like crazy.

"Mamma!" I scream, clawing my fingernails at the planks to get a better grip. Pain shoots straight up my arms. "Mamma!"

The water is a monster tearing at me to let go. A few minutes later, I can't feel my legs no more.

"Mamma!" I scream over and over again. I don't know how long I been hanging on to the cypress branch and the piling. Feels like hours and hours. Water shoots up my nose and down my throat, choking me, but I keep screaming so someone can hear me. Hoping someone's passing by on the road.

Then, like a dream, I hear my name come floating out of the darkness. "Shelby Jayne!" Is it real or are my ears playing tricks on me? Then I hear it again and I start crying, but I can't tell who it is.

"Mamma!" I scream again, but I'm gettin' a sore throat and can hardly get the word out.

Through the blinding rain, I catch a glimpse of something yellow. Like the light from a lantern.

Now someone's yelling my name over and over and I try to shout again, but nothin' comes out but a whisper.

The lantern gets closer and closer, and now I hear the sound of a boat engine. From out of the rain and the darkness the lights on the prow of a flat-bottomed fishing boat come into view and I watch as the boat turns and runs alongside the pier.

Another lantern is lifted high, swinging along the railing of the boat and searching the water. That's when I start sobbing harder. Behind the lantern is Mirage, my mamma, hanging over the side of the boat. Rain drums against the lantern, trickles down her face. Her eyes are dark, her skin white as a sheet. "Shelby Jayne, Shelby Jayne!" she screams. "I see her! Down there! Stop the boat!"

As soon as she spots me, my mamma don't wait for nothin'. She thrusts the lantern at someone in a yellow rain slicker and throws a ladder over the edge. The boat shudders as it scrapes along one of the bridge pilings.

For a split second, I see Mirage in the glow of the lantern as it swings crazily in the wind. Then she climbs up on the boat's railing and throws her legs over the edge.

A man's voice shouts, "Hey, stop! Stop! She's goin' in the water!"

Before anybody can pull Mirage from the edge, she leaps right off the side of the boat and into the water with a splash. Her head goes under, and then comes back up immediately. Her arms slice through the water as she comes toward me. Never knew she could swim.

"She's gone overboard!" yells the man through the fog. "That woman jumped! Man overboard! Two down! Two in the water!"

"Mamma!" I yelp as my cold, numb hands suddenly slip from the branch.

Instantly, I start to float away, screaming again, but Mirage grabs my hand and pulls me through the water toward her. The grip of her arms is fierce and tight and I melt like butter against her chest. The rushing water pounds against me and I feel so limp, my arms and legs swirling in the water like they don't even belong to me no more.

"Shelby, baby," Mamma murmurs in my ear. "I got you, I got you. Hold on to me. I'm gonna get us over to this other piling. These broken planks you been hanging on to are about ready to go."

I reach up and put my arms around her neck. The water is whipping fast and strong, but I'm in the crook of her neck. Her arms encircle me as she moves us along the branch to a firmer piling down the pier and away from the broken planks.

When I look up, two men in yellow slickers and hats lean out over the side of the boat to throw two life preservers out to us. As soon as the rope reaches Mirage's outstretched hand and she wraps it around her fist, a second boat pulls up on the other side of the pier. This boat is huge and its horns are blaring into the night. Suddenly, there are blazing lights everywhere and people shouting.

It's the Coast Guard or the Water Patrol or something.

Mamma puts the second life preserver over my head and helps me adjust it. One-handed, she ties the length of rope around my waist, tugging the knot to make sure it's tight. "I'm gonna let them pull you up, *shar*. You okay?"

"I'm scared," I tell her because I don't want her to let me go. I want her to stay with me forever.

"You can do it, baby, you're all right. Just let the rope carry you. You don't gotta do nothing; they got you. The rope's tied to that big boat. You ain't goin' nowhere but inside that boat."

Her dark eyes look into mine, and I see her lips trembling, and I can't help starting to cry all over again.

She presses her cheek against mine and whispers in my ear, "You okay, *bébé*?"

I nod again, but just cry even harder.

She hugs me tight and cold water pounds between us, blasting right up my neck. "I love you, *bébé* girl, I love you. Always have, always will."

"I love you, too, Mamma." Next thing I know, I feel the pull of water rushing over my whole body as I'm sucked out of the bayou. I'm in the air, over the edge of the boat, and a minute later I'm lying on a bench. People rush around putting blankets on me and shouting but I can't understand a word they're saying.

My stomach lurches and water comes dribbling up out of my mouth. Feels terrible, but a minute later I start to feel more normal, even if the boat is rocking side to side.

Rain's coming down in great sheets, but not too much later, Mamma is lying next to me on some sorta table or bench. She's got a gash on her head that's bleeding, trickles of red running down the left side of her face, but she reaches out her hand to mine and squeezes my fingers, then holds my hand to her cheek.

She's smiling and crying at the same time. "Shelby," she whispers, and her voice is raw and croaking. "You could have drowned so easy. What were you doin' on that pier?" She stops to gulp back a sob and I can't stop myself from watching her, studying her face, memorizing her features. I know for certain that she really is the girl in the locket.

Mamma strokes my face with her fingers. "This afternoon," she starts to say, "you mentioned a girl named Gwen. I know who you're talkin' about. She was my best friend in all the world. My friend for life. That pier is where she drowned years and years ago."

"I know," I say, thinking about Gwen's golden hair floating in sunlight. I think about her smile as she popped out from behind the angel. And then I see her disappear in that crack of lightning and I know that she didn't have to drown again. That she made it. She is gone, crossed over at last to where she won't be lost any longer.

"Oh, baby," Mirage says. "Seein' you holding on to that branch as the boat came up, I thought I was gonna break apart into pieces if I watched you go under." My mamma's eyes look old and sad and relieved all at the same time. Her arms shield me from the storm, and then we're crying together, rain and tears mixing up.

"It's a miracle we found you, a blessed miracle. But you're gonna be fine, *bébé*. You breathin' okay?" Her hands rub my back and I cough again, more water dribbling out. There's a nasty taste in my mouth.

"My stomach hurts."

"Expect it does, but you're gonna be fine."

"You're bleeding," I tell her, looking at her face in the dim glow of the lanterns.

She wipes at her forehead, and blood comes away on her fingers. Just then one of the Water Patrol men comes up with a medical bag with a red cross on it. He opens it up and gets out disinfectant and bandages.

"Couple a stitches, ma'am," he tells Mirage. "Even after I clean this up you need to get checked out by a doctor. No signs of concussion, but I think you should make sure."

"I'm not worried about myself, jest my daughter."

"We took her temperature and blood pressure and she's already gettin' that water out of her stomach. Other than that, she's a tough little girl. Survived all that time in the water and hardly a scratch on her. No signs of hypothermia, either."

"She's brave and strong," Mirage says, gazing at me. She hasn't stopped looking at me since she jumped into the bayou and kept me from going under. I give a shudder when I think about how I'd let go right when my mamma jumped in. Right now I hurt so bad I can hardly move a finger underneath all the blankets. But I'm finally warm.

One of the officers shouts back at us, "We're ready to move out of here. You all sitting tight, ma'am?"

The medic doctoring Mirage shouts back, "We're good. Go on!"

I feel the surge of the boat's engines and the bulk of the ship turning away from the broken pier.

As we lie on the bench together, Mamma pushes the damp hair off my face. "Who were those men in that other boat? The one you jumped overboard?"

"Couple hours ago when you disappeared 'round the bend in my boat, I ran back in the house and called a neighbor a few miles down the swamp. Always offers help in case I have an emergency. Never had to take him up on it before now. I was terrified I was going to lose you all over again."

Her voice chokes up and I feel her arms tighten. "Tell me why you run off like that, Shelby Jayne! What were you doin' comin' out here in this storm? You made me crazy with worry."

I try to find the right words that won't make her think I've gone loony. "Just trying to find Gwen. I showed you those notes before I ran away."

"You dropped one of 'em on the kitchen floor after you shot out the door."

I give a start, not realizing I'd left one behind. "Which one?"

"The note she wrote to me the night she died. I left it in its blue bottle. Never wanted to see it again long as I lived."

"So you did see the note the night she drowned? And you were there on the pier, right?" There's the most peculiar sensation in my gut when I think about seeing my own mamma when she was a girl shooting past me on the bridge as she ran away from the Truth or Dare game and those taunting kids.

I give a start and suck in my breath. If Mirage hadn't run, she probably would have gone in the bayou that night. She might have drowned when she was only twelve. Instead, Gwen drowned.

"I remember every note Gwen and I used to hide in them blue bottles," she whispers. "I was there that night. And I ran. I've hated myself ever since for deserting her. Night of the worst storm ever recorded on this part of Bayou Teche. Gwen's parents came home to chaos and police boats and ambulances. The whole town was out there on the banks cryin' and prayin'. I'll never forget it long as I live."

"Was that storm worse than tonight?"

I can feel her trembling. "Tonight's a pretty close second."

I wonder if she'd believe me that I saw it all happen. That I've seen Gwen as a ghost.

"Gwen's parents were in New Orleans closin' on the house they'd just bought. Her daddy got a new job over there. She and me were both heartsick that she had to move away. We was babies together. Our mammas were the best of friends, both of 'em *traiteurs*. I should never have left her there. I shoulda been there to help her. To grab her and pull her home with me. Or jump in the water when — when —" She stops for a moment and presses her lips together as tears start slipping down her face again. "I wasn't there to save her. Or stop her from drowning."

"She's the girl who got hit by lightning, isn't she? The night the bridge broke apart."

Mamma leans back to look at me. "How do you know these things?"

"I've seen her," I tell her, and I can't help still being a little bit afraid that she'll send me to a mental hospital. "In the graveyard, at her house."

Her eyebrows draw together in a frown of confusion. "You mean that old house out on Deserted Island?"

"Yeah, I been there, too. It's still there. I've seen her bedroom. Her sister's room, too. Maddie."

Mirage lets out a shocked gasp. "It's so strange to hear you say Maddie's name."

"Did they find — ?" I stop, hardly able to say the words. "I watched Gwen disappear. Did they find her — ?"

"Yes, baby, they dragged the bayou and found Gwen. After the funeral, the DuMondes' grief was so terrible they took Maddie and moved away fast as they could. That's why the bridge is still broken all these years later. Never saw 'em again. Always wondered what happened to that family."

My mamma pulls the wool blanket tighter up under my chin. "Thought I was gonna go crazy seein' you in that water, prayin' to God you could hang on. Never been so scared in my whole life."

"I saw the lightning and felt like I was burning up. I watched the bridge fall into the bayou, too." My own guilt starts rising up inside my chest, like I'm drowning, also. "I tried to save her before the lightning, but she just disappeared. I couldn't save her."

Mamma makes a choking sound. "Neither could I, *shar.* Neither could I."

"But why did I see her?" I ask her. "Was I supposed to save her? Do something different to stop it?"

"I don't know, Shelby Jayne. Never knew ghosts were real, but maybe they are. But I do know we can't go back and undo things. Sounds like her spirit was restless, sad." She gives a sudden, choked laugh. "Jest like me. Maybe she came to you because I wouldn't never go out there again. Never have gone out to see her grave all these years, and I haven't visited her house, either. And yet she wanted to give me one last message."

"She already did," I tell her softly.

"What do you mean, baby?"

"One of the blue bottle notes in Gwen's handwriting — handwriting that looks ghostly and different from all the other notes — says, 'I can't find you! Are you lost?' I think she *has* been looking for you."

"See why I gotta move, Shelby Jayne? My heart feels like it's breaking all over again."

"But, Mamma, she was always happy when she talked about you. She told me she had a best friend she loved more than anybody in all the world."

"Really? I don't understand then. What does she want me to do?"

"Maybe she wants you to know it's not your fault. Maybe she don't want you to move away. And maybe I had to help her cross that bridge one last time cuz she needed help finally crossing into heaven."

My mamma wipes at her eyes. "If that's true, then this time we know she made it. *You* found the notes, Shelby Jayne. *You* ran out there in that storm even though it was dangerous. Even when it meant you might drown yourself."

"The notes didn't make much sense at first, but I figured

out which were written by her, and which were written by you."

My mind races as I suddenly think about the scrapbook locked away in the cupboard in Gwen's old house. Odd prickles race along my skin. I wonder if it's still there. Maybe I actually saw the *real* notebook, not just a ghost one.

Mamma shakes herself inside the wool blanket. "Maybe Gwen does want me to stop feeling guilty, Shelby Jayne. Maybe I been carryin' somethin' I shouldn't a been all these years. Maybe —" Her voice drops low. "Gwen gave me a second chance. A chance to save you."

CHAPTER NINETEEN

THE WATER PATROL BOAT DROPS US OFF AT THE SWAMP house, docking next to an Inter-coastal Ambulance that's already arrived. A paramedic keeps trying to check Mamma's cut and see if she needs stitches, but she keeps saying she's fine and to go on.

One of the men on the patrol boat tells me to keep the blanket he gave me, so I keep it wrapped tight around me, since I'm shivering in my sopping clothes. Feels like I've been wet for hours and hours. Every muscle in my body aches and throbs.

Soon as I get off the boat, my legs give out and I slump right down to the grass. All my strength just leaks right out of me.

"I think we need to have the paramedics check you out, too, Shelby."

"I'm fine. Just tired." I think that cold water pounded at me so hard and for so long, it took all the life right outta me.

Before I can get up again and walk up the porch steps, another boat comes roaring up the bayou. It stops and docks right at our very own bank. It's not a very big boat, just a small motorboat with only one person inside. The man jumps out, ties up the rope, and runs toward us.

It's my daddy.

"Philip!" Mamma cries, letting out her breath in a big whoosh. "You made it."

"Mirage," he says, and his voice is scratchy and hoarse. "Drove as fast as I could from the airport." Then he spots me all wrapped up in my blanket. "Shelby!"

I run toward him and jump right into his arms. His hug never felt so good in all my life.

While Daddy carries me up the steps, the paramedics take Mamma inside the living room on a stretcher and then transfer her to the couch.

"I'm good," she insists over and over again. "So much better now that I'm home with my family."

My family. Except we aren't really a family anymore. Just

the thought of all that's happened the past year makes the knot inside my throat grow big and lumpy again.

After the ambulance boat leaves, Daddy insists on steeping lemon in hot water in the kitchen for all of us.

"It'll chase away the chill from that bayou dunking you both got," he says.

The teakettle is soon whistling and I'm feeling warm and sleepy. I got bruises all over from banging against that pier for so long and my skin is tender, my bones sore and achy.

Rain keeps drumming against the roof like it's not gonna stop for forty days and nights.

Mamma declares, "I do believe we might float away like Noah's ark. Going back into town tonight is out of the question, Philip. You can sleep right here on the fold-out couch."

Watching them, Daddy pouring the hot lemon tea, Mamma curled up in a blanket, I get a funny feeling inside my chest. So many things are churning away in my mind, but I don't know how to put them into words.

"You got some bad bruises, Shelby Jayne, but at least they'll heal," Mamma tells me. "Now that you and I are together, I hope we can heal *us*. You're not running away from me anymore. I'm gladder than I've been in a long, long time."

"You jumped in the water and saved me," I say, and I don't realize I'm thinking out loud until I say it. "You could have drowned, too. Those men didn't want you going overboard."

"Pretty sure they were afraid they'd be fishing two bodies out of the bayou the next day." She shakes her head. "There wasn't no time to wait or to throw a line. I could tell you were ready to slip right away from that piling. I'd do anything for you, *bébé*. Anything."

I think I really do know that now for sure, and suddenly the swamp house grows fuzzy and blurry around me.

"You're gonna have a bad scar, too," I say, pointing to her forehead. There's a little bit of red seeping through the bandage. "Do you have any healing recipes for that? I mean *traiteur* recipes. In that book. In the kitchen."

"Oh, Shelby Jayne," she says, looking at me, her eyes tearing up again. "I got a salve that moisturizes the skin. Like vitamin E oil. Good for preventing scars. Got some other things to speed up the skin's healing, too."

I nod, thinking about how I'd like to take a closer look at that *traiteur* recipe book. It always looked more interesting than I wanted to admit. Almost like she can read my mind, Mamma says, "I'd be honored to have you make me a healing spell."

Raindrops chatter at the windows and my heart does a funny little jump inside my chest. A healing spell. My first one. For my own mother.

And then it hits me that I've just had the strangest thought in my whole life. My *first* healing spell. As though there might be a second.

"Shelby," Daddy says, "why don't you take a bath and get ready for bed, then come into Mamma's room with us? I already started the water for you."

After I collect my nightgown, clean underwear, and a pair of socks, I step into the bathtub filled with hot water and bubbles, eager to soak away the moldy, leafy bayou smell. It's in my skin, my nose and mouth, even in my throat from swallowing so much of it and coughing it up again.

I scrub my arms and legs and wash my hair, then kneel underneath the faucet to let the clean water rinse out all the shampoo.

After I dry off and pull on my nightgown and socks, I stick my wet hair into a ponytail.

My heart skips two beats when I think about the charm bracelet I stuffed into the pocket of my wet, dirty jeans earlier. Snatching them off the floor, I dig my hand into both pockets, pulling out the soggy blue bottle notes and the charm bracelet which is intact. I sink to the edge of the tub, feeling a huge sense of relief. What if I'd lost it? Lost Gwen's notes, too?

The relief makes my eyes well up as I lay the notes out on my bed to dry. I smile at the baby gator charm as I put the bracelet around my wrist and make sure it snaps good and tight.

When I step into the hallway, Daddy says, "Come say good night to your mamma."

"My two favorite people," Mirage says when I walk into her bedroom.

I look at the black stitches on her forehead where the paramedics tended. Her hair is tangled and her face is pale, and my mind is bursting with a thousand thoughts. I keep seeing her jump straight into the bayou for me. No second thoughts, no fear. Just pure love.

Daddy sits in the chair next to the bed. "I do believe we gotta make us some shrimp gumbo tomorrow. It'll cancel out all this cold rain tonight." His voice is soothing and I just want to crawl onto his lap and cry for a while, I'm so glad to see him.

As I get up on the bed and sit close to Mamma on the pillows, she lifts the bracelet away from my wrist, fingering the delicate charms. "Remember when I said that every charm tells a story? This is the story of me. A story of you. A story of

Gwen. A story of friends and a story of mothers and daughters."

I put my head against her shoulder and stare at the charms swinging on the beautiful old silver chain. The charms of a girl, of a friendship, and of a family that once loved one another. And then I can't help hoping that maybe that family loves one another still.

Mirage wipes her tears, laughs at herself, and then suddenly her arms fold me up tight. "Oh, Shelby Jayne, I'm so blessed to have you. Blessed to be alive. Blessed to have my beautiful baby girl safe and here forever."

Hot tears start rolling down my face.

Daddy leaves his chair and sits on the bed, scooting closer to me and Mamma. His arms go around both of us at the same time and then we're all of us crying together.

I can feel their breaths close to mine, our hearts beating together. I'm warm and safe, and my heart swells up inside my chest, growing bigger like it's going to lift me clear off the bed and I'll start floating away.

"I'm sorry, Mamma," I tell her, my voice all choked up. "I'm sorry for all the mean things I've done and said. I'm sorry for all that time hating you."

She presses her forehead against mine and our eyes lock together. "Nothin' to be sorry for, *shar.* It's my fault for leaving you, for not trustin' in your daddy's love. Not trustin' in myself to keep us a family. But we're all of us learnin' to love again. First time in a long time."

Daddy's big arms squeeze us tighter still, and I see tears flowing out of his eyes, too. My heart feels like it's going to burst for sure.

"I almost lost both of you tonight," my daddy says and his voice is rough around the edges, like the words are having a hard time coming out. "I'm thinking there's some things I want to change about me, about this job that takes me across the world. Changes I want to make about our family."

He reaches out to clasp Mamma's hand. They smile at each other and a peculiar tickling starts to rise in my stomach.

Mamma says, "I have a present for you, Shelby. Been waitin' for the right time to give it to you, and I think that time is finally here. Pull open that nightstand drawer and find the box with the purple water hyacinths painted on the side."

I lean over to open the drawer, pulling out the beautiful little jewelry box.

"Open it," Mamma says in an excited whisper.

I snap back the lid and there's a shiny new charm nestled

inside. When I lift it out there are three silver hearts dangling from a tiny loop of chain.

"See how the hearts all lock inside one another?"

I nod, looking at it closely. All three of the silver hearts fit inside one another, like a puzzle. Except it's not a puzzle at all. It's beautiful and perfect, the hearts separate and distinct but linked together.

"This here charm is our family," Mamma tells me. "A heart for each of us. You, me, and Daddy."

"Let me help you attach those hearts to the bracelet," Daddy offers.

"Put it right in the middle," I tell him.

He fits the tiny silver hooks together so the three hearts dangle from the bracelet and then slips it over my hand again and snaps it closed. I hold up my wrist and watch the charms swing together.

Mamma leans back into the pillows. Her face is starting to bruise and I'll bet it hurts somethin' fierce. Those knotted stitches show how my mamma saved my life.

My heart stops racing and my stomach quits churning as I think about everything that's happened. "I think it was those blue bottle notes that brought Gwen back."

Mamma gives me a wistful smile. "Charm bracelets and blue bottles are powerful things, *shar*, and anything's possible.

Memories and grief locked up for years and finally let loose."

I'm relieved to see that the charms are all safe, even the gator charm. Nothing got swallowed up by the bayou when I fell in, although there's water in the tiny blue bottle and the rolled-up note looks soggy.

The most important thing is that my charm bracelet is full of stories, full of faith, and full of my family and me.

Most of all, it's full of love.

EPILOGUE

After I jump out of the boat and tie the rope around a cypress knee, Mamma and me hold hands as we walk toward the Deserted Island house.

"Can't believe I'm actually here," Mamma whispers as sunlight falls through the oak leaves and stains the path. "Used to come here every single day when I was a girl, but it's been almost twenty years now."

"Does it look the same?"

"Mostly, but the trees are bigger, the path weedy and overgrown."

Actually, the path seems more overgrown to me, too, and it's only been a few days. Which makes me wonder. When I came here with Gwen was I going back to *her* time — or was she coming forward to *my* time?

When we get to the clearing Mamma stops and just stares and stares.

The house has aged years and years since I was here with Gwen just a few days ago. The walls have collapsed a little bit more, the porch is sagging in on itself, the paint on the clapboard peeling, the roof shingles moldy and caving in around the chimney.

"Better be careful," Mamma says as we pick our way through overgrown bushes and weeds that are taller than me. The air is filled with the thrum of crickets and clouds of gnats.

We manage to get around the broken boards on the porch and push at the front door, which creaks as it swings wide. "If the fire department was here, they wouldn't let us near. Stay together and watch your step so we don't crash through a board."

Even though it's the middle of the day with plenty of light, the interior of Gwen's old house is a dusky twilight due to the filthy windows and dingy wallpaper.

I watch Mamma staring around the living room, her eyes following the stairs leading up to the second floor; I see the memories and emotions flitting around on her face. Shock, disbelief, sorrow, and sadness. "This house used to be like my second home," she says.

I tug on her hand as we go up the staircase. The steps are actually in decent shape but we carefully creak up each one.

Moments later, we're standing in Gwen's old bedroom, empty of furniture. Mildew stains drip down the corners from rain and the dormer window that's open a few inches.

"Probably some vagabond or hermit passin' by," Mamma murmurs. There were signs in the kitchen that someone had stayed here over the years. Trash and a ripped-up sleeping bag. Pieces of charred wood left in the stove. Coffee stains in the sink, crumbs, and mouse pellets.

A peculiar shimmery feeling runs from my little toes all the way to the top of my head. I'd been to Gwen's house with her right after her parents moved away, when the house had leftover furniture and dust.

Somehow, she and I had straddled time, half in hers, half in mine. She really had been hovering between her old home and heaven, trying to leave, confused and lonely, but tethered like a deflating balloon to Bayou Bridge.

"I remember Gwen's secret cupboard," Mamma says, walking over to the closet in the corner near the slant of roof. "We built it with her daddy's help."

She opens the closet and peers inside, bumping her head against the low ceiling. "It's smaller than I remember, but it's there. Reach in, Shelby Jayne, and open it. I know it's empty, but I jest have to look anyways."

I duck under her arm and pull at the little door with the brass knob. Pull and pull. "It's stuck."

"Probably swelled up with all the damp."

Then I remember the trick Gwen used the day she showed

the secret cupboard to me. I curl my hand into a fist and pound the edge of the frame. The door pops open.

My mamma lets out a cry of surprise. "That's right. The door never fit quite right in its frame."

She turns to gaze at me, a look of bewilderment on her face. "You really did see her, didn't you?" She shakes her head in disbelief, and then her voice goes real soft. "Too bad Gwen's scrapbook ain't here to look at. I'd give anything to see it again. Probably her family took it with them when they moved."

She glances around the dusky room. "Better get on out of here now."

An odd feeling starts to rise deep inside my gut. On a whim, I reach clear into the chamber, hoping there aren't snakes or spiders. I feel dust and cobwebs, my fingers tangling up in the stuff.

"Shoulda brought a flashlight, huh?" Mamma says, trying to peer over my shoulder.

My fingers touch something hard. And real! The corner of a book and the corner of something else. A box of some kind.

"Mamma! There is something! There really is!"

"You ain't jokin', are you, Shelby Jayne?"

I reach my arm in even farther, all the way up to my armpit, and inch it out. All at once, Gwen's scrapbook is sitting in my hands. "Look! It really *is* here!"

Mamma's got tears in her eyes as I put the photo album in her hands. She blows dust off the decorated cover and peeks inside. "Oh, my, oh my, Shelby Jayne. I can't hardly believe it. Why didn't her family take it with them?"

"Maybe they forgot about it in their hurry to move."

She goes quiet, looking into my face.

"What are you thinking, Mamma?"

"This has gotta be one of the reasons Gwen's spirit stayed here, tied between her angel grave and the broken bridge and this house. She knew this was still here. And she wanted me to know it. This scrapbook was actually a project she was working on to surprise her parents for Christmas, but she died more than two months before. Wonder if it's possible to find her family all these years later and take it to them. . . ." Her voice trails off as I go to shut the secret chamber.

But then I recall that I'd felt more than one item inside the cupboard, so I reach in again, my stomach leaping like a mullet. Inch by inch I wiggle my fingers to get around the corners and finally pull out a small box. *Gwen's jewelry box.*

"Oh, lorda mighty," Mamma breathes, her face going white. "She always kept this in the middle drawer —"

"— of her bureau," I finish. "You open it."

"No, you open it. My hands are shakin' somethin' fierce, *shar.*"

Slowly, I insert my small key charm to unlock the box and

then lift the lid, expecting it to be empty. Surely, Gwen's sister, Maddie, would have taken the few beaded bracelets and earrings that used to be in here.

And the box is empty, except for one item.

As soon as Mamma sees it, she bursts into tears.

Gwen's charm bracelet is lying inside. My heart pounds so hard I can't even hear myself think as I touch the gator charm and the owl and the locket and the key and the topaz birthstone, hanging from the silver chain. "Her charms!" I cry out.

"And this here's her Cajun fleur-de-lis and *traiteur* box — and her blue bottle." Mamma hugs me tight against her, and a burst of emotion fills up my eyes.

The bracelet is exactly the same as I remember when Gwen wore it around her wrist. "It's been sitting in this jewelry box all these years?"

Silently, Mamma nods, then pulls the bracelet out of the box, straightening out all the little charms along her palm. "I always thought Gwen was wearing her bracelet the night she drowned. Always figured it was on the bottom of the bayou, buried in the mud and silt, or swallowed by a gator."

"Her family must of forgotten to check Gwen's secret chamber."

"Probably figured the same thing I did. That the bracelet was lost in the bayou that night."

I run my finger along the row of pretty charms. "Before she went out in the rain to play Truth or Dare, she took it off and put it in here for safekeeping. Remember her note calling you to come to the bridge that night?"

Mamma bites at her lips and shakes her head. "We'd planned to play Truth or Dare the next rainstorm that hit. Thought we'd be daring and tough. Prove we weren't afraid."

Taking a gulp of air, I lift my eyes and Mamma looks up at the very same time. "You think she wants us to do something with her charm bracelet?"

Mamma nods. "I do think so. Maybe this is another reason she was hanging on to this old world. She didn't want the house to fall apart or get bulldozed down. Her most important possessions lost forever."

"I think she wanted you to find them, Mamma. I think she wanted you to know she's okay. And she was worried you'd leave Bayou Bridge before you found her book and bracelet."

Mamma presses the bracelet against her lips. "Shelby Jayne, I think you're right. And you set it all off. Like a chain reaction. Soon as you pulled out that very first blue bottle note."

We hold hands even tighter as we walk back to the boat. A few minutes later, we're kneeling in front of the stone angel monument and Mamma is running her hand along the inscription of Gwen's name.

She closes her eyes, then leans her head back, like she's feeling the sun as it flits back and forth behind the clouds. "Oh, Shelby Jayne, I don't know what to do. Should I bury the charm bracelet down in the dirt beside her?"

I chew on the inside of my cheek and notice that the hard lump that's been there for a year is starting to go away. I think about everything that's happened, about Gwen and Mamma and me and all the pieces of Gwen's life — and that's when a piece of the puzzle suddenly clicks right into place. And completes the picture.

"Not yet," I tell her excitedly. "I think there's another reason Gwen has been haunting the graveyard and the bayou — and me."

Mamma raises her eyebrows, but doesn't ask what I'm talking about.

"I still need to lay it all out in my mind first."

She nods, patient, and her lips are smiling just a little bit despite the tears in her eyes.

A gusty wind rises over the water and twilight is coming on, earlier than usual as October rushes forward.

Mamma rises to her feet. She reaches out to take my hand and I have so much emotion inside me that it's leaking out my eyes. "Let's get on home before we get wet, *bébé*."

A light rain spatters the sidewalks as I get to school Monday morning.

I brace myself as I spot Tara and Alyson coming out of the bathroom.

When I touch my bracelet with my fingers, all those charms give me strength and I figure those girls can't affect me no more.

Holding my head high, I breeze past them like they're invisible. Even their gossipy whispers don't do nothin' at all. Like a fly just buzzing around and then gone on the next breeze. I've got stories they'll never know. And ghost secrets they'd kill for.

Stopping at my locker, I dial the combination, get out my math book, and slam the door.

Beside me, another locker three doors down slams shut at the exact same moment.

I look up and laugh as I realize that our movements are exactly the same at the same time. Like a coincidence.

It's the girl, Larissa. I think back to when we bumped into each other the day I ran away from school.

I remember the ragged jeans, the skinny legs, the scars on the side of her face.

I take a breath and get ready to ask her the question I've wanted to ask ever since she warned me away from the cemetery bridge. "Did you get those scars from falling off that broken pier into the bayou?"

I have a feeling nobody has ever bothered to want to know the truth before.

She watches me with her quiet brown eyes and nods. She stands there, not moving, not running away, her eyes holding mine. "Fell. Pushed. Don't rightly know exactly how I ended up in the water. All I know is I hit those jagged boards, them rusted nails."

"Were there gators coming after the blood in the water?"

She nods, but doesn't speak.

"How'd you get out?"

She lifts her shoulders. "They did drag me out over the pilings, pulled me back onto the pier. But I was stupid. Too chicken to leave. Too dumb to know they didn't really care about me, although they pretended to at first."

I think about that. How Mirage ran away, afraid. And how I did the very same thing, even though I was brave enough — or scared enough — to grab my charm bracelet first when Tara snatched it away from me. How Larissa let herself get bullied. And how Gwen was the tough girl. She stayed when she should have run. Stayed and it cost her her life.

I never see Larissa with anybody else. No group of friends, not even one single, special, best friend. She glances down, her hair sweeping the edge of the textbook she holds against her chest.

"Um, I'm Shelby. You know I moved here a couple of months ago."

"I know. I was new last year. Used to live outside Jeanerette. My parents bought that old antique store. Bayou Bridge Antiques."

I catch my breath, clutching my own textbook.

"I saw you come into the store with your mamma. Back when you first got here."

"Really?" My heart starts to make a funny thumping in my chest.

"I was in the storeroom unpacking boxes."

"That day I was there," I began, "I saw the most wonderful doll collection."

"Oh, I love those dolls! Although *some* people might think we're too old for dolls."

I shake my head, hardly able to speak, but remembering. Remembering Gwen's house and the doll in her bookcase. "Oh, no," I tell her in a rush. "I don't think you can ever be too old for dolls!"

"My favorite is an old porcelain doll in a beautiful rose-colored lace dress," Larissa says. "She has golden curls and a tiny chip on her chin. Sometimes I make up stories to explain how she got that little chip. It's my mamma's doll. She got it when her sister died, but my mamma was only nine when it happened."

I stare at her and my legs go weak. As I lean against the locker, the peculiar buzzing in my ears returns, stronger than ever.

Larissa says, "Sorry, once I get started talking, I end up telling my whole life story. My mamma said I can get the porcelain doll out one of these days and hold her. If I'm very careful. Um, would you like to come back to the store sometime?"

I can scarcely speak. "I'd love to come. I know that doll. I mean, I used to." I stop, not sure how to explain.

Tiny frown lines wrinkle Larissa's forehead. But then she smiles and her smile is one of the prettiest things I've ever seen. "How could you know it?"

I take a deep breath. "I think we were meant to meet. I mean, it's a long story." I stop again, then ask, "Do you believe in best friends?"

Larissa nods, biting at her lips. "I think so. I hope so."

"Do you believe in *traiteurs*?"

"Of course. My grandmother is a *traiteur*. But she's been gone a while now."

I laugh and feel myself blush, tears filling up my throat.

"I've got an idea," Larissa says, her voice growing less timid. "Would you like to come over one day this week? We could take the porcelain doll out of the case and look at her together."

"I'd love to." And all I can think about is showing Larissa and her mother Gwen's hidden scrapbook and her charm bracelet and all the memories that have been lost for so long. "Um, can I ask you a question?" This is the hardest part and I'm not sure if Larissa will hate me for mentioning it.

She studies me carefully, waiting for me.

"Would you ever want to come over and let me and my mamma give you one of her special healing creams? For those scars, I mean. It's not fair those kids did that. . . ." My voice trails off. "Well, you know."

"My parents want to take me to a special doctor one day. When we got some money again, that is."

My heart twists inside my chest as I think about the new scar my own mamma has now after jumping into the bayou to rescue me. "I think she might have just the right healing spell for you. To erase scars, I mean."

A slow grin starts to spread across Larissa's face. "How about let's make up a magical cream that will erase those girls?"

I start giggling at that, and I'm pretty sure I've just found my new best friend in Bayou Bridge.

✳

Later the rain clears up and the sun comes out bright and lemon yellow. After I get home from school, I go out to the back porch while Mamma starts dinner.

Miss Silla Wheezy follows me as I jump down the steps, rubbing against my legs while Mister Possum Boudreaux chases a lizard down by the elephant ears.

Sunshine sprinkles across my shoulders as I walk over to the blue bottle tree, golden light bouncing off all that blue glass, making it sparkle like it's got magic.

My eye catches one of the blue bottles at just the right angle — and there's a note inside! My thoughts go crazy and my gut flips upside down. Could it be another one of those lost notes from Gwen?

Stretching up on my toes, I slip the blue bottle off its branch, then shake it upside down to get the note out.

Quickly, I unfold the slip of paper and smile. The words are written in my mamma's familiar handwriting.

We're having an early supper, shar, so hurry and wash up. Taking a glazed yam cake over to the Moutons' down the bayou. I hear their mamma is sitting up and talking on her own now. It's cause for a celebration — and I want you to meet their daughter, Livie.

A warm and exciting feeling washes over me — because I came out here with a blue bottle note of my own.

I slip the note from Mamma into my pocket, then take out the note I wrote a few minutes ago in my bedroom.

Frowning at the massive, sparkly blue bottle tree, I wonder which bottle to use to be sure she finds it.

I take out a piece of string with nine knots I found in one of the cupboards, put it around the neck of one of the bottles, then tie the ends good and tight so it don't slip off. Finally, I hang the bottle with the string on the very front branch, just like a Christmas tree ornament. No way Mamma'll miss that. I'll bring her out here after we finish eating and nonchalantly walk her past the right bottle.

I know why she never put up those strings of Christmas lights she bought at Bayou Bridge Antique Store. She'd left all those notes from Gwen inside of the blue bottles, afraid to take them out, afraid to leave them, afraid to even go close. If only she'd known that Gwen was hovering on the edge of time and waiting for her best friend to set her free.

Think I'll get my daddy to help me string them lights up as a surprise for her.

The cat's throaty purring is driving me bonkers. "Okay, okay, Miss Silla Wheezy, I'll pick you up, you lazy old thing."

Holding the cat in the crook of my arm, I unfold the note I

wrote and double-check the message written in my neatest cursive.

Meet me at the Bayou Bridge Antique Store after school tomorrow. I have something wonderful to show you, and it's the best surprise ever!

I fold the note back up and pop it through the neck of the blue bottle, then tap the glass so it sways through the air on its branch.

Mission accomplished. I can't wait for tomorrow. Not sure I'll sleep all night long.

Getting down on the cool grass, I lie under the shade of the blue bottle tree, the warmth of Miss Silla Wheezy curled on my neck. Drumming her raspy purr straight into my chest.

Mister Possum Boudreaux goes flying past me like he's gone nuts. He darts through the elephant ears, rustles up the cattails. Then stands stock-still on the bank, staring out at the afternoon fog curling away across the water.

I sit up with a start as the shimmery image of a girl in a pirogue paddles across the water. Her golden hair is flying in an invisible breeze. My throat gets a huge lump and my eyes sting with tears. But in a good way. Gwen's oar dips into the water and she disappears into the fog. I know she's gone for good. But there are more messages to find in the blue bottles. Other stories I'll hear someday.

When I look up into the blue sky of all those bottles shimmering in the crack of sunlight overhead, I think about how bottles and messages and healing charm bracelets worked some mighty miracles.

I think about Larissa and my daddy and my mamma, and I know there are still more amazing things to come.

Most especially, I think about how bottles and charms worked the miracle of erasing my own scars. The scars I've been carrying too long on the edges of my heart.

ACKNOWLEDGMENTS

A bayou full of love and thanks goes to my husband, Rusty, my sons, my mother, my sisters, as well as Tracey Adams and Lisa Ann Sandell for your endless support, love, and belief in me as I made it through the crazy-fast book deadline and came out smiling and sane on the other side.

I'm so grateful to the Scholastic team, including: the incredibly amazing art director Elizabeth B. Parisi; as well as my fantastic publicist, Amanda Vega; production editor extraordinaire Starr Baer; the fabulous associate editor Jody Corbett; and talented copyeditor Monique Vescia.

Huge thank-yous to my super helpful readers: my very wise and intuitive son Jared, wonderful friends Nancy Hatch, Marilyn Prewitt, and Cindy-Rae Jones who keeps me on my Southern toes and off the fainting couch.

I'm very grateful to the many special *traiteurs* I was privileged to meet and who spent hours talking to me. Deborah LeBlanc, Alan Simon at Vermilionville (Cajun & Creole Heritage Park), Becca Begnaud, Annie and E.J. Suier, Roberta Daigle, and Eula Berthelot, who keep faith, hope, and charity alive in the small towns of Louisiana.

Much appreciation to Glen Pitre and Michelle Benoit of Côte Blanche Productions whose amazing documentary, *Good for What Ails You* inspired me many times over and who welcomed me to their home with warm hospitality.

A heart full of love and affection goes to very special friends, Elward and Olive Stephens on Four-Mile Bayou, and to John Heald who introduced us.

ABOUT THE AUTHOR

Kimberley Griffiths Little is the author of *The Healing Spell*, as well as a dozen short stories that have appeared in numerous publications and the critically acclaimed novels *Breakaway, Enchanted Runner,* and *The Last Snake Runner.* She is the winner of the Southwest Book Award.

She grew up reading a book a day and scribbling stories, while dreaming of one day seeing her name in the library card catalog. In her opinion, the perfect Louisiana meal is sausage gumbo and rice, topped off with warm beignets, although crawfish étouffée runs a close second.

Kimberley lives in a solar adobe house near the banks of the Rio Grande in New Mexico with her husband and their three sons. Come visit her at www.kimberleygriffithslittle.com.